THE WARRIOR CITIZEN

A Soldier's Journey to Iraq and Back

R. Jeremy Harrison

iUniverse, Inc.
New York   Bloomington

For the service members and their families who have
sacrificed so much in the Global War on Terrorism
thank you

TABLE OF CONTENTS

"I believe that every right implies a responsibility; every opportunity, an obligation; every possession, a duty." --John D. Rockefeller, July 8, 1941.

Preface

SINCE THE BEGINNING OF TIME, man has been at war. The reasons for each battle have varied from land and power to freedom of religion and relief from persecution. However, the effect of each war on the warriors has been relatively the same, although looked at differently throughout time. They would go back to their homelands with the expectation of returning to life as they once knew it. But the reality of this hope was that each individual who went home after war would never be the same as the person who left for war. The enduring question has always been, why?

We as human beings have this misconception that the ability to endure adversity and come out unscathed is inherently stored within us, that an inner strength exists which can help us rise above any challenge without any consequence. Unfortunately, this is not always the case. We are born with the ability to learn from events that occur throughout our lives but are rarely prepared for every situation that may arise. As a result, there are those of us who search for a lifetime for the answers to questions that confront us every day, only to find that the needed solution does not exist within us.

As children, we learn from our families. We learn how to walk, talk, laugh, cry, tie our shoes, eat, and so on. As time goes by, we continue to learn from friends, teachers, coaches, our own children, and many other individuals involved in our lives. So as we grow older, these learned behaviors, actions, thoughts, and beliefs become instinct, and we react to situations according to what we know. But we sometimes fail to recognize that certain events may arise where we find ourselves without the tools necessary to persevere. As a result, problems may arise, problems that can affect us for the rest of our lives, as well as affect the lives of those around us.

This is at times the case of our brave men and women who are fighting on the battlefields throughout the world today. They face fear, loss, sadness, sickness, injury, and sometimes even death. These issues, if left unaided, can lead to a lifetime of hurting.

Veterans often dig through their toolboxes of learned coping skills trying to find a resolution, only to find that the right tool for fixing the problem is not in the toolbox. It seems as though the drill instructors, senior officers, and ranking professionals, who preach repetition so physical reactions become reflex, often fail to teach possibly the most important skill: how to emotionally deal with the repercussions of combat.

Not having the adequate understanding of how combat stress can affect veterans' lives can lead to disaster. Our men and women who serve overseas deserve to know what can happen to them and what they can do to endure the potentially lifelong struggles that may exist once they try to return to normal lives.

After the Vietnam War, many veterans did not receive the necessary treatment for the problems they were having at the time. Many of those problems were symptoms of posttraumatic stress disorder, or PTSD, as it is often called. Consequently, many chose to take their own lives, others turned to life on the streets, and a large percentage relied on drugs and alcohol. The fact remains that the appropriate attention was not given to them.

Services are now in place for the veterans to get the treatment that they may need, but many are choosing not to use what they are entitled to receive. As a result, many veterans returning from Iraq and Afghanistan are turning to the same self-medicating as the Vietnam veterans. Many veterans are again taking their own lives. Marriages are falling apart, and many veterans are committing acts that lead them to jail. And this is often because they fail to seek the attention they so desperately need.

I am a combat veteran, and I know what I went through before seeking the help I so urgently needed. Currently, I treat combat veterans and their families. I educate them about what can happen as a result of being exposed to the trauma that is war, and I give them the tools to help cope with whatever problems may exist. The number of veterans who need help increases every day. Many are living the same life as Jason in this book. But the help is out there, and life can be great again. It is just a matter of updating that toolbox we call our brain.

The War is Over

IT HAD BEEN ANOTHER ROUGH night for Jason, an evening filled with heavy drinking at a local bar, a late night cab ride home with always faithful Frank (the regular graveyard shift driver who by now gets Jason home without asking any directions), and finally a staggering walk into the house and up the stairs to the bedroom, where his wife, Shannon, was lying awake reading a book, waiting impatiently. But she never said anything. By now she was at her wits end with this unacceptable pattern of behavior from her husband. Jason walked around the bed, took off his clothes, crawled under the blankets, and quickly passed out, beginning his customary erratic sleep and horrifying nightmares.

No one could have seen this coming, not even Shannon. It didn't seem possible from this man, who only a short time ago was a highly revered citizen and hero in his hometown. From the day he returned from Iraq, his life began a steady decline.

Friends said that Jason was always one to partake in a few drinks every now and again, but they never would have expected him to succumb to the ills of alcoholism. Jason would disagree that he had developed an alcohol problem, but would not deny that he had done his share of partying over the past few months. Whenever someone gathered enough nerve to question him about his drinking, he would always respond by saying, "I deserve to do whatever I want."

Jason, although he was only twenty-nine years old, garnered a formidable reputation as a physician and was a widely respected community member. He was born and raised in a relatively small town, and upon graduation from medical school, returned home to practice, even though he was offered numerous job opportunities in much larger cities. But it was for his latest achievement that he had become such a hero in the eyes of his peers, the same experience many believe led to his ultimate demise. Jason, only six months ago, returned from a twelve-month combat tour of Iraq, where he was a member of an army reserve transportation company that was responsible for running supply missions throughout Iraq and Kuwait. His friends and family knew that it was because of what he experienced in Iraq that he developed his drinking problem, but Jason never talked about it. His company suffered several casualties, and for a community with a population of less than twenty-five hundred, the losses affected nearly everyone.

The night passed, and when Jason woke up, ready to begin another day, he noticed almost immediately that something felt different today, and it wasn't the headache or his dry mouth. He slowly arose from his bed, careful not to move too abruptly, and headed for the bathroom. On his way out of the bedroom, he stopped for a glance in the mirror. "Way to go idiot," he said to himself in a soft voice. "You wasted another one." He then took a step, and as he turned, he paused to look down at a picture on the dresser that was taken while he was in Iraq. It included two of his closest buddies, each smiling. It was the last picture taken before that dreadful incident that changed his life forever.

Although Jason had this picture on his dresser since his return from Iraq, today he actually sat down and held it in his hands. Sitting on the corner of the bed, he stared at it for about ten minutes, remembering that day in Iraq when it seemed as though everything was going to be okay. *Why did this have to happen? Where did it all go wrong?* On this day, the anniversary of that horrific day in Iraq, Jason remembered the events as if they happened yesterday. Jason never let go of his feelings of guilt. *I wish there was more I could have done. I miss my friends,* he thought to himself. He then stood up, gently placed the photo back on the dresser, and proceeded to the bathroom.

Standing over the sink, Jason looked at himself in the mirror. His eyes were glassy and his skin was quite pale, clear remnants from the night of too much boozing. He slowly began crying. As he recalled details of the ambush that took his friends' lives, his crying became more intense, and he continued sobbing for several minutes. Shannon, who was downstairs folding clothes, could now hear Jason crying.

"Are you okay?" she shouted.

Jason did not respond, which was usually the case whenever Shannon asked him almost any question these days.

She then yelled a little louder, "Jason, are you okay?"

Again she received no response. She shrugged her shoulders and continued folding the clothes.

A few minutes passed, and when she realized she could no longer hear Jason making any noise, she went to the bathroom to check on him. She trudged up the stairs, loud enough so he could hear her coming, as if he would respond this time. She grasped the doorknob and turned it to open the door, but it was locked, which was very unusual. *Jason never locks the door,* she thought to herself. Suddenly, she heard a loud cracking sound, which sent her into a fit of hysteria.

"Jason! Jason! No!"

She began pushing and pulling on the doorknob, but could not get the door to open. Shannon then remembered a trick that Jason once showed her to open this door when it was locked, when she accidentally locked herself out. She ran into the bedroom, grabbed a safety pin lying on the dresser, and ran back to the bathroom door. After jiggling and dropping the pin a few times, she finally got the door unlocked and pushed her way into the bathroom.

"No! Jason!"

Her worst nightmare had come true. Jason was lying on the floor in a puddle of blood, the result of a gunshot wound to the head. She frantically ran out of the room and called 911. She then went back into the bathroom, fell to the floor, and held Jason in her arms. When the emergency crew finally arrived, it was too late; Jason was gone.

Although Shannon knew that Jason had some problems, she never expected this to happen. What was it that had led Jason, a respected doctor and well-liked man, who was seen as a hero in the community, to this point? What happened that was so bad that he saw no other choice?

Shannon read a lot of material and watched many news stories about veterans returning from war and developing mental health problems, even some about them taking their own lives. But even though she knew he had problems and needed help, she never thought Jason would make this type of decision. Not her Jason. She could not understand the impact of the events that took place in Iraq, and Jason never really talked much about specific feelings and thoughts related to them. But none of that mattered now. Jason was gone. So many questions unanswered, and so many emotions unknown. Neither Shannon nor anyone else who knew Jason expected this outcome.

Chapter 1 : The Beginning

ON JANUARY 16, 1991, AT precisely 6:38 PM EST, the United States initiated what turned out to be a swift military campaign to remove Iraqi forces from Kuwait. Just five months prior, Iraqi president Saddam Hussein approved the invasion of his southern neighbor on the accusation that they were overproducing oil and stealing it from one of Iraq's southern reserves. It did not take long for the Iraqi forces to seize control of the small country. Despite American and coalition troop levels rapidly increasing in Saudi Arabia, along with numerous diplomatic attempts made by both the United Nations and the United States to persuade the Iraqi government to peacefully remove their forces from Kuwait, the government of Iraq refused. As a result, with approval from both the UN and the Congress of the United States, President George H. W. Bush authorized the use of combined air and ground forces to free the people of Kuwait from the occupation of the Iraqi troops. This turned out to be the largest military operations implemented by the Unites States since the Vietnam War, as well as the largest activation of the reserve components since the Vietnam Tet Offensive of 1968, authorized by President Johnson.

Although the ground action was short-lived (the total length of the ground campaign lasting less than a week), the power and pride of the United States was evident. Within a week of the mutually agreed upon cease-fire, U.S. combat forces began returning home. Parades were held around the country honoring the troops for their efforts in the desert. And because of the large contingent of reserve components, even the smaller towns held ceremonies and parades for their local troops. It was a proud time, a time when Americans truly embraced their armed forces and showed respect for what they had done. Almost every community was impacted in some way. People of all ages knew this was a time to be proud of being an American.

As time passed and all of the troops returned home from the Middle East, Americans went back to their normal lives, as the excitement from the success of the war had faded. Although this was the case for many, not all Americans would let this war pass by and forget the impact that it had on this great nation. One young man in particular, Jason Henson, saw something special during that memorable parade in the faces of everyone watching. When his small community's reserve unit returned home from a tour in the Middle East, everyone was so proud, as if they had personally contributed to the war effort. It was from that moment that Jason felt a desire and an obligation to enlist in the army with the idea that one day he too could be welcomed home as the brave men and women of the 132nd Transportation Company had been.

Jason dreamed of one day becoming a doctor in hopes that he could give something back to the people of the community that he grew to know so well over the years. The tiny town of Harrisville, Pennsylvania, had embraced Jason ever since he was born. His father, Ray, was the town physician, and Jason was often in his father's office when he was not in school, entertaining the patients as they waited in the lobby. He had a knack for making other people laugh, often mocking his father and pretending to be a doctor himself, but he was bright enough to recognize when it was time to stop. Sometimes, when there were no patients, Ray would show his son some of the equipment that he used and teach him how to use it. Jason was a quick learner, and by the time he reached his teenage years, he was familiar with just about everything used in a doctor's office. It was clear to almost everyone, including Jason, that one day he would fill his father's shoes. Jason knew by the time he was sixteen that he would be going to college to earn his degree in medicine and become the practicing physician everyone expected him to be. But even though Jason knew this was the chosen path for him, the events leading up to and following the war in the Persian Gulf changed his view about what he would do with his life. So at the age of sixteen, when most teenagers are consumed with their looks and getting their first car, Jason was making up his mind that he was going to join the army.

During his senior year in high school, Jason spent countless hours searching for and applying to various colleges and universities in and around Pennsylvania, trying his best to find the perfect school. Although Jason knew his career path, he was uncertain of exactly how to go about pursuing it. As a result, Jason made frequent visits to Mr. Stein, his guidance counselor and an army veteran himself, to try and put together some sort of plan.

In addition to meeting regularly with Mr. Stein, Jason would also eventually have meetings with another influential person in the guidance office, Staff Sergeant Paul Anderson, an army recruiter. Each time Jason sat waiting in the lobby, he would listen to SSG Anderson and the other service branch recruiters as they used every trick in their book to try and persuade as many of the graduating men and women into joining their particular branch. During his final semester, Jason made at least three trips each week to see Mr. Stein, and most of the time the recruiters were there as well. As time passed, the recruiters recognized Jason, but he never made eye contact with any of them. Even though he knew he wanted to join the army, Jason wasn't sure he was ready to make the commitment. However, Jason's presence on a regular basis didn't go unnoticed for long. Because it is the nature of the job, SSG Anderson finally broke the silence between the two, and on the day Jason was actually going to say something, SSG Anderson beat him to the punch.

"I notice you're in here a lot," he said to Jason.

"Yeah, just trying to figure out what I'm gonna do after I graduate," Jason replied.

"What are you thinking about?" SSG Anderson asked with a grin.

Jason, anxious for the day when the recruiter would ask him that question, quickly responded by stating, "I want to be a doctor, a family physician to be exact."

"A very admirable choice. Your family must be proud."

"They are," Jason said, "Especially my dad. He has his own practice here in Harrisville."

"Who is your father?" the recruiter asked.

"Dr. Ray Henson," said Jason.

"I know him. I've been to him a bunch of times, especially when I was a kid. How's he doing?"

"Great, just fine," replied Jason.

The two continued chatting about being from the same town and discussed some gossip about some of the local people. Before long, a rapport was established, and the two began discussing exactly what Jason had in mind upon graduation.

SSG Anderson asked Jason where he was going to go to school.

"I'm not sure," Jason said, "My dad is going to pay for half of the tuition, so I want to find a good school that I will be able to afford to pay half of. I know I can get loans, but I don't want to be paying for them for twenty years. I've wanted to join the army reserves, probably since I was a sophomore, so hopefully some of the money from that will help too. I hear they give some money for school."

The recruiter's face lit up like the star on top of a Christmas tree when Jason said he thought about joining.

"They sure do, Jason. Why don't we set up a time for you to come to my office after school and we can talk about it?"

Jason, butterflies flapping away in his stomach, nodded in compliance and said he could come after school tomorrow. The two shook hands and parted ways.

Jason then turned to his counselor, who was standing there as the two shook hands. He asked Jason if he was ready. They proceeded to the office. As Jason was sitting down and Mr. Stein was shutting the door, he asked Jason, "What was that all about?"

Jason, nervous and excited at the same time, told him about his dream of joining the army, going back to the days of the parades after Operation Desert Storm. Mr. Stein, although very proud of Jason for his accomplishments and goals, was a little hesitant to get excited for Jason and this potential decision.

"Jason, I admire you for wanting to make this type of decision; it's honorable. But have you thought about the negative aspects as well?"

"What do you mean?" Jason asked with a curious look on his face.

"Well, Jason, you're aware that I served in Vietnam, aren't you?"

"Yes."

"I don't talk about it much, but I lost quite a few friends over there. And it hasn't been easy trying to deal with that."

Jason listened intently as Mr. Stein talked about his days in Vietnam. He was amazed to hear that he was an infantryman and spent many days fighting in the jungle.

"I never would have guessed it," Jason said to him.

"Why is that?"

"Well, I guess when you see movies like *Rambo*, well, you just don't look like him."

"I'm sorry to inform you, Jason, but most Vietnam veterans don't look like him," he replied in a defensive tone. "He was created for a movie."

"Sorry," Jason stated quietly.

"I'm sorry, too. This isn't why we are here. It's just hard to think you could be going to war some day. The way that the Gulf War ended, it's just bound to start up again. I'll support you in whatever you do, you know that, and I'm proud of you for doing this. It's just hard sometimes. I've gotten to know you so well, and I'd hate to see anything bad ever happen to you. I'm proud of you, buddy."

"Thanks," Jason replied with a smile.

The two then began discussing college options, as they usually did, and then Jason left to finish his day.

On his way home from school, Jason, overwhelmed with emotion from the day's events, pondered what the near future would have in store for him. He thought about what Mr. Stein said, and that scared him a little. But he knew this was a dream of his, and nothing would stop him. He pictured himself in a parade, waving to everyone welcoming him home from some war that may never happen. The whole idea was inspiring, and he couldn't wait to tell his parents about it. The more Jason pondered these thoughts, the more he began to feel a sense of pride.

Upon arrival to his house, Jason, so excited he barely put his car in park before he got out, ran to the house, threw the door open, and immediately went to his parents, who were sitting across from each other at the kitchen table, discussing their day, as was typical for them.

"What is it?" Jason's father asked, sensing the excitement in his demeanor. "Well, I finally did it," he replied.

"Did what?"

"I talked to a recruiter today."

Although his parents knew that this was a dream of Jason's and were proud of him for it, they seemed a little distraught at hearing this. His dad began scratching his head, and his mother immediately looked out of the window, then at the floor, and then back at Jason. They were hesitant to respond, but finally his mom spoke.

"So what did you talk about?"

Jason dropped his backpack, sat down at the table, and began telling them about the details of the discussion with the recruiter.

When Jason was finished explaining, Ray, who looked like a puppy whose bone was just taken away, asked, "So if you do this, when do you plan to leave, and when are you going to start college?"

Jason explained that no plans had been made but that he would probably leave after graduation, with plans to start school in the spring.

"What are you going to do in the fall?" his dad asked.

"Well, I was thinking about getting a part-time job and maybe helping you around the office from time to time."

"Okay, Jason, if this is what you want to do, your mother and I will support you all the way. Just make sure that this is exactly what you want to do," Ray said, looking at Angie for approval.

"There's no doubt in my mind that this is what I want to do," Jason responded without hesitation.

Jason's mom said nothing throughout the discussion, as was usually the case when emotions were involved, but when she realized that Jason was sincere about doing this, she shed a tear and said to him, "I love you, and I am so proud of you."

Jason gave her a hug and was off to his room to further contemplate the decisions he was about to make.

That night, Jason could hardly sleep. He lay in bed, staring at the ceiling, pondering the major changes he was about to endure. *I'm really going to do this,* he thought to himself. He pictured in his mind the parades for the troops and how proud they must have felt as everyone around was clapping and cheering, knowing that one day he could be one of those troops. Feeling good about his decision, Jason finally fell asleep. When he got out of bed in the morning, he felt like a new person, as if he already was a hero. Today was a new beginning, and things were now different, because he knew he was meeting with the recruiter and that this was a major step in solidifying his decision to join the army.

Jason arrived at school a little late. Amongst all of the excitement from yesterday, he couldn't remember where he put his keys. It turned out he never took them out of the car, and that was the last place he looked. When he arrived to class, he began thinking that he wished he had never found his keys, as the day seemed to drag along very slowly, and he could think about nothing else except for the dismissal bell at the end of the day, which would release him to go see SSG Anderson. That time finally came, and Jason headed to his car. He was starting to get a little nervous but was excited at the same time. He got in his car and headed straight for the recruiter's office.

When Jason arrived, the recruiter was standing outside, smoking a cigarette and talking with some of the other recruiters. He introduced Jason to each of them, and then they headed to the office. They sat at the recruiter's desk, which was located in a small corner of what appeared to be a rather large office. As SSG Anderson pulled some paperwork out, Jason looked around the office, gazing at the various posters and pictures hanging on the wall, and took notice of the other potential recruits in the office, who were staring around just as he was, probably just as nervous.

"Are they signed up already?" Jason asked.

"No, they're here completing paperwork, just like you."

The two men continued discussing some of the benefits of joining, which included some money for college, a very important factor in Jason's decision-making process. However, it really did not matter to Jason what was discussed. His mind was already made up. Nevertheless, he did ask a few questions pertaining to different jobs he could get, as well as some of the things that take place at basic training. As the two completed their discussion, SSG Anderson began situating the papers Jason needed to sign, the first of a few phases he would have to complete before finally being sworn in as one of the newest members of the Unites States Army.

Typically, the recruiter would set up a time when a potential new recruit would have to take the Armed Services Vocational Aptitude Battery, or ASVAB test before the recruit would sign any papers. This test helped to determine to what type of job each new recruit would be best suited. But Jason had taken the test earlier in the year when it was offered at his school, something that was commonplace at most high schools.

About two hours had passed, and the two of them had finally completed the paperwork and all questions had been answered. Jason was finished with everything that had to take place with the recruiter that day. The next phase would occur at the regional Military Entrance Processing Station, or MEPS. This is where the new recruits went to fill out more paperwork, get a complete physical, decide what career they wanted to pursue, determine when they would be ready to leave for basic combat training (BCT), and get sworn in as an official army recruit. At that point the process was complete. The next step was training.

Jason and the recruiter decided on a date to go to MEPS and finally parted ways for the day, "See you soon, soldier," SSG Anderson said.

Jason simply grinned and waved.

As Jason left the office and exited the building, he felt a sense of pride he had never experienced before, and he held his head up high with a slight touch of arrogance. He could not wait to tell everyone what he had decided to do, although most people who knew Jason would not be surprised.

When Jason got home, his parents were sitting on the couch, watching television, anxiously awaiting his arrival. They could tell by his smirk that something was up, and they knew he had enlisted.

"Well," Ray said, "let's have it."

Jason told them everything that happened at the recruiters' office that day. He even told them, with a quaint smile on his face, trying to hide his excitement, that SSG Anderson called him a soldier. Although Jason was beaming with excitement, his parents looked the opposite.

"What's the matter?" Jason asked.

Ray responded, holding back tears, "Nothing, buddy; we're just so proud of you."

"You're all grown up," Angie said, not concerned with refraining from crying.

Both of his parents stood up at this point and gave Jason a hug.

Ray then asked, hesitating, not wanting to detract from the current mood, "So what about school?"

Jason paused. The last couple of days, Jason completely neglected to take school into consideration. This abruptly brought him back to reality.

Now that Jason had made his decision about the army and completed everything necessary before going to the MEPS, it was time to focus on college.

Jason had several meetings with Mr. Stein, trying to determine what schools would fit into his plan. In the past, he advised Jason to apply to several schools, which would give him several options from which to choose. Well, as it turned out, and as no surprise to anyone, Jason's high test scores and grade point average led to acceptance at every school to which he applied. However, that made the process of elimination that much more difficult. To narrow down the number of schools, Jason decided to look for a few specific variables.

First, Jason wanted a school recognized for having an above-average medical program. Second, he had to determine which ones would meet his financial qualifications. Next, he wanted a school that was not too far from home so traveling to reserve drills on the weekend would not become a hassle. Finally, Jason came up with a unique scenario to help eliminate some schools. He wanted to find out the percentage of students at each school that were active in the reserves and National Guard, as the ones with the most probably had a good system set up to meet their needs. If nothing else, he might end up knowing several of the other reserves, who might be in his unit. So after several meetings with Mr. Stein, long discussions with his father, as well as trips to the schools on his list, Jason finally determined where he was going to go: Penn State. Everything was falling into place.

With most of his important plans made, Jason could finally relax a little and enjoy the rest of his senior year doing what everyone else was doing: hanging out with friends and going to a few parties. Graduation seemed to be approaching rather quickly, and Jason knew it was time to get to the Philadelphia MEPS. He called SSG Anderson, and they arranged a day when they could go and complete the final phase of the recruit process before leaving for boot camp. They had decided to go on Thursday of the next week, April 20th, three weeks before graduation.

By this time, Jason was getting a little more nervous, more so than ever before. He decided to sit down and have a talk with his dad and discuss some of his feelings.

"Dad," Jason said.

"Yeah, buddy."

"I've been having a lot of mixed emotions about all of these decisions. On one hand, I'm excited about getting into the school I want and going to the army, but I'm also nervous. My whole life is about to change."

Ray, who was always reassuring, responded, "Well, Jason, you're right. You have had to make a lot of big decisions. But do you feel that you made the right ones?"

Without hesitation, Jason responded, "Absolutely."

"Well then, I've always had confidence that you will make the best decision for yourself. And I personally think that you have made some great choices. It's just all happening at once. Everything will work out great. Trust yourself. You, son, will make a difference."

With that being said, Jason felt better already.

"Thanks, Dad. I just needed to hear you say those things."

Ray always seemed to have a way of putting things so Jason would feel good. One thing Jason always remembered his dad saying was, "Follow your heart, Jason, for it is the guide to happiness in your life." Ray reiterated that message on this day, and Jason fought hard to fight back tears, but to no avail. Jason finally realized the impact his decisions would have on him, his family and friends, and his community. But he felt as if he were on a mission, a mission to do things that would positively impact his community, that same community that embraced him as a child.

Ray smiled and gave Jason a hug.

"I'm so proud of you, son," he said as he too shed a tear.

"It's all because of you, Dad. You taught me everything I know."

Angie heard the entire conversation from the other room, where she was making dinner, and as they finished talking, she entered the room, smiling from ear to ear but crying at the same time. She walked towards them and gave each a hug. No words were necessary. Her expressions said it all. After all of the emotions had settled from this heartwarming moment, they all went back to their business, not forgetting what had just taken place.

Jason called up some friends, and they decided to go out for the evening, knowing that this would be one of the last opportunities to spend some time together before moving forward with their lives. They reflected on their times together and laughed about some of the crazy things they had done over the years, like the time when they went mailbox bashing and ended up wrecking the car, and when Jason was caught hitting cars with snowballs. They also discussed the decisions they had made about their future and what life might have in store for them. After several hours passed, they parted ways and all went home. The rest of the weekend was pretty normal, although Jason knew this would be his last weekend before completing the recruit process and that things would be different from that day forward.

As the school days came and went, Thursday the twentieth quickly approached. The big day was here. SSG Anderson was at Jason's house to pick him up at 7:00 AM sharp. It took less than two hours to get to the MEPS. SSG Anderson accompanied Jason into the building and showed him where he had to report, and then he left.

"Good luck, Jason," he said as he walked towards the elevator.

"Thanks."

Jason knew that at the end of the day, when they saw each other again, all final decisions would be made, and he would officially be ready for basic training.

There's a saying in all branches of the military, one that has continued through time and will more than likely be around for many generations of servicemen and women to come: "Hurry up and wait." This statement means exactly what it sounds like: quickly get to where you have to go, but sit and wait when you arrive at your destination. Well, for Jason it was no different. Because there were so many people who had to go through the same stages, the entire day was full of hurrying to your next station and waiting in line for your turn. Everything was pretty well organized, so Jason knew exactly where he had to go and when he had to go there.

The process that takes place at the MEPS is not unlike line work in a factory. There is the initial phase, the assembly line, where the product is born, or in Jason's case, where all recruits are gathered, aligned, and briefed on the day's activities. Then there are the various stages that the product must go through and pass before finishing at the end of the line, the point at which the product is ready for final inspection and then sent to its ultimate destination for sale and use, not much different for a new recruit being given the stamp of approval and ultimately being sent to basic training.

As the day passed, Jason began to feel more and more like he was not a person but a *thing* that had to pass inspection. But remembering his discussions with SSG Anderson, he understood that this is how it often works in the military. You are a piece of the machine that functions day-to-day and enables the military to be productive and successful. Well, this day seemed to last forever, beginning with all the paperwork that had to be completed. Then Jason went through all of the phases of the physical (which include hearing and eyesight tests, flexibility and motion tests, blood work, a urine test, and so on), and then some more paperwork. By the end of the day, Jason probably signed his name and wrote his Social Security number (one of the most important things for a person to know in the military, as it is often used in place of or in addition to names on documents for verification) close to fifty or sixty times. Jason, as expected, passed through all phases of the physical and paperwork process with flying colors. In fact, his results were some of the best of the day. There was one more station for Jason to complete, which to him and most other new recruits was the most important and exciting phase of the day: picking their job, determining when and where they will go to basic training and advanced individual training (AIT), finding out where they will be stationed, and settling on what bonuses and college money they will receive.

Jason, waiting impatiently for his name to be called to make his final decisions, was set on what he was going to do and where he would be stationed. Although he had thought about different jobs and possibly being stationed in a city outside of his own, Jason remembered why he decided to enlist in the first place and knew he wanted to be a part of his local unit, the 132nd Transportation Company. His name finally called, Jason, giving a firm, "Yes, sir," continued to the office to finalize his plans.

Before they advanced any further, the man working with Jason said to him, "I know you're new and all, but I'm not an officer, so don't call me sir, okay?"

Jason, red-faced, apologized and asked what to call him.

"Sgt. Higgins," the man replied. "You'll learn the rankings soon enough, so don't worry about it."

Jason nodded in compliance. They continued to go over Jason's qualifications and what he had in mind for the military.

"Anything in particular you would like to do in the military?" Sgt. Higgins asked.

"Well," Jason explained, "I've always wanted to be a member of the 132nd Transportation Company in my hometown. I remember the day they returned from the Gulf War. Our town had a parade for them, and it was at that time I realized I wanted to be a part of that unit."

As Jason was telling the story, Sgt. Higgins was reviewing his test scores from the ASVAB.

"Why the reserves and not active duty?" he asked Jason.

"Well, I was accepted to go to Penn State. I want to be a family doctor and would like to begin next spring."

"Jason, you have some great test scores, and the army has a great medical program. With these scores, you could choose pretty much any path you want."

"I appreciate that, sergeant, but this is what I really want to do. I want to do something different in the army from my regular career, and I really want to be in the 132nd."

"Okay. Thought I'd try. So let's take a look and see what we come with," Sgt. Higgins said, sighing as if he were disappointed.

He went from screen to screen, looking for the information on what Jason wanted to do.

"Found it," Sgt. Higgins said.

Sgt. Higgins informed Jason that he was eligible for a three thousand dollar bonus, the Montgomery GI Bill (money for college), and a ten thousand dollar student loan repayment.

Jason, grinning as he listened to what he could receive, asked, "So are there any openings in the Harrisville unit?"

After taking a few minutes to find that information, Sgt. Higgins confirmed that there were a few openings. Jason could barely contain himself. Everything was falling into place.

"There's one stipulation, though," Sgt. Higgins affirmed. "You have to take the slot now to solidify your position, and that also means that you will have to leave for basic training right after graduation."

"Oh no," Jason responded. "My friends are already making plans to go to Myrtle Beach for senior week two weeks after graduation. If I take this position, I won't be able to go."

Sgt. Higgins replied, "Yeah, but if you choose to wait and go to training a little later in the summer, you could lose your spot in that unit and may not make it back in time to start school in the spring."

Jason only needed a few moments to ponder this decision. For over two years, he had been anxious to join and get into his home unit.

"Well," Jason said, disappointed that he would not be able to go to the beach, "let's do it."

And with that, the contract was drawn up and Jason once again had to read paperwork and sign his name and Social Security number several more times.

"That's it, Jason. We're done here."

Sgt. Higgins stood, and Jason followed suit. He reached out to shake Jason's hand. "Good luck, Jason. Welcome to the army," he said.

One last step had to take place for everything to be solidified. It was now time to be sworn in as a soldier in the U.S. military.

"Thanks for the help, Sgt. Higgins. Take care," Jason said, trying to hold back his excitement.

Jason proceeded down the hall to wait for the order to be sworn in. Just before he was called, Jason looked to his left and saw a familiar face. It was SSG Anderson coming to pick him up. Having done this many times before with other recruits, SSG Anderson knew at what step Jason would be.

"Well," Jason said, this time not holding back that smile, "I got everything I wanted, and I'm going to be with the 132nd, just like I'd hoped."

"Congratulations," SSG Anderson replied. "You deserve it. Now go make it official."

Jason's named was called, along with six other recruits, to go into the room where the swearing in took place. This was it, the moment he'd been waiting for, for over two years. The room was quiet. The room was entirely white, with the exception of the

American and military flags posted in the corner and the blue carpet with the national seal on it. Nothing else was in there—not that it was needed.

As they stood in line, nervous and excited at the same time, a man walked through the door. He introduced himself as Colonel Armstrong. He began telling the men about the courage and bravery that each of them represented and that their country would be proud of the sacrifices they were making. This speech sent chills up Jason's spine, his sense of pride now stronger than ever before. The colonel then called the men to attention, and as they were standing as still as you could imagine, with their right arms raised, he told them to repeat after him.

Jason stated, "I, Jason Henson, do solemnly swear that I will support and defend the Constitution of the United States against all enemies, foreign and domestic; that I will bear true faith and allegiance to the same; and that I will obey the orders of the president of the United States and the orders of the officers appointed over me, according to regulations and the Uniform Code of Military Justice. So help me God."

And with that, they were dismissed. Jason left the room and met with SSG Anderson.

"Well," Jason said, fighting back tears, "I did it."

"Congratulations. I'm proud of you, and I know your family will be, too. Now let's get home so you can tell everyone about it."

The drive home was relatively quiet. Jason was going over in his mind what had taken place that day. He was also exhausted. He soon fell asleep, and when he awakened, he was in his driveway.

Jason got out of the car and thanked SSG Anderson for everything and told him he would see him at school. He went into his house and headed for the living room. By the time Jason returned home, it was about ten thirty at night, and he knew if his parents were still awake, that was where they would be. He quietly entered the room to find both of his parents asleep, his dad on the recliner and his mom on the couch. He gently shook his father's shoulder, careful not to scare him.

His father slowly opened his eyes, and when he realized it was Jason, he said, "Ang, get up!"

Although it was late and all of them had to get up early in the morning, they stayed up for about another hour and discussed what happened at MEPS.

When the conversation concluded, Ray and Angie wiped the tears from their eyes and Ray said, "Son, I'm proud of you. You're really doing this."

His mom nodded in agreement with Ray and gave Jason a hug. They finally retreated to bed, although none of them fell fast asleep. Ray and Angie lay in bed discussing the decision their son had made.

"I'm not so sure about this, Ray," Angie said with a concerned voice.

"Well, he's a smart kid," Ray responded in a defensive tone, "and he's been determined to do this for a long time. Nothing we say would change his mind, and quite frankly, I think he has made very good choices."

"Well I never said I disagree; I'm just nervous," Angie replied. "He's our only son, you know, and I'm his mother. I think I can be concerned."

"Okay," said Ray, "you've got a point. We have to stick together on this and support him. That's what's most important. It'll be tough, but we'll make it okay."

"He sure has grown into a fine young man, hasn't he?" Angie asked with a proud voice.

"He sure has. I think we've done just fine with him. Let's get some sleep. Good night."

"Good night."

Meanwhile, Jason lay in bed reviewing all of the things that took place throughout this semester of school. *What a crazy year this has been,* he thought to himself. And with that, he finally fell asleep.

He woke up the next morning, exhausted from the previous day's events and the little amount of sleep he managed to get. His mom was already awake, and when she heard Jason moving around, she went to his room and told him he could stay home from school today if he wanted. Jason, excited to tell his friends and Mr. Stein about yesterday, quickly responded in the negative.

He then jumped out of bed and headed for the shower. When he was done and dressed for school, he went downstairs to find his mom had prepared a big breakfast for him: eggs, pancakes, bacon, hash browns, and toast.

"What's all this?" Jason asked with a huge grin on his face.

"Well, I figured you would need a little boost this morning. I know you're exhausted."

"Thanks, Mom; you're the best."

Jason finished his breakfast and gave his mom a kiss, and then he was off to school. He arrived at school a little early, hoping to catch his friends before class. He found Paul and Tony (his childhood friends) and told them how things went yesterday, and informed them that he would not be able to go to the beach. Disappointed but happy for him, they both gave him a friendly punch in the arm and told him they'd be thinking about him while they're basking in the sun on the beach. Jason laughed, as did Paul and Tony, and the three of them headed for class. Jason went through the motions of the first part of the day, anxious and only thinking about what Mr. Stein might have to say. When Jason finally got to go to the counselors' office, he saw Mr. Stein talking to SSG Anderson and knew they had already discussed it. Jason, a little disappointed, walked up to them.

"So, I guess you heard?" Jason asked, looking at Mr. Stein.

"Yeah, and I'll tell you what, Jason; I couldn't be more proud of you. You stuck to your word and decided to join the 132nd."

Jason nodded. SSG Anderson asked Jason what his parents thought.

"They're happy. They were a little sad, but said they were proud of me."

"I knew they would be," SSG Anderson replied.

Mr. Stein asked Jason to come to his office to talk about it. Jason said bye and continued down the hall.

"Well, Jason, how do you feel about your decisions?"

"I feel great, but I am little nervous."

"Well, that's normal. You'll be fine," Mr. Stein replied nonchalantly.

They discussed the details of the contract, and Mr. Stein also included some advice for Jason pertaining to boot camp.

"Just remember, Jason, don't ask questions, and don't ask questions."

Jason laughed at this piece of advice, as did Mr. Stein.

"No, really, it's not that tough; you just have to pay attention to details and take care of yourself. The rest will fall into place."

"Thank for the advice, Mr. Stein. One more thing: is it hard to keep up with the physical fitness part?"

"Trust me," Mr. Stein said, smiling, "They'll make sure you get into shape." Besides, you're in good shape anyway."

"I know," Jason replied. "I guess I'm just nervous."

Mr. Stein let Jason know that was normal and reassured him he would do fine. The two wrapped up the discussion and Jason headed for the door.

"Jason," Mr. Stein said with a tranquil voice, "I'm proud of you, too, and I know you'll do great."

Jason nodded and headed out the door, realizing this was probably the last time the two of them would get together for any length of time regarding this subject.

During the next couple of weeks, Jason spent a lot of time studying for finals, working out at the gym, and spending time with friends. One week before he had to leave, he received an unexpected phone call. It was from his childhood girlfriend, Shannon, who had moved away just before they started high school. When that happened, Jason was devastated. In fact, he didn't have another long-term girlfriend the entire time he was in high school.

"Shannon?" Jason asked with a surprised voice.

"Yeah, it's me."

Jason had not talked to Shannon in quite some time and was shocked to hear from her. He had no idea where to start the conversation.

"I heard you decided to join the army."

"Yeah, how'd you know?"

"My dad told me. I guess he called one of his buddies from back there, and he told him."

The two of them talked for a little over an hour, which to them felt like minutes. As the conversation came to a close, Shannon asked if she could write to him while he was gone.

"Sure," Jason responded immediately. "I'll write you with the address when I can."

Jason was so anxious and nervous talking to her; he never even asked what her address was. He didn't remember until after they got off of the phone, and when he realized, he became upset. Apparently, she was thinking the same thing, as she called back within fifteen minutes.

After getting her address, Shannon said to Jason, "I almost forgot to tell you, I'm going to Penn State starting in the fall."

Jason stayed silent.

"Jason, you there?"

"Yeah, I'm here," Jason responded in a soft, excited voice. "Me too, starting in the spring," Jason explained to her.

This too stunned her. Although she was excited by this news, she tried to reply as if it were no big deal.

"Wow, I mean, that's great. Maybe we can get together some time."

"That would be great," Jason said.

Not knowing what to say next, as they were both in a state of shock, they hung up again. Jason immediately told his parents and then called Paul and Tony tell them about what took place. They too were happy for him; they knew he never truly lost feelings for her.

The week seemed to fly by for Jason. He completed all of his exams, passing all of them. He graduated, packed everything he needed to take with him, said his good-byes to everyone, and spent his last night with his mom and dad. They had dinner together: lasagna and garlic bread, Jason's favorite. They talked all about what would happen in the next couple of days. Afterwards, Jason and his family watched some television together, continuing to discuss every little detail, and finally they all went to bed.

Jason couldn't sleep. It was finally here. Time to go to training. Jason was so nervous, not knowing what to expect when he arrived at Fort Leonard Wood, Missouri. SSG Anderson, always punctual, was at the house at 7:00 AM Jason packed his bags in the car, gave his mom and dad hugs and kisses, and was off, not to return for another several months. When they arrived at the airport, SSG Anderson showed Jason where to go and said his good-byes as well.

"Good luck, kiddo."

"See ya," Jason replied.

Well, here he was, at the airport. He was now all alone and feeling a little depressed but excited as well. Jason checked in and turned over his bags. He then went through security and got on the plane.

As he sat there, waiting for the plane to depart, he looked out his little window and softly said, as if he were talking to someone, "See you in a few months."

Chapter 2 : Basic Training

THE PLANE TOOK OFF, AND Jason was on his way. The flight was a little more than three hours, so Jason decided to get some sleep, which was no problem considering he had almost none the night before. After arriving at the airport in St. Louis, Jason retrieved his bags and headed towards the office that the military had set up at the airport for incoming troops. Following his sign-in, Jason joined the other new recruits standing outside the terminal. Their bus finally arrived, and now they were off for another three-hour trip, this time to the base. No one talked, and no one slept. Everyone just stared out of the windows, not really looking at anything in particular, just reflecting on their journey and feeling nervous about what was coming their way. They finally arrived at the base. The driver informed them that they had arrived and they would be getting off at the inprocessing center in just a few minutes.

When they arrived at the center, a man dressed in army camouflage came directly to the bus and climbed up the stairs, staring with the meanest look Jason had ever seen. This guy was massive. He was probably about six foot five inches tall and weighed at least a rock-solid 215 pounds. Quite the intimidating specimen, and by no means the most pleasant.

"Get off of my bus, now!" he shouted.

And so it began.

The reality of the decision that Jason had made quickly materialized (or as those in the army might say, the "Oh, shit!

factor"). As the recruits frantically filed off of the bus, exhausted from their day's travels, they were told to stand in a straight line and not to move or speak. Scared shitless, no one moved or said a word.

What in the hell did I get myself into? Jason thought to himself.

As he stood there, frightened and tired, he listened as the man in uniform shouted at them.

"Listen up," he said to them. "My name is SSG Brown, and you will address me as Staff Sergeant, Got it?"

Collectively, they replied frantically, "Yes, Staff Sergeant."

"I will be in charge of you maggots for the next week while you are inprocessing, got it?"

"Yes, Staff Sergeant!"

"Now, respond as your name is called."

SSG Brown proceeded to do a roll call, as was customary when new soldiers arrived. All were present and accounted for. He introduced some other people who were standing with him. He told the recruits that these people would be assisting him while the recruits were under his watch. Once everyone was introduced, SSG Brown made an announcement.

"For the next week, we will be preparing you for the first phase of basic training, which will include getting all of those wonderful shots some of you may have heard about, and there will be plenty more paperwork for you to fill out. During this time, we'll be getting you acquainted with some of the basics of being a soldier, and you'll also get your uniforms. Furthermore, and this is my favorite part, we are going to be introducing you to a little thing called PT, or physical fitness. Any questions?"

There's always one in the crowd.

"Staff Sergeant Brown, when do we get to sleep?" Rule number one: never ask this question.

"So, you a little tired?"

"Yes, Staff Sergeant Brown."

"Well, we have a cure for that. It's called the push-up. And I'm guessing that since one of you is tired, all of you may be a little tired as well," he said sarcastically. "Now, everyone, drop and give me twenty!"

None of them hesitated. The bags dropped almost simultaneously as they looked for a clear spot to do their pushups.

"I can't hear you," SSG Brown said.

So the troops began counting off. "One ... two ... three ... four ... five ... six."

Now, contrary to what many people believe, not everyone who joins the military is athletic. Actually, there are many who have never done anything more physical than play dodge ball in their junior high gym class. So, after six, the numbers started dragging out a little bit. For most of them, twenty pushups was nothing, even after the lengthy travel and exhaustion they felt. But for those unfortunate few, the ones who were probably going to spend a lot of time in this position, ten seemed like a more realistic number. Several began to stand as they finished their twenty.

"What do you think you're doing?"

"I'm done, Staff Sergeant Brown," one of the soldiers replied.

"I never told you to get up. Now get back on the ground, all of you!"

Everyone stayed on the ground until all thirty-five of them were finished or couldn't do anymore.

"What a disgrace," SSG Brown said, appalled but not shocked. "My grandmother can do more than twenty pushups, and she's seventy-six years old."

As the week went by, Jason began to think that SSG Brown's grandma was Wonder Woman, because she could do more of everything than any of the recruits could do.

"On your feet!"

Exhausted, everyone slowly repositioned themselves in a standing position back in line. SGG Brown told the new soldiers to go in the building and sit quietly where his assistants tell them to. They filed in and sat, quiet as mice. By this time, Jason (and everyone else) was completely worn out. It was almost twelve thirty at night, and it appeared there was no bedtime in sight. One of SSG

Brown's assistants came over and stood in front of where they were sitting.

"My name is Sgt. Ramirez, and that's how each of you will address me. Got it?"

"Yes, Sgt. Ramirez."

"Now, for the next seven or so days, you will be spending all of your time in and around this building, completing everything necessary before we send you off to boot camp. Understand?"

"Yes, Sgt. Ramirez."

"Up and down this building, there are rooms on both sides of the hallway, and that's where all of the work will be completed."

SSG Brown interrupted. "From here on out, everything you fools do will be done in the order in which you are told, not what you think might be right. Got it?"

"Yes, Staff Sergeant Brown."

Sgt. Ramirez continued to tell the new recruits about the rules and regulations for what was to take place over the next several days. When he was done speaking, he called them to their feet. Finally, they were told they were going to their new house to get some sleep. This *house*, as he liked to call it, was nothing more than a raggedy, old, open-bay building that had bunk beds lining both sides of the walls and a community shower. By the time they got into their racks, it was almost 2:00 AM. Most everyone fell fast asleep, but not Jason. He lay in bed, letting all of the day's events settle in, contemplating if he had made the right decision. It took little time for him to realize that, although the next nine weeks were going to be living hell, it was all just a step towards reaching his ultimate goal. This gave Jason a little bit of comfort, at least enough to let him fall asleep.

Well, this night's sleep (and the next several weeks') was short-lived.

"Wake up, wake up. Rise and shine. It's time to get up and get dressed," SSG Brown and his loving companions shouted collectively before the sun was even up.

"You have fifteen minutes to get dressed and be outside in formation," SSG Brown ordered.

Not even realizing what time it was, they all jumped out of bed and got dressed as fast as they possibly could. Unfortunately for all of them, there were a few knuckleheads who insisted on taking a shower. Twenty minutes had passed before everyone was finally standing in formation.

"Well, running a little late, are we? I got a cure for that. Drop and give me twenty," SSG Brown insisted.

Again some struggled, so all of them had to stay down until everyone was finished.

"On your feet!"

SSG Brown was standing tall, looking fully at rest and ready for another day of yelling at new troops. *This guy needs a hug,* Jason thought.

"Well, it's 0600 already. That's 6:00 AM for those of you idiots who don't know military time."

Jason couldn't believe it. *Four hours of sleep?* he thought. *This is crazy.* But it was true, and he would learn to get used to it.

"It's chow time," SSG Brown shouted.

In formation, of course, the group was marched to the chow hall, and when they arrived they were given the guidelines for their behavior inside: sit down, shut up, eat, get up, get back outside and in formation, and wait for everyone else to do the same. After chow, they were given instructions on what was going take place over the next several days and how it would happen. The group then moved to the building they were in last night and began the long and tenuous process of soldier preparedness.

Basically, this week was not much more than an extended week at the MEPS. Paperwork (which seemed endless), shots, purchasing basic supplies (soap, shampoo, deodorant, etc.), getting all of the necessary military clothing, more paperwork, the infamous haircut, pushups, learning basic commands, eat, some sleep, finalizing all of the paperwork, and rechecking everything that had been completed during the past week. All of this took place in what seemed to be a very short period of time.

Finally, the recruits were able to make their first phone call before loading up the cattle trucks and heading down range, where basic training would begin. The purpose of the phone call was to let family members know that they were about to leave for camp and that they were doing okay. They were given two minutes each to place a call. When Jason's turn came, he rushed to put in the calling card information and dialed his home number. Fortunately, his dad answered the phone immediately.

"Dad?"

"Yeah, Jason, it's me. Are you doing okay?"

"I'm fine. We only have two minutes, so I just want to let you know that things are okay. We've been doing inprocessing all week and are leaving to start boot camp soon. How's Mom?"

"She's good. She says she loves and misses you."

Jason, swallowing hard and trying to hold back tears, replied, "I love you guys. I'll call again sometime soon. Tell my friends I'm doing just fine."

"Will do, buddy," Ray said, holding back his own tears. "I'm proud of you, son. Good luck."

"Thanks, Dad. Bye."

And with that, Jason fell back into formation and waited for further instructions. After about another ten minutes, everyone was done with his or her phone calls and back in formation. SSG Brown then informed them that the cattle trucks were on the way.

Cattle trucks were used for the transporting new *boots* (slang term for recruits until they finish boot camp) as a tool of degradation, as if they were not human but a herd of animals. The trucks arrived after a couple of minutes, and the boots loaded up.

As if they needed any motivation, SSG Brown and his psychopathic accomplices were screaming at them, "Hurry up!" and "Pack it in!"

Jason rushed into the truck as quickly as he could while carrying two heavy duffle bags. When the truck was finally packed and on its way, Jason looked at the guy standing next to him.

"Man, it's hot in here," Jason said, "you'd think they could at least have some air-conditioning in these things. I can hardly breath."

The soldier hesitated for a second as he struggled to get a grip on his bags, and then responded, "Gotta love it. Packed in a truck like sardines with all of this crap—no air, can barely breath—and all this in the state of Missouri," he said, pronouncing *Missouri* like *misery*, "one of the hottest places to be in the summer. Boy I'm glad I joined the army."

Jason simply nodded and tried as hard as he could not to think about his current state of affairs, as hard as that was. He knew this was just part of the process, and in the end, it would all be worth it.

The three cattle trucks carrying the troops, about forty on each, finally came to a halt. But there was no movement. Everyone stood impatiently, waiting for something to happen. Finally, the doors opened, and what took place next was for some the scariest moment of their lives. There were several drill sergeants standing outside each of the trucks, screaming, name calling, cursing, and spitting (unintentionally) at everyone as they filed off of the truck and into a building, where more drill sergeants awaited. "Get of my truck, you worthless pieces of shit!" one of them yelled.

Jason's turn came, and when he got out of the truck, he immediately made a *big* mistake. He looked one of the drill sergeants in the eyes—only those eyes were about six inches above his.

"What the hell are you looking at?" The man made of cinderblocks screamed.

"Nothing, sergeant," Jason said, quivering as he struggled to hold his two duffle bags.

"Is that so? You think I'm nothing?"

"No, sergeant," Jason said, sounding like a five-year-old who was just caught stealing candy.

"Well, guess what?"

"What, sergeant?"

"Get down and push the pavement!"

Jason commenced doing as he was told. It was clear to Jason and everyone else around him that this push-up crap was going to be a regular treat. As he lay parallel to the ground, Jason looked around, noticing about fifteen other recruits doing the same. Now he didn't feel so bad, at least psychologically. After about thirty pushups, Jason was told to get moving. He joined up with the rest of the newly formed company inside a building, which was actually a gymnasium. As he entered the room, he noticed drill sergeants scattered all around the room, screaming at various individuals as they emptied their bags. In fact, that's what everyone was doing— emptying their bags.

The drill sergeants were making the troops go through all of their stuff and informing them of what they could and could not have, not hesitating to point out things that could embarrass them. Jason made the mistake of laughing when a female drill sergeant held up a pair of bikini underwear that one male troop had in his bag. Jason's three seconds of giggling led to many laps around the gym. This process in the gym was not something unique to his group. Each time new troops arrived, they were sent to the gym, where they were told to dump their bags and take out things that are not allowed at boot camp. Essentially, they could only have basic personal hygiene items and military clothing. Everything else went into one bag and was locked up in storage until basic training was completed.

Not only were bags being checked, but there was also a lot of PT going on. In fact, the military likes to use the word *smoking* for this kind of PT. It's non-stop moving for an extended period of time. For those who are not in shape, this process often leads to muscle failure and vomiting. Smoking takes place almost every day throughout basic training, but gets less intense as time goes by. It goes a long way towards improving physical fitness.

This initial smoking lasted for about two hours, and when it was over, they were taken to their barracks. They would maintain residence in the same barracks throughout the duration of basic training. They had a brief one-hour period to put their stuff away in their wall lockers and take a much-needed breather. These barracks were set up not unlike college dormitories. There were about ten rooms to a floor, and two community bathrooms, or latrines, on each. Each room housed eight troops and consisted of four bunk beds, which at this time had no linens. That would come later.

Jason lay on an empty bed, trying to relax both his mind and body, as an opportunity for this had not really occurred since he left home. Well, that too was short-lived, as the one hour lasted about fifteen minutes. Typical of early training phases, the drill sergeants liked to keep everyone on their toes. The recruits stood in formation when they got outside, anxiously awaiting instructions. The drill sergeants were standing around as well, until one of them, the big guy who screamed at Jason when he got off of the truck, came walking out of the front door, as if he were the king amongst his people. Basic training was officially under way. Today was the first of many miserable, hot, tiring, and depressing days to come. Such is the life of a soldier at boot camp, where you are broken down to next to nothing and built back up to be a soldier.

The big man stood in front of them, looking from side to side as if he was sizing up the company. By this time, the ninety-seven men and twenty-two women had broken down into three equal platoons, one platoon being a person short of forty.

"Listen up," the big man said with a deep, bellowing voice. "My name is Sgt. First Class Thomas," he said, his accent about as Southern as they come, "and I will be your acting company first sergeant for your entire stay here at the Wood. These other sergeants will be here as well to assist me and all of you in getting you trained in what it takes to be a soldier in the United States Army."

This statement alone sent chills up Jason's spine. SFC Thomas continued.

"Most of you will get through these next eight weeks with no major problems; but there's always a select few who don't have what it takes and are forced to say good-bye while the rest of you go on. We're gonna do a lot of soldier skills training, a lot of physical training, or PT, as I like to call it, and then we're gonna do a lot more PT, and then some more training. Do as you're told, speak only when spoken to, follow the rules, and you just might make it all the way. Screw up, and I get mad. And when I get mad, so do these other fine soldiers here working with me. The result of that: not good."

SFC Thomas informed the new recruits how the barracks would be broken down and who would be rooming with whom. So all of the items that were unpacked earlier—you guessed it—were packed up again. The recruits also learned which of them would start out as the squad and platoon leaders. Each platoon had four squads, and each squad had ten soldiers, except for one. Three platoons meant three platoon leaders and a total of twelve squad leaders. And since nothing was known about any of these new troops, SFC Thomas asked for volunteers. Now, if there is one thing that anyone should learn in the military, no matter what branch of service that may be, *do not* volunteer. It's a recipe for trouble, especially in this situation. Of course, there were those eager few who jumped on the chance to take these leadership positions, but they wouldn't last long. Any time anyone screws up, the squad leader and then the platoon leader are responsible for that person. And since everyone was new at this, there were bound to be screw-ups.

After all of this was established, SFC Thomas completed roll call, with the squad and platoon leaders writing down the names of the soldiers in their squads. Following roll call, everyone was put back into his or her places in formation. The platoons were then given ten minutes to get their stuff moved from their current locations into their new rooms and lockers. Mass chaos ensued. Imagine 119 people trying to get to four different floors (the females had their own floor) using two doors, and then packing their stuff and trying to move from floor to floor with all of their belongings. Well, it is impossible, and the drill sergeants knew that. At the end of ten minutes, all of the drill sergeants were in the building, screaming at everyone to get outside. As everyone filed out of the doors, they were given orders to go straight to the big yard in front of the building (a place with which they would become all too familiar) and get into the front leaning rest position (push up position) and commence counting. *Smoking* was in full effect.

For the next thirty minutes, SFC Thomas and the others were yelling about not being efficient and punctual, using several expletives in between. By now, the troops were really struggling to perform the exercises.

"On your feet," SFC Thomas shouted. "Fall out to your rooms."

They were finally given ample time to get situated and take a breather in their new rooms. This was the first time that Jason and the others had an opportunity to talk the entire week. They talked about some of the things that had occurred and how bad this training sucked. They also talked about where they were from and why they joined the army. Jason was able to remind himself why he was here and enduring this torture, as many put it. Shortly after their discussion, they filed back outside and into formation in preparation for movement to the chow hall. Many of the troops had a difficult time eating, as their stomachs were bothered by all of the PT. But not Jason. He sucked his food down and was ready for more, but that wasn't going to happen. In boot camp, you get what you eat and eat what you get, or something like that.

Again they filed out into formation and waited for instructions. Once together, they were told that they would be getting their bed linens and learning how to make their racks. *Make my rack?* Jason thought to himself. But this isn't what most non-military types would think. This is a big thing in the military, and there is only one way to do it: the right way. They went to the linen building (there's a building for everything on a base), drew their linens, and then headed back to the barracks, where they were given a class on the proper way to make their beds. It seemed easy enough, but it was a little tedious. Every layer had to be a certain way, and every fold had to be a certain way. Once they were taught how to do this, they had to go in, do it themselves, and then get inspected.

Well, everyone finished, and no one passed inspection. They would eventually learn to do it right. There's a pattern that develops during the beginning phases of boot camp. Nothing is ever done right or on time. It's the old philosophy that practice makes perfect. Well, in boot camp, there is a lot of practice for everything, from shining boots, to marching, to doing first aid, to shooting an M-16 A-2 rifle. The thought is that in the end, everyone will be successful and be doing everything the same, or close to it. There is no individualism in the military.

After the first week, the soldiers were able to make a phone call home to say they were doing fine. Again they were given two minutes, so there was little time to say anything else. Jason called Ray, and they had the same conversation as the week before, only this time Jason sounded a little more worn out, as to be expected. Soldiers in basic training are allotted some time to write home most evenings and are allowed to receive letters in the mail as well.

During the second week, Jason's name was called during mail call. It was a letter from Shannon. He couldn't wait to get it open. When they were dismissed, Jason rushed to his rack and ripped open the letter. In it, Shannon wrote how nervous she had been about calling him, but she was glad she did. She stated how proud of him she was and that she couldn't wait to see him when he returned. Jason momentarily forgot about how rough things were going so far and pictured himself back home, sitting on a couch, watching a movie with Shannon, laughing about the good old times, and talking about their future together. He could hardly contain himself. He wanted to yell out with excitement, but realized that probably wasn't the best place. His life was moving ahead as he planned, and Shannon coming back into his life was a bonus.

Jason was awestricken. He couldn't believe everything that was happening to him. It was surreal. He was finally at basic training after two years of waiting, he got into a good school close to home, and now the only girl he ever loved was communicating with him and he was going to see her when his training was completed. After reading this letter, Jason took a shower, got his clothes ready for the morning, and went to sleep, getting his best night's sleep in a few weeks. Morning came quickly for Jason, but today felt like a new day. As if he did not have enough motivation before the letter, now his level of determination and pride had increased even more.

Over the next several weeks, the recruits did a lot of PT and sat in on a lot of classes, from map reading to first aid to how to talk on an army radio. Everything was done until everyone was on the same page and understood how to do it, and then it was on to the next new task. There was little time to sleep and a lot of time to train and do PT. PT was done daily, and there were periodic PT tests that each soldier had to pass. These consisted of push-ups, sit-ups, and a two-mile run. There were not too many people who passed the first couple, but by the end, only a few did not pass. Jason was no exception. He always finished with one of the highest scores. As the weeks of boot camp passed by, a lot of positive things were happening for Jason.

First of all, he was being recognized by the drill sergeants as a great soldier and natural leader. They were especially impressed with his medical knowledge. Second, Jason was very well liked amongst his peers, and he made a lot of new friends. Two of them were actually going to be in his unit when he returned home and another was going into the medical program at Penn State. It did not take long before Jason was appointed as the platoon leader, a position he maintained throughout the duration of boot camp. Finally, and maybe most important to Jason, Shannon continued writing to him expressing all of the feelings she had for him and the excitement she felt about seeing him when he returned.

With basic training graduation around the corner, Jason was feeling better than ever. During the last couple of weeks, the drill sergeants eased up a little on the soldiers and would even have conversations with some of them from time to time. One evening, as Jason was shining his boots, another soldier came into Jason's room and told him that SFC Thomas wanted to see him. It was almost never a good thing when a drill sergeant wanted to see you, especially the first sergeant. Jason nervously hurried to SFC Thomas's office.

"Private Henson reporting as requested, drill sergeant," Jason said, clearly nervous as his legs trembled a little.

"At ease, private. Take a seat."

Jason sat down in a chair across the desk from SFC Thomas.

"Private," he said in a calm tone, "I don't usually do this, but I brought you down here to tell you that I have been quite impressed with you. I've done many cycles of basic training, and I can't remember any recruits who performed with so much energy, passion, and determination as you have. You are going to make one hell of a soldier when your training is done."

Jason, stunned with what he was hearing, hesitated, but responded. "Thank you, drill sergeant," Jason said, fighting back a smile. "I've wanted to be a soldier for several years, and I'm proud to have the honor of doing so."

SFC Thomas, not knowing the appropriate follow-up, replied, "Keep up the good work. You can go back to what you were doing. Dismissed."

Jason stood, and off to his room he went. This was the exclamation point. If he ever had any doubts about making this decision, they were now gone. Jason never told anyone about that conversation, not even his dad. This was his memory, and his alone.

With graduation just four days away, the troops were busy getting everything done so they could be ready. The next few days would consist of cleaning equipment, turning stuff in, practicing for the graduation ceremony, and continuing PT. Physical training never stops in the army. Next, the troops were allowed some time to use the phone, and this time it was for more than two minutes. Jason called his father first and solidified plans for graduation. Ray and Angie were flying to Missouri to see their son graduate. After plans were discussed and Jason caught his dad up to speed on what had happened so far, he abruptly ended the conversation. Since this was the first opportunity to use the phone for an extensive amount of time, there was one other person he wanted to call. After he dialed the numbers and the phone began to ring, the butterflies began flying in his stomach.

"Hello," a soft voice said at the other end.

"Shannon? It's Jason."

"Jason, oh my gosh. How are you?"

Although the two of them corresponded through several letters, this was the first time they had a chance to talk directly to one another. After Jason answered, the two of them spent the next half hour discussing their letters and catching up on what life had been like over the last couple of months. It was clear that when Jason returned home, this friendship was going to turn into something more, but neither of them said that directly over the phone. The two ended by saying they would talk soon. Jason was floating. He knew he had his old love back.

Graduation day was finally here. Ray and Angie arrived the day before and had a couple of hours to spend with Jason. At dinner, they discussed community gossip, and Jason talked about some of the crazy things that took place during training. After dinner, Ray and Angie went back to their hotel and Jason to the barracks. The next day was great. The ceremony was beautiful, and basic training was finally over. Jason was able to spend a few more hours with his parents but had to report back that night, as he had to report for Advanced Individual Training, or AIT, tomorrow. It was an emotional evening, but everything was very positive. They parted ways over a few tears of joy. It wouldn't be long before they would be seeing each other again. For now, however, it was good-bye.

Chapter 3: AIT (Advanced Individual Training)

USUALLY WHEN A RECRUIT FINISHES boot camp, he or she must pack again and go through the same process leading to Fort Leonard Wood, which consists of driving, waiting, flying, waiting, driving again, and finally arriving at the new base for inprocessing. But Jason was lucky. His AIT was right there on the Wood. Motor Transportation Operator Training was located right down the road from Jason's current barracks, so he only had to walk a short distance to get there. Plus, he had a few buddies with him, Privates Bay and Rose, which made the transition easier. Together, the three privates walked to the new training area, and within minutes, they were checking in and setting up their rooms. Although they had to report that day, which was Friday, they were not going to start actual training until Monday. Because they were early and not many other trainees had arrived yet, the three of them were able to room together. They were sitting around on their bunks when they heard someone walking down the hallway towards them. It was a drill sergeant.

"What the hell are you three punks doing?"

Jason spoke for them.

"We just arrived, drill sergeant, from right down the street."

"Did you check in?"

"Yes."

"Well, you won't be sitting around here all weekend. Come with me."

Some things never change, Jason thought to himself.

The drill sergeant showed the privates where the shed was and told them to get in there and get to work. No specific directions were given, but the three soldiers understood clearly when they opened the shed doors. There was about every outdoor tool imaginable packed in there, and so it was clear that *area beautification* was what the drill sergeant had in mind.

The three of them, along with everyone else who sporadically showed up for AIT, spent the rest of the weekend cutting grass, trimming weeds , picking up garbage, and raking. It wasn't too bad. They were able to work at their own pace, plus they had a couple of opportunities to use the phone and go the Post Exchange, or PX, to get some new supplies.

The weekend went by quickly, and by Monday morning, there were about fifty soldiers in formation. Even though AIT is not as strict as BCT, there are still a lot of restrictions and a lot of yelling. While there were not as many soldiers at AIT as in basic training, initially there was the same amount of drill sergeants. That number would gradually decrease as time passed.

Just like BCT, there was a drill sergeant who came to the front of the formation. If there were a mascot for the army motto, "mean, green fighting machine," this guy was it. *Incredible Hulk, without the green skin,* Jason thought.

"My name is Sgt. First Class Henderson, and I'll be in charge of you until you complete AIT. Just because you finished BCT doesn't mean you're now a soldier. You still have to show me and my staff that you are capable of doing this job. And don't think it's as simple as driving a truck. There's a lot more that comes with it."

He introduced his staff and then ordered everyone to march down the gravel road to a nearby one-story, rectangular, aluminum building, where, inside, they would learn exactly what the next six weeks would entail. SFC Henderson was right: there was a lot more to it. Not only were they going to learn to drive the various military cargo trucks, but they would also learn basic mechanics, road signs, tactical movements, and other specifics pertaining to driving in a combat theater. For Jason, the next several weeks were actually rather fun. It was not unlike taking a driver's license course, except on a larger scale, with a few more obstacles. As expected, he picked up on most things right away and quickly found himself in a leadership role again, assisting the instructors with the troops who were having a difficult time. SFC Henderson took a liking to Jason and let him know that.

"Private Henson, come over here," SFC Henderson yelled to Jason.

"Yes, sergeant," Jason replied as he ran across the parking lot through the line of trucks.

Before Jason could get a breath and say a word, SFC Henderson stated, "Henson," with his deep, bellowing voice, "every now and again we get someone through here who excels beyond our expectations. Well, son, this cycle you're that person."

"Thank you, sergeant," Jason replied, trying to hold back a smile.

"I don't want that to go to your head now; you need to keep it up. And don't expect any special treatment."

"No, sergeant."

"I just thought you should know. Maybe it'll be some extra motivation. Our army needs good leaders. Now get back to work."

And with that, Jason headed back to the trucks. He had a newfound motivation for getting the work done and helping the other troops. He was now in the spotlight, and he couldn't afford to screw up.

The first five weeks came and went, so it was time for the final test week. There would be written, oral, and hands-on testing. This process was more of a learning and review process, as soldiers who make it to AIT are almost guaranteed to pass, and the instructors make sure of that. Jason and his fellow soldiers passed with flying colors, and by week's end, they were all experts (at least in their minds) on every truck they trained with. Although there was a graduation ceremony, it was not as boisterous as graduation from BCT. The company commander gave a speech about the importance of motor transportation operators in the army, and then they were pinned with a ribbon signifying completion of AIT. Soon, they were released, and Jason was well on his way to returning to the little town of Harrisville, Pennsylvania, now a soldier and excited to get on with his life.

When he arrived at the airport, his mom and dad were waiting for him with open arms.

"Welcome home, son," both of them said as they hugged him.

"It's good to be back."

"You look great," his mom said.

"Thanks, Mom," Jason said with a smile. "They worked our butts off."

"Well, now you can relax a little," Ray responded.

"I can't wait. Let's get out of here." Jason said, eager to get home.

They grabbed Jason's bags and headed to the car.

Jason could hardly contain himself. He couldn't wait to show off his new uniform and tell his stories. He especially couldn't wait to see Shannon.

As they got closer to home, Jason noticed some signs hanging from the houses and telephone poles. He missed what the first few had on them, but the next one he saw read, "Welcome Home, Jason. We're So Proud of You!" The next one said the same thing. And the next one, and the next one.

"Who did all of these?" Jason asked.

"A lot of people got involved," Angie replied. "So many people are very proud of you."

"This is awesome."

As they arrived at the house, Jason noticed a lot more cars than usual for that area. But he didn't think much of it as he headed for the door.

Ray reached over Jason and unlocked the door. "Welcome home, son. I love you," his dad said to him.

Jason turned the knob and walked in.

"Surprise!"

Jason stepped back, startled by the unexpected welcome.

"Welcome home, Jason," several of the people shouted.

Jason walked in with a huge smile on his face.

"Thank you," he replied.

Several of his friends and neighbors had gathered at the house to surprise Jason and make sure they let him know they were proud of him for his service. He was a popular guy, and a lot of people cared for him and wanted to show it.

As he shook hands and gave hugs, he struggled to hold back tears. After the greetings, everyone headed for the kitchen, where lots of good food and drinks awaited. The party lasted a few hours before the last person was gone. It was a good day. Jason was back, and he was now ready to serve his country, both publicly and militarily.

Jason spent the next several days resting, watching television, doing a little bit of PT, and catching up with his friends and family. He also discussed some of what he had been through for the past fifteen weeks. Although everyone was elated to see Jason and know that he was doing okay, after a couple of days, the excitement wore off and it seemed that everyone went back to their usual business. This was a little depressing for Jason, but he understood. Besides, Jason was ready to get back to everyday life. But before doing so, he had one more visit to make. Looking his best in his army dress green uniform, Jason drove to his old high school to pay a visit to Mr. Stein. He also figured that SSG Anderson would be there, knowing his recruiting never stopped.   When Jason arrived at the school, he entered through the main doors, chest sticking out and head held high, and reported to the main office to get a pass to go to the counselors' office. As Jason approached the counselors' office, he noticed that SSG Anderson was in there, talking to a student. Jason quietly walked up to them.

"Don't listen to a word he says," Jason said sarcastically.

"Hey, Jason. How you doing?" replied SSG Anderson.

"I'm great."

"Looking good."

"Thanks."

SSG Anderson finished his discussion with the student and then began talking with Jason, getting all of the details of his experience. Mr. Stein came out while they were talking and shook Jason's hand.

"Good to see you, Jason. You look great."

"Thanks. Good to see you, too, Mr. Stein."

For the next forty-five minutes or so, the three of them talked about their experiences at boot camp, basically ignoring the fact that two of them were there for a job. As they finished up and said their good-byes, Jason thanked them for their advice and went on his way. This would be the last time the three of them were together for quite some time.

Jason completed his day by doing a little shopping and stopping in his dad's office for a visit, which Ray always appreciated. Jason retired to his house for the evening and began contemplating his next move. When Ray returned from work, he noticed that Jason was preoccupied with something, as he sat in the recliner with a perplexed look on his face.

"What's on your mind, Jason?"

"Well, I was just thinking about what I'm going to do until school starts and was wondering if I should call Shannon."

Jason had not yet told his dad about their correspondence during BCT and AIT.

"I thought you were going to help me around the office," Ray said, remembering the comments Jason made before leaving.

"You mean I really can?"

"Sure. I'll even pay you a little bit. Just give me a couple days to get things set up."

"Great, Dad. Thanks."

"Now, what's going on with Shannon?" Ray asked with a snide grin.

Jason told his father about all of the communication they had and the feelings they expressed to one another.

As any excited, caring father would, Ray asked Jason, "What in the hell are you waiting for, son?"

"I don't know. I guess I'm a little nervous."

"Jason," Ray responded assertively, "You just went through fifteen weeks of intense military training, and you're afraid to call a girl?"

Jason thought about that response, pausing for a moment. "You're right."

Jason called Shannon, and the two of them had a great conversation. In fact, they made plans to get together over the holidays for a date. Over the next couple of months, Jason and Shannon spent a lot of time on the phone, reminiscing about their days together. Because all of his friends were away at school, this was about the only thing Jason spent time doing besides working for his dad. He was getting bored, and he was anxious to see Shannon. Between returning home from AIT and getting started at school, Jason did have a couple of weekend drills with the reserves, and even though he was excited to get that part of his life started, his focus was elsewhere. He couldn't stop thinking about being with Shannon again.

The holidays finally arrived, and Jason and Shannon got together as planned. They got along like they were never apart. In fact (as if it needed to be said), they decided to try dating again to see how it would work. And why not? They got along great before and were now going to be at the same school. The holidays came and went, and it was now time for Jason to begin the next phase of his life.

Chapter 4: College Life

RAY SET JASON UP WITH a two-bedroom apartment in State College and helped him move in. Once things were settled, Ray gave Jason a little bit of spending cash, wished him luck, and was on his way. Shannon arrived shortly thereafter, and they spent the rest of the evening together. They couldn't be happier. The two of them spent the weekend before classes began touring the campus, and Shannon showed Jason where his classrooms were located. Afterwards, they headed back to Jason's apartment to finish setting up the place. Shannon spent the rest of the weekend at Jason's place, something that would become the norm.

Monday arrived, and Jason was finally beginning classes in college. He was so excited, although that excitement wore off as he learned how difficult his curriculum would be. Nevertheless, he constantly reminded himself that if he could make it through basic training and AIT, he could get through anything. Well, he was right. He passed all of his classes his first semester, all As except for one B. Additionally, things between him and Shannon were going great. This year was definitely getting off on the right foot.

That summer was his first summer of true freedom. This was the first time he was out on his own with no parental control. Every kid's dream, right? Well, the summer wasn't as great as Jason had hoped, and he would soon find out that although the reserve drills were only one weekend a month, the training always seemed to interfere with something he wanted to do. In addition to missing his family reunion and Shannon's family reunion, he also endured another blow because of his two-week training. Shannon and her family invited Jason to go to Florida for ten days for their vacation. As it turned out, that ten days coincided with Jason's first annual training in Fort Chaffee, Arkansas. So while Shannon and her family were basking in the warm sun on the beaches of Miami, Florida, Jason was spending a lot of time driving around in a five-ton truck with no air conditioning in one-hundred-degree weather. Not ideal, but it was all part of being a soldier.

Jason's first annual training was not all bad. He did learn a lot about tactical driving, and he did get to have a little bit of fun. At one point, they played war games using the multiple integrated laser engagement system, or MILES, gear, which is just like laser tag. Jason got to be on the attacking force. He loved it. However, it was not nearly as exciting and fun as Miami would have been. Nevertheless, he did get through training, and when he was done, he returned to his apartment in State College, where Shannon was waiting for him. They spent most of the rest of the summer together, going to movies and dinner, heading back home to visit family, and simply lounging around, enjoying the time they had together. The fall semester approached rather quickly, and it was back to the grind, as some students might say.

Over the next few years, everything seemed to go as planned. Jason and Shannon were doing really well as a couple and excelling in their education. Most of Jason's drill weekends consisted of mainly the same thing: driving the various vehicles, doing PT, and keeping up on basic military training, such as first aid and weapons qualification. His annual two weeks of training were basically the same as his first year. The first week was always spent in the field, living as a soldier would in a combat environment (tents, field chow, port-a-johns, and foxholes), all the while practicing driving trucks and playing war games. Over the next two years, Jason began to feel the monotony of being a reservist, wondering if it was ever going to be as exciting as he had once hoped. But he kept going strong and fulfilled his commitment to his utmost capabilities. In fact, as was the case since the beginning of BCT, Jason was always recognized as a leader and a great soldier, so much so that he attained the rank of sergeant in less than four years, and staff sergeant wasn't too far off. School was basically the same, where Jason shined in all of his classes. He had a knack for his chosen path.

Shannon was completing her studies towards becoming a teacher and was going to graduate in May of 1997. Jason still had a long way to go, but he was nearing the end of his undergraduate degree, with one more semester to go. During spring break of 1997, Jason and Shannon went to visit her family in Ohio. While they were there, on a night when Shannon and her mother were preparing dinner, Jason and her dad, Allen, sat outside on the back porch swing, shooting the bull, enjoying the cool evening breeze and the beautiful city skyline. Allen noticed that Jason appeared a little nervous, as he kept looking down and twiddling his fingers.

"What's wrong, Jason?"

"Well, Mr. Miller," Jason said anxiously, "I wanted to ask you a question."

"Well, what is it?"

"You know how much Shannon and I love each other."

"Yeah," Allen responded, as if he knew what was to follow.

"Well, I wanted to know what you think about me asking her to marry me."

Without hesitation, Allen responded, "I think that would be wonderful."

Jason was so excited. "Thank you, Mr. Miller. You won't be disappointed."

The two of them were called in for dinner shortly after this discussion, and not a word was mentioned. Jason and Allen could barely contain themselves. Over the next couple of days, Jason and Shannon spent a lot of time studying and completing papers for school. When Friday finally arrived, they headed back to school. Jason wasn't going to pop the question until Shannon graduated, but he wanted to get asking her dad permission out of the way.

Graduation quickly arrived, and Shannon was finally done with school. Both of their families attended her ceremony, and everyone went to dinner afterwards. Although Jason had always imagined asking Shannon to marry him in a romantic fashion, he now felt compelled to ask her with their families present. Well, as they sat at the table having a few drinks, Jason knew he had to make a move. As the dinner progressed, Jason grew more nervous. In fact, at one point, he knocked over a glass of water and bumped his chair back into a passing waiter, not paying attention to what he was doing. His mind was completely occupied with what he was about to do. Finally, Jason decided to ask the question.

"Can I have everybody's attention please?" Jason nervously asked, trying to be quiet enough so those at his table would be the only ones to hear him.

Everyone stopped what they were doing and looked towards him, their eyes feeling like laser beams to Jason.

He looked around, hoping no one else in the restaurant was looking, as he was already extremely nervous. He then moved his chair back and got down on one knee beside Shannon. She knew what was happening and began to cry. By this time, several patrons in the restaurant were watching, too.

"Shannon, you know how much I love you, and I couldn't think of a better time than this to ask you if you would like to spend the rest of your life with me. So, will you marry me?"

Without even taking a second to think, Shannon blurted out, "Yes." She wrapped her arms around him.

Cheers, claps, and whistles came from throughout the restaurant. Jason and Shannon's mothers were crying along with Shannon, and their dads were clapping. Everyone was ecstatic. Aside from Jason's few nervous miscues, the evening was perfect. The rest of the evening was spent mostly discussing wedding ideas and what Shannon's intentions were now that she has graduated. Although she had already made her decision, she had not told her family that she planned to go to graduate school for teaching. While they were excited for her to begin her career, they were happy just the same to hear this news. What a night this turned out to be.

The following summer, aside from wedding planning, was not much different than the previous few. Jason decided to take a couple of classes to get ahead, and Shannon did the same. His training this year was back at Fort Chaffee, so nothing exciting would happen there, with the exception of a few heat casualties. School started and seemed to end just as fast. Jason had his graduation ceremony in December and was to begin medical school in January, so it wasn't as exciting as when Shannon graduated. The next couple of years went by as everyone would have expected. Jason did great in school and was promoted to staff sergeant, one of the fastest promotions to this rank in his company's history. Time was flying by for the both of them, as they were so busy with all they had going on in their lives.

It was now the fall of 1999, and Shannon was going to graduate with her master's degree. She was hired almost immediately at a nearby elementary school, and now both of them felt it was time to get married. Since one of them was now working, which was what they were waiting for, they could plan a wedding and look for a new home.

During this time, another big decision had to be made. Jason's initial six-year active enlistment in the reserves was completed, so he had to decide whether to enter into inactive reserve status for two years or stay active. Well, the decision was not as complicated as they thought it would be. Because Jason had some schooling left and they could use the money, he decided to maintain active status for the final two-year period rather than go to Individual Ready Reserve. That way, he could continue to use his GI Bill money.

Since Jason knew that his annual training was going to be in July of 2000, he and Shannon went ahead and made all of the wedding plans for August following his training. Although they made most of their plans together, the finishing touches were done by Shannon and her mother. Angie had her say as well. These were exciting times. Jason only had one more year of school and then his residency, they were going to get married, Shannon had a full-time job, and everyone in their family was doing great.

Summer came quickly. By now they were cramming in wedding plans, frantically trying to ensure they got everything they wanted and all of it was in place. But with the help of their families, everything worked out great. When Jason returned from his training in Virginia, it was time to get married. Although this was a huge step for them, they had been together so long that they were very comfortable with the decision. All of their friends and family made it to the wedding, and everything turned out beautifully.

Everyone involved did their jobs without error. The decorations in the church were done by a professional wedding planner, so everything looked great. Shannon's dress, which was altered a little from the time her grandmother wore it, looked like it was made for her. And Jason, of course, was as handsome as ever in his black tuxedo with baby blue tie and vest. They had their reception at the fire hall in Harrisville, the main event center for anything happening in the city, so not only did the people who were invited show up, but many people throughout the city also showed up just to congratulate them. No one seemed to mind. The party went on for several hours as everyone sang, danced, took pictures, and ate. Everyone had a great time.

The reception ended around 11:00 PM, at which time the newlyweds left to catch a plane for their honeymoon in the Bahamas. For what seemed like the first time in years, the happily married couple was finally going to get a break and spend some time focusing solely on each other. It couldn't have turned out better. Aside from a couple short rain showers, the weather was a sunny eighty to eighty-five degrees every day, and the food was to die for—fresh seafood and fine wine whenever they wanted. Perfect.

The dream vacation finally came to an end, and the newlyweds returned to their recently purchased home, which was located halfway between State College and Harrisville; that way, neither one of them would have to drive too far to get to where they needed to be. Jason knew he would eventually be working for his dad, a little less than thirty minutes away. Their life was heading in the right direction.

Jason was approaching his final year in the reserves. Although he didn't get the parade that he dreamed of, he did fulfill part of his dream by completing an enlistment in the reserves. But was that enough? Throughout Jason's final year of classes, he and Shannon had several discussions about what he should do. Shannon, as usual, told him she would be supportive of whatever decision he wanted to make, although deep down she really wanted him to get out. She was ready to focus on a family and didn't want to worry about him going somewhere. However, she knew how much Jason loved the army, and she didn't want him to be upset with her. Although he typically listened to what Shannon had to say, Jason felt her support alone was not enough. He needed more input. So he decided to go home alone for a weekend and seek the advice of the one person who had almost always been able to help him make the right decisions: his father.

Jason and his dad sat at the kitchen table for hours talking about this and every other decision Jason and Shannon had to make. Although his dad was well aware from the countless discussions throughout the years, Jason explained again to his dad his dream of being deployed.

"Dad, you know that joining the army was a dream of mine for several years, and I'm happy with the ways things have turned out. But the plans I had have not been entirely fulfilled."

"I know, Jason, but plans don't always work out as we'd like them to. Besides, you put your time in, more than most people would do. And now you have a wife, and maybe soon kids. I'm not telling you not to reenlist, but you have reasons, good reasons, not to. But I also know how stubborn you are, and deep down I know you'll reenlist anyway. And that's okay. But realize, you've done enough, and then some. I'm proud of you no matter what you do."

"I know, Dad. I appreciate that. But I think I need to give it one more shot. Maybe do a year or two at a time. See how it goes."

"Not a bad idea," his dad agreed. "A little at a time."

Jason returned home and informed Shannon of his decision.

"Shannon," Jason shouted as he entered the front door.

"Upstairs, honey," she replied. "In the bedroom."

Jason ran up the stairs, excited to tell her about what he had decided.

"Well," Jason said, "I've made my decision."

Shannon put down the shirt from the pile of clothes she was folding and sat on the bed. "Well, let's have it."

"I think you'll be happy," Jason said to her.

"Yeah, well?"

"I've decided the best thing for the both of us right now is to do one more year and take it from there. It will coincide with the beginning of my residency. Besides, we can use the money right now, and it will give us some time to think about what to do next."

"I can live with that," Shannon responded. "Maybe next time you will consider my thoughts a little more."

Jason, not used to hearing this tone from Shannon, thought about questioning her attitude, but quickly realized that he did make the decision sans her input. "Okay," he said with a smile. "It's a deal."

Jason gave her a kiss and left the room. The decision was final. Now he could focus on his final year of school, with one less thing to worry about, at least for the time being.

The spring semester went by quickly, and finally his time to shine had arrived. Jason was done with classes and could now get out there to do his residency and start practicing with his father. His family was very excited for him. Jason couldn't be happier. A third trip to Fort Chaffee, Arkansas, for annual training in nine years couldn't even bring him down. He was now on a mission. He was going to prove to himself and everyone else that this was the right career path for him. In his mind, and quite frankly in the minds of many other people, taking over his father's family practice was inevitable. He grew up in that office. He worked his butt off in school to get to this point. At last he could begin the work he always wanted to do.

The summer passed, and the first phase of Jason's residency went as expected. He quickly gained a reputation at the hospital as a quick learner with a great personality. He had the ability to make everyone laugh, even during difficult times. By now, Jason realized that this was the right choice for him. Realizing the importance of being a doctor and the responsibility that he was going to soon be taking on, he made the decision to finish up this year in the reserves and call it quits, with no regrets. But something happened just after summer ended that made Jason reconsider that decision.

In fact, what happened would ultimately change Jason's life and the lives of many other people forever.

Chapter 5: The Time Has Arrived

JASON SOMETIMES HAD AN OPTION of what shift he wanted to work at the hospital. He would often choose to work the midnight shift so he could be home when Shannon woke up in the morning and when she got home from school. He would sleep while she was away. The week that began September 10, 2001 was no different. That Tuesday, Jason finished his shift at 6:30 AM and headed home to make Shannon breakfast: a bagel with cream cheese, oatmeal, fruit, and some coffee. He was home by 7:00 and had her breakfast on the table by 7:15. They sat together at the kitchen table and discussed Jason's night at work. It was a rather slow night. Shannon had to be at the school by 8:00, so she was usually out the door by 7:45. Today was no different.

After Shannon left, Jason sat on the couch to watch the morning news. As usual, he dozed off by the time the weather segment was on. But something on the news woke him up. At around 8:46 that morning, there was a break in the news. The reporters announced that at precisely 8:45 AM, an airplane crashed into the north tower of the World Trade Center. For some reason this announcement woke Jason from his sleep. As they were discussing this, at 9:03, just eighteen minutes after the first crash, the reporter stated that another plane crashed into the south tower of the World Trade Center. By this time, Jason, as well as most of America, was glued to the television and knew this was no coincidence. Within the hour, all airports, bridges, and tunnels in the New York area had been ordered to close. America was being attacked. At 9:30,

President Bush, speaking from Florida, announced that America had suffered an apparent terrorist attack. Within fifteen minutes, at 9:43 AM, another plane crashed into the Pentagon, and less than thirty minutes later, another one went down in a rural area in Pennsylvania. As the details of the events of that morning began to unfold, Jason could only think of one thing, and this one thing was probably on the mind of every person serving in the armed forces at the time: *We're going to war.*

Shannon called Jason after the last plane went down.

"Are you watching the news?" Shannon asked.

"Every minute since the first plane hit," he responded.

"I can't believe this is happening," Shannon said. "Can you?"

Jason did not respond.

"Jason," Shannon shouted, "are you there?"

"Yeah, I'm here," he assured her. "Shannon, I need to get off of the phone. I'm going to call my unit to ask if there is something I should be doing."

"Okay," she replied. "Make sure you call me when you know something."

"I will," Jason said. "Talk to you later."

Jason hung up the phone and immediately called the armory. Apparently, he wasn't the only one calling the center, as it took him almost thirty minutes to get through. His unit administrator answered and, knowing the reason for the call simply stated that everyone was now on alert status, but no action needed to be taken as of yet. This wasn't enough for Jason. He called some of the guys in the unit to talk about what was happening. They all thought that America was going to go to war, but no one knew yet who was responsible.

After talking to a couple of the guys in the unit, Jason called Shannon back and informed her of what he was told. They abruptly ended the conversation, as they knew communication lines would be tied up and Jason was anxious to find out any news from his unit. Obviously, Jason did not get any sleep this day, but he couldn't have even if he had tried. The day passed, and no calls came in. When Shannon came home, she threw the front door open. Jason was on the couch, watching CNN. Shannon began asking several questions before Jason could answer one. She was panicking, shaking, and pacing.

"What did you find out? Can you believe this is happening? What are you going to have to do? How many people have been hurt?" Shannon was asking these questions as if she were running an auction. "What should we—"

Jason interrupted, "Slow down, Shannon. Relax. I can barely understand what you are saying. Take a breath, for crying out loud."

Shannon took a long, deep breath and sat down on the recliner next to the couch.

"We don't know anything yet," Jason explained. "We've been put on alert status, so we just have to be reachable by phone. I doubt we have to do anything."

Although Jason said this to ease her anxiety a little, he really had no idea what he and his unit might have to do.

"Maybe reenlisting wasn't the best idea," Shannon blurted out.

There was no response.

For the first time, she realized the seriousness of the situation. The rest of the evening was spent speculating on what could happen. Would Jason be activated? Where would he go? What would he do? No one knew for sure. It was now just a waiting game.

By the time Jason had to go to work that night, it was clear that there were going to be no more plane crashes, at least for now. The airports were shut down and security was at its highest level. It was very unclear, however, if any further attacks were imminent. Exhausted, Jason made it through the night, and when he came home in the morning, went straight to bed. The unit had not called his house, and there had been no further attacks, so he felt it safe to assume that he did not have to get ready to go anywhere, at least not yet.

Jason fell fast asleep, and he awoke to Shannon coming home. She went upstairs to see if he was awake, and when she realized he was, she went into the room.

"Any news today?" Shannon asked.

"Not yet," he grumbled. "I've been in bed all day, anyway."

"Well," Shannon continued, "it has been verified that the hijackings were planned by Osama bin Laden and Al Qaeda. And, apparently, that last plane was heading for the White House but for some reason didn't make it. President Bush said we will respond."

Jason didn't respond to this. He reached for the remote and turned on the television.

"What are you thinking, honey?" Shannon inquired.

"If the president knows who did this, then he has to be planning a revenge attack. I'm sure the news will be talking about that. Who knows what's going to happen?"

"I'm going to go do a few things for school," Shannon said to Jason as she rose from the bed. "What do you want to do for dinner?"

"Whatever," Jason responded.

Shannon changed out of her work clothes and headed out of the room to the office. Jason continued watching the news from the bed for a while. He eventually made his way to the couch. Jason listened intently as Secretary of Defense Donald Rumsfeld called on all men and women of the armed forces to be ready for what the coming weeks and months will hold. Hearing this, Jason realized that the possibility of him going to war was real. The thought sent chills up and down his spine.

Over the next two weeks, more information came to the forefront about the terrorist attacks. It was clear that Osama Bin Laden was the mastermind behind the attacks and that the terrorists had trained in camps in Afghanistan, where the ruling party, the Taliban, was supporting them. It would not be long before the United States retaliated.

Jason had to continue his residency, but it was tough for him to focus as his thoughts were constantly filled with what the near future might bring. During his first drill weekend after the attacks, the leadership made it clear that the intensity of the training was going to dramatically increase. Even though reserve units frequently trained for their particular specialty, they rarely trained as if war and a possible deployment were imminent, with the exception of the war games at annual training in the woods.

They were now faced with the task of getting all of the soldiers trained at the highest level possible and ensuring everyone knew everyone else's job, as well. Because Jason was a staff sergeant and had been in the unit for over eight years, he was considered an expert within the unit and had a major role in ensuring everyone was ready. He was up to the task. Every drill weekend was now vital. Time was precious.

Over the next several months, Jason was very busy. He was working full time at the hospital, and when he was not sleeping, he was planning for the upcoming drill weekends. In addition, he also had to make sure that all of his personal affairs were in order, like his life insurance, will, power of attorney, and finances. In addition, he wanted to spend as much time as possible with his family. This was a stressful time for both Jason and Shannon. The uncertainty was dreadful. Both of them were distracted at work, they were having a tough time sleeping, and they argued a little more; and the worst part was that nothing was certain. Jason might not be going anywhere.

As the New Year rang in, the United States was busy in Afghanistan, taking out elements of the Taliban regime. At the same time, rumors were flying about a possible invasion of Iraq. Although there was no clear evidence that Iraq was a threat to the United States, it was believed that they had weapons of mass destruction and could use them against the United States or our assets in other countries.

By late winter and early spring, Jason, as well as about every reserve and National Guard member and their families, was becoming very stressed about what was becoming more and more evident. If the country was going to war, every person in the services would play some role. President Bush was frequently on the television, keeping America up to date as to what was going on in the War on Terror, as it was now being called. He frequently warned other countries that we were not going to sit and wait to be attacked again, that we were going to seek out and destroy the enemy before they could strike. This included the Iraqi regime. Saddam Hussein continued to deny that he had weapons of mass destruction. United Nations' weapons inspectors were in his country, searching for any signs of these weapons, but continued to come up empty-handed. Still, President Bush was insistent Iraq had the weapons and was continuing to make threats.

By the end of the summer, when Jason was finishing his residency, many of the reserve and National Guard units were making preparations. Many were put on active duty orders even after they had their annual two-week trainings, to get together everything they would need for a deployment. This would include loading their vehicles on trains for shipment overseas, buying supplies that may be needed while deployed, getting up to date on all of their shots, and updating all of their paperwork to include wills and life insurance. While it was becoming clearer that a war was imminent, everyone was still being told nothing was certain— not yet, anyway.

Jason had finally completed his residency in the middle of the summer and was ready to begin his practice. Although he was constantly thinking about being deployed, he knew he had to maintain his civilian life and continue to perform his daily tasks, just as any ordinary person would do. Even though this was tough for him to do, Jason began practicing with his father and quickly became a fixture in his office. When he was not working, he spent most of his time at home glued to the television, as was the case with most of the people in the military. Jason's increased level of anxiety was recognized by Shannon. He ate less, talked less, watched the news more often, and was on the phone with his military buddies more, as well. Whenever she would try and talk to him about it, it always led to an argument. Jason denied that the potential of going to war was bothering him, but those who knew him best could see that it was clearly distracting him.

The thought of going to war was weighing heavily on Jason's mind. President Bush's speeches about the threats against the United States were becoming a regular piece on the news, and it seemed as if he was not going to back down from Iraq. Additionally, the war in Afghanistan was at full throttle, and several American soldiers had lost their lives. However, Americans were being reassured that victory would occur and America would prevail in the Global War on Terror.

Before Jason's October drill weekend, he received a phone call from his platoon sergeant, First Sergeant Williams. He informed Jason that although no orders had been received as of yet, it appeared that the 132nd Transportation Company was going to be put on active duty status for a couple of weeks to make the necessary preparations for possible deployment that many other units had already made. Jason was silent. His face didn't register what he was hearing. Shannon was in the room and asked him what was going on. First Sergeant Williams asked Jason if he heard what he said.

"I hear ya, top. I'll inform my squad to be prepared."

With that, the conversation ended. Shannon could tell by the pale color of Jason's face that it was not good news.

"We're being activated," Jason said quietly, not knowing what response he would get.

"What? What do you mean, activated?" Shannon asked frantically.

"It's okay," Jason said reassuringly. "We're only being put on active duty orders for a few weeks, just to make sure we have everything ready to go just in case we do get called to go somewhere. It's just routine."

Shannon was speechless.

"Don't worry, Shannon. It doesn't mean anything," he reiterated.

Jason knew that it was more than this, but he wanted to keep Shannon as calm as possible. She wasn't buying it. Shannon began sobbing.

"I don't know what I would do without you. I hoped the day would never come. Now what?"

Jason gave her a hug. He didn't know what to say.

Shannon knew when she married Jason that it was always a possibility, but like the significant others of many servicemen and women, she thought it would not happen to her. Well, it was happening. And it was happening to hundreds of thousands of military families around the country, and around the world. Jason did his best to reassure her, but nothing he could say would make her feel better. They spent that evening at home together, discussing the possibilities if something should happen. When they finished their conversation, Jason called all of the members of his squad and informed them of the message from 1SG Williams. Jason and Shannon were not going to be the only ones not sleeping well that night.

Jason went to work the next day and informed his dad about the phone call.

"Dad," Jason said with a low tone.

"Yeah, son."

"I'm going to need some time off."

Ray's stomach immediately dropped.

"It finally happened, huh?"

"No," Jason responded. "It's not what you think."

Ray didn't say a word. He listened intently as Jason continued.

"I got a call last night from my first sergeant. He said we received orders to be on active duty for a few weeks just to make sure everything's ready, just in case we get the call."

"Do you think that will happen soon?" Ray asked softly.

"I really don't know, Dad. But we have to be ready."

"Well, buddy, I'll do whatever I have to do to help you and Shannon out. Just let me know. We'll have some of the appointments switched around. I'll be fine here. Do what you have to do."

He gave Jason a hug. Jason met with a few patients early but then had to leave to get ready for drill, pack his bags, and make some more calls.

Jason and Shannon didn't talk much that night, but the emotions were evident. Although the plans were not definite, Shannon spent most of the night crying, not knowing how she would handle Jason being away. When Jason was finally packed and ready to go, they went to bed without any further discussion.

Jason didn't get much sleep that night, and he was up before the alarm rang. He got out of bed and headed for the shower. Shannon was awake, too, not sleeping much herself, and she went to the kitchen to prepare some breakfast. When Jason was dressed and ready to go, he went to the kitchen and sat at the table to eat. Again there was little discussion, but Shannon did tell Jason to call her if he received confirmation of being activated for deployment readiness. Jason assured her that he would and finished his meal. When he was done, he kissed her and headed out the door.

Jason arrived at the armory a few minutes before seven, just in time for the start of the non-commissioned officer meeting. Upon walking into the meeting room, he immediately noticed that something was up.

"Our orders just came in, SSG Henson," one of the guys said to him.

Expecting this to happen, Jason simply replied, "I figured."

As everyone sat for the meeting to begin, the company commander, Captain Hillock, called the meeting to order.

"The unit is going to be put on active status for the next three weeks in order to load equipment, get needed supplies, update all paperwork, and begin receiving shots. Even though all of this is happening, it's only preliminary. It does not mean that we're being deployed, only getting prepared."

The sergeants just looked at each other. Some were smiling, others looked scared, while some, well, their expressions showed nothing in particular. For most of them, this was all brand-new. There were some who were deployed during Desert Storm, and they were fine, but others weren't quite sure how to take this news. Jason, however, was ready. He had been thinking about this for a long, long time. It was time to focus, even if they were not sure they were going anywhere.

It is not uncommon for this process to take place without getting deployed. In fact, most reserve and National Guard units went through this practice, even the ones that did not go anywhere. However, most units that had to go through this procedure assumed that they were getting ready to go to war.

Usually, these meetings lasted only about thirty minutes or less, as the weekend itinerary was the normal topic of discussion. But because they were going to be on active duty for the next several weeks, the meeting lasted over two hours.

When the other soldiers in the unit showed up, they were simply told to hang out until the meeting was over. The soldiers knew what was happening. After the NCOs completed the agenda for the next few weeks, they left the meeting room to inform the soldiers of the news. There were mixed emotions throughout the platoon. Some were excited, others appeared upset, while many had no idea how to react. Once the information was put out, everyone was given an opportunity to call home to inform his or her loved ones about the news. Jason immediately called Shannon. Before she even picked up the phone, she knew who was calling. She took a deep breath and answered.

"Hello."

"Shannon, you there?"

"Yeah."

"I can barely hear you. Are you okay?" Jason asked.

"No, I'm not okay. I know why you're calling."

"No, no," Jason responded. "It's not what you think. We're only getting activated for the three weeks we talked about. That's all."

There was a moment of silence and then Shannon responded, "Well, you have to do what you have to do."

"Listen, babe, I know this is hard for you. We have to get through this. It's just three weeks."

"For now," she responded.

"We'll see. But I have to go. The other guys have to call home, too. Don't worry; it'll be okay. I love you."

"I love you, too," she replied.

Shannon hung up the phone and continued to sit on the couch, staring at the floor, pondering what was going to happen next. Jason got back to work.

The rest of the workday consisted of discussing what was going to be happening over the next three weeks and what the soldiers had to do to make sure everything got finished. They were let go early that day so they could go home to do whatever they had to do to be prepared for the duration of the activation. Since Jason did not live too far away, it would be easy for him to go home a few days a week, so when he went home, he only had to pack a few things. When he arrived home and opened the front door, he saw Shannon sitting on the couch, watching the news.

"Hey, honey," Jason said softly. "How are ya?"

"I'm fine," she replied.

"Do you want to talk about this?" Jason asked as he approached her.

"I think we better," she replied. "I'm not sure exactly what to say or think or do. I'm really confused."

"That's okay," Jason assured her. "This is new for us. We'll figure it out. It'll be fine."

"Fine? Maybe for you, but I'll be here, alone, trying to take care of everything by myself."

"Shannon, right now, all that's happening is that we're getting ready. We have plenty of time to sort out everything so we're both prepared if I go. Besides, there are a lot of families around here that will have soldiers with me, you know that. You can all help each other out, and my parents most definitely will help. And that's if we get deployed."

"You're right," Shannon responded. "I guess I'm getting ahead of myself. But I have to be prepared, right?"

"Yes, and you will be—we will be. For right now, though, I have to go pack some things. We'll have some lunch later and then go to my parents. I told my dad to expect this, but I want to tell them it's for sure. And I'd rather do it in person."

"Okay," she said.

Jason kissed her on the head and went upstairs to pack his things. When he was done, he went to the kitchen and prepared lunch. He made chicken breast and broccoli, their favorite. Following lunch, Shannon got ready, and they headed to Harrisville.

By the time they arrived, Ray and Angie already knew.

"Hey, Dad," Jason said.

"Hey there, you two," Ray responded.

Angie came in from the kitchen, where she was cleaning up from their lunch, and immediately went to Shannon and gave her a hug, followed by one for her son.

"I guess you know already?" Jason asked them.

"Yeah," his dad said. "It doesn't take long in this neighborhood."

Jason could tell by his mom's puffy eyes that she had been crying, but he said nothing of it.

"It's only for a few weeks for now," Jason told them. "Nothing has been said—not even speculation."

"Isn't that part obvious, though?" Ray sarcastically asked.

"Who knows, Dad," Jason replied. "But for now, we need to focus on this training time. I'll be around a good bit while we're activated, so I'll keep everyone up to date with what we find out. In the meantime, we do need to think about the next few weeks."

"So what do we need to do?" Ray asked.

"For now, nothing," Jason said. "But Shannon will need your support and some help if we do get deployed."

"Well that goes without saying, son," Ray replied.

"We'll figure it out over the next few weeks," Jason said, frustrated over not really knowing anything for sure. "For now, let's just enjoy some time together today."

Shannon remained silent the entire time. She didn't know what to say or ask. All she could think about was being home alone. But she didn't say anything else about it today. She didn't want to seem selfish.

"You want to play some cards or something?" Shannon asked.

"Good idea," Jason responded. "Let's play some Euchre and forget about this stuff for a while."

And that's what they did. They played some cards and tried not to focus on the impending future. Jason and Shannon stayed until after dinner and decided to go home to be together alone. Jason had to report back in the morning. The remainder of the night was relatively quiet. Jason was busy watching the news and planning in his mind for the coming weeks of preparation, thinking about what his soldiers were going to need to do and what materials they may need to obtain if they get deployed. They went to bed around ten.

When Jason woke up, about six o'clock, it was time to go again. He gave Shannon a kiss, finished packing his things in the car, and headed out the door. Back at the unit, most of the soldiers had arrived early, anxious for any fresh news and to get started on their preparations.

Over the next three weeks, the soldiers were very busy. They had to get all of the trucks ready and moved to the train yard, where they would be loaded up and sent to a shipping yard for a trip overseas, most likely to Kuwait. They had to pack up all of the equipment that they had, including tools, tents, and tactical gear, and put it in shipping containers to go wherever the trucks were going. They also had an opportunity to purchase any other materials they may need, such as building materials and news tools that could be used on the battlefield. They also had to meet with an assortment of people throughout their command to get their paperwork updated. This would include powers of attorney, life insurance, wills, and various other forms that were necessary for deployment. In addition, they spent a lot of time training up on basic combat training: first aid, chemical weapons training, and map reading, among others.

The three weeks seemed to fly by, and before they knew it, everything was gone and everyone was now ready for deployment. Problem was, there was no new information put out and nothing had changed. So at the end of the three weeks, all of the soldiers went home, where they would anxiously wait for that phone call telling them it was time for deployment.

Jason did his best to live his life as if he was not going to get deployed, but he found that very difficult to do. At the office, patients would frequently bring up the subject, curious to know his thoughts about the possible war. Ray would also ask him, almost on a daily basis, how he and Shannon were doing and if he had heard anything new. As for he and Shannon, times were tough. They were both very stressed out at the possibility of Jason being deployed and not receiving any confirmation otherwise. As a result, they would often argue over little things, such as the garbage not being emptied, who was going to cook, or whose turn it was to go to the grocery store. Until this situation had arisen, arguing was not something with which they were very familiar.

The next couple of months, which included the holidays, went by very quickly. When Shannon and Jason were not at work, they spent much of their time discussing (or arguing about) what may or may not happen. Watching the news had also become commonplace in their home. In the past, Thanksgiving and Christmas were usually fun and exciting times for the both of them and their families, but this year was much different. Everyone realized that this may be the last time they would celebrate these holidays together before Jason left for somewhere in the Middle East. Although not much was said on the subject, the potential for deployment was at the forefront of everyone's minds.

The holidays passed and there was still no word on deploying. By this time, shortly after the New Year, 2003, troop levels had greatly increased in Kuwait, and the potential for war was becoming more evident. It appeared as though it would only be a matter of days before the president would decide to invade Iraq. He was making it quite clear that he was not going to back off unless Saddam Hussein and his regime stepped down.

Jason's unit had drill during the weekend of January 11th and 12th, and he figured that if they were going to get the call before the war started, this would be the weekend. The anxiety that both Jason and Shannon were feeling was very clear throughout the week. They put off doing regular household chores and went out to eat most nights. Jason was exercising a lot and watching the news in most of his free time. They were both also taking more time off of work.

By Friday evening, Jason and Shannon were mentally and emotionally drained. Because of the excessive stress that they have been experiencing for quite some time now, they were simply ready for some news, good or bad. There wasn't much conversation at the Henson home throughout the evening. In fact, this had become the norm for them, other than the times that they would argue or bicker at one another. Both were very exhausted, and by nine thirty, they were asleep.

Jason arose early, at about six o'clock, and he was quickly out of bed and into the shower, clearly anxious to get ready and be off to the armory as soon as possible. After showering, he threw on his uniform and headed to the kitchen. Typically, he and Shannon would have had breakfast together, but he was ready before she got out of bed. He fixed a pot of coffee, and when his thermos was full, he went back to the bedroom to kiss Shannon good-bye.

She mumbled good-bye, and Jason was out the door and off to drill. When he arrived at seven, almost everyone was there, even though the meeting was pushed back to seven thirty. It was obvious they were early for the same reason. But as he approached some of the troops, glaring at them as if to get some response about deployment, one of his buddies said, "Nothing yet, sarge." Jason nodded and headed into the building towards the meeting room. All of the NCOs were there, pacing around the room, waiting for some sort of news. The only thing Jason was told was that the commander had been on the phone for about fifteen minutes, but with whom no one knew. Everyone eventually sat down and waited for the commander to come into the room.

At precisely 7:10 AM, on the morning of January 11th, 2003, Captain Hillock walked in to the meeting room and stated that he had some very important news. Immediately, Jason's stomach filled with butterflies.

"Well," the commander stated, "we got 'em. We're going to the Middle East."

There was an array of responses at this time. Some cheered while others cried. Some sat there, frozen in their seats. Jason was speechless. Although he felt a little relief that he finally knew for sure, he couldn't quite figure out how he was supposed to feel. Almost instantly, he thought about the parades he saw when the first Gulf War was over, and a smile overcame his face. Then he thought about Shannon and what her response was going to be when he told her the news. While thinking about all of the things that this news meant, both good and bad, he suddenly felt overwhelmed with a sense of pride. Even though Jason has been told on numerous occasions how proud of him others were, this feeling of pride was nothing he had ever felt before. He suddenly began to cry, but immediately forced himself to stop, remembering the crowd around him.

Then the commander spoke, and everyone was immediately silent.

"Our company is going to be vital to getting the mission accomplished. You can't get anywhere without transportation."

A faint laugh went throughout the room.

"I'm very proud of each of you," he continued, "and I'm proud of this company. We have strong history, a history that includes many worldwide missions. This outfit has meant a lot to the members of this community, and they stand behind us, without question."

These comments sent cold chills up and down Jason's spine. But the next statement the commander made was devastating.

"Now for the bad news," he said with a very sympathetic voice. "We are going to be on active duty beginning Tuesday, and we are leaving for training at Fort Leonard Wood on Wednesday, before flying overseas. Yes, that's correct—Wednesday."

We only have four stinking days to get ready, Jason thought to himself. He would later find out that this became common for many deploying units. They were given almost no time to make final preparations. Captain Hillock then informed them that he was going to tell the rest of the unit and then let them go home until Tuesday evening, when they would say their final good-byes to their loved ones, whom they would not see again for an undetermined amount of time.

Jason cried the whole way home. He cried because he was excited, he cried because he was nervous, and he cried because he was really doing what he set out to do when he was just sixteen years old. But most of all, he cried because he knew that this was going to devastate Shannon and that soon he would be away from her—and quite possibly never see her again. When he arrived home, Shannon was standing at the door, sobbing. She already knew. When Ray heard, he called to see if Shannon was okay, assuming Jason was already home. She gave him the biggest and longest hug she had ever given him. They were both speechless. As they made their way inside, they began discussing the details of his orders.

Ray and Angie arrived about an hour after Jason got home, and they were as emotional as Jason and Shannon. They discussed the specifics of what had to take place over the next few weeks and what each family member could do to help. Jason had to make sure that Shannon had all of the contact information for their personal affairs, the unit and family support group leader, Red Cross, and his commander and first sergeant's wives. He had shopping to do for things such as personal hygiene items and undergarments. He also wanted to buy some tools, such as a flashlight and holder for his belt, a multi-tool, binoculars, and various other small camping supplies. He wanted to be prepared, over prepared if necessary. Jason also wanted his parents to have the same contact information as Shannon, just in case. He also talked to his dad about some household chores and upkeep to help Shannon, such as cutting grass from time to time and changing oil in the car and other basic car maintenance. Jason asked him and Angie to just stop in and check on Shannon once in a while. Ray assured Jason that he would.

They also discussed where he might be going and what he might be doing. Although he did not know for sure, he told them that he would be in a safe place, away from the fighting, doing his best to alleviate any extra anxiety. After lunch, Ray and Angie left, and Jason and Shannon began the discussion that every departing soldier hates to talk about.

"Shannon, I need to discuss something with you, and it's not going to be easy," Jason said sensitively. "I don't expect anything to happen to me, but the reality is that it might."

Shannon did her best to try and hold back tears, but at this point, it was impossible. She had been so emotional for several months now. This was the tip of the iceberg, the last thing she wanted to discuss.

Jason showed her the papers for his Service Members Group Life Insurance. "I took out this policy to help take care of you if something bad should happen to me. All of the instructions are here. I don't want to get into any more details about it; I just want you to know it's here. My will is also here, and the directions are clear. Just put this stuff away somewhere. Hopefully, you'll never need to look at it."

Shannon continued crying off and on throughout their conversation, and Jason said nothing about it. He knew that regardless of what he said, she was going to cry anyway. They also discussed other logistical matters, but Shannon did not hear much past the first part of the discussion.

Once all of the aspects of the deployment were discussed, they tried to have a normal weekend. They went out to dinner and then visited family and some friends, but not for too long, as they wanted to spend as much alone time together as possible. They spent the rest of the evening and most of the next day lying around, reminiscing and talking about the positive side of this deployment. They felt this would bring them closer together and that they could learn to appreciate their time together more.

Jason and Shannon spent the next two days getting things ready for the deployment. Jason went over the specifics of the orders with Shannon several more times, being sure not to miss anything. The rest of the time was spent packing and writing down information that either one of them may need, such as points of contact and emergency procedures. By Tuesday morning, everything was in place and all necessary preparations had been completed. Jason and Shannon went out to a nice lunch and then returned to pack the car for departure. Ray and Angie arrived at their house as they were packing and helped them get the rest of the stuff done. It was finally time to go, and Jason's parents followed Jason and Shannon to the armory.

When they arrived, they had difficulty finding a place to park. It seemed as if everyone had brought their families to send them off, and it appeared as if more than half of the community was there to bid them farewell. As the family members stood around, talking and crying, Captain Hillock called for everyone's attention.

"Ladies and gentlemen, thank you for being here today to show your love and support for your friends, family, and community members. I know this is a very difficult day, with many more to follow. But keep in mind, these soldiers have trained hard together and are very good at what they have to do. We will look after one another and take care of one another. I will personally do my best to ensure the safety of every soldier here. This is a monumental event for this company and this community. We will make you proud."

A loud army "Hooaaaahhhh" was belted out by the soldiers. The commander continued to pass along some information for the family members about support groups and contact numbers should an emergency occur, and he then gave everyone fifteen minutes to say their good-byes. At this point, there was not much to say that hadn't been said already. Ray helped Jason load his bags on the bus and then gave him a hug, telling Jason he loved him. Angie followed suit, crying intensely. Jason then turned to Shannon and gave her a long, hard hug.

"I love you so much, Shannon Henson," Jason whispered to her.

Shannon was sobbing, but was able to reply, although it was broken up, "I lo-love you too. I'm gonna miss yo-you so much."

"Me, too. I have to go now. I'll call you as soon as I can."

Shannon said nothing else. She just cried. Jason loaded his stuff onto the bus, and all of the other soldiers soon followed. As the busses pulled away, Jason looked out of his window to capture one last glimpse of his family. He struggled unsuccessfully to hold back his tears. When he could no longer see his parents or Shannon, he turned back in his seat. It was time to focus.

Chapter 6: Back to the Wood

JASON WAS SILENT ON THE bus ride to the airport. It was finally setting in that he would not be seeing Shannon or his parents again for a long time, something he had never been faced with before this moment. During the bus ride, the troops were given information about the process that was going to take place over the next few weeks. They would go to Fort Leonard Wood, Missouri, a place that most of them were familiar with from BCT and AIT, to do some training and get needed supplies for their journey overseas. They were also told that it still wasn't certain where they were going, but deep down, everyone knew. Everyone was going into this assuming that they were going to Kuwait, and after about a week, that would be confirmed.

After what seemed like a long bus ride to the airport and a long flight to Missouri, Jason and the troops again boarded another bus for a three-hour trip to the base. Once there, they were set up in barracks, where they would be staying for the next few weeks. They set up their areas and were given the evening off to get settled in, make some phone calls, and get some rest. Jason naturally called home to reassure Shannon he was okay and to make sure that she was doing okay as well. The tears were shed again, but nevertheless, they were able to have a nice conversation. Jason returned to the barracks after the call and got some sleep.

The next few weeks were very similar to basic training and AIT, only not quite as intense; everything was done in a condensed version. Every evening, they were given updated information as to what was going on in the news, but it was mostly the same: no weapons of mass destruction were found, yet President Bush was not backing down. After about two weeks, Jason, and just about everyone else, was getting restless. They were tired of doing the same old training. Frustration was mounting over the continued training in the freezing weather, especially since they knew they were going to the desert. *Why would the Department of the Army order us and so many other units to train at Midwest, Eastern, and Northern bases in the middle of the winter?* Jason wondered. Nonetheless, the troops were there in the snow, training and eager to leave.

During the third week, irritated, depressed, and cold, the soldiers were finally given the information they were waiting for. Captain Hillock called a formation and informed the troops that they were leaving for Kuwait in two days. There was not much reaction to this statement. The soldiers knew it was coming and by now were just ready to go. They were all given a chance to call home and tell their families they were leaving but were not able to tell them where they were going, as directed by the commander. Of course, they told anyway, and Jason was no exception. He talked to Shannon for about ten minutes and his dad about the same. He then headed back the barracks to get his gear ready for the trip.

The next day was spent in briefings about what to expect when they arrived in Kuwait. When they were finally done with the briefings, they were sent back to the barracks to get some sleep, as they were going to leave first thing in the morning. But because of the anticipation, no one could sleep. When the next day arrived, they loaded up the busses again and went to the airport. Departure time finally came, so they filled the plane and were off for the Middle East, eager to get things started.

Chapter 7: Kuwait

IT WAS A LONG FLIGHT. It took about nine hours to get to the layover point, which was in Frankfurt, Germany, and then another three hours to Kuwait. They finally arrived in Kuwait at around 3:00 AM on February 14th, Valentine's Day. They were told to stay on the plane until they received further instructions. After about thirty minutes, the commander came over the loudspeaker with instructions. He proceeded to tell them that when they exited the plane, there would be a table set up near the busses where they were to show their identification cards and then hustle onto the bus. The process was to take place expeditiously so any potential threats would not have targets in clear, standing view. But as Jason exited the plane, nerves on end, he wondered why he and his fellow soldiers were to move so quickly when there was a table set up with people checking IDs. If it were so dangerous, wouldn't they be covered? Nevertheless, Jason did as ordered so as to not receive any flack.

When he got on the crowded bus and sat down, the reality of the situation began to set in. It was hot, damn hot, even at three thirty in the morning, and the windows on the bus were closed with the curtains drawn. Everyone was being told to move rapidly as if to avoid any danger. He was beginning to realize that this was for real. As the busses filled and everyone in the unit was loaded on them, a final roll call was taken. The busses then moved out and would not stop until they reached the base, where the unit would take up residency until further orders were given.

They arrived at Camp Arifjan around 6:00 AM. Before entering through the gates of the base, each soldier had to get off of the bus, show his or her ID again, and clear his or her weapon to ensure none were loaded. When Jason got off of the bus, he quickly glanced around, checking his surroundings. He noticed lots of warehouse-style buildings, plenty of fencing, guard towers, and a lot of military vehicles. After proving that he was who he said he was and that he wasn't on the verge of shooting someone, he got back on the bus and sat.

When everyone had completed the base entry procedures, the busses began moving again and eventually stopped at one of the warehouse buildings. Everyone exited the busses and offloaded the bags. A formation was held, and the unit was informed that the building they pulled in front of was where they were going to be staying until given further orders. They were also given some basic base rules: they were to carry weapons and gas masks at all times and not salute in certain areas. They were given times and locations for eating, among other things. Following formation, they were told to move into the building and set up their stuff.

The warehouse was about the length of a football field and was packed full of soldiers, allowing each person a space slightly larger than an army cot, which is seventy-seven-inches-by-twenty-eight-inches. There was no extra room; the place was as packed as a can of sardines. In addition, there was no air-conditioning, so it was very hot. Once they were set up, the commander gave the troops the rest of the day to relax, get some sleep, write, and get familiar with the base. Jason used the time to set up his cot, unpack some of his gear, get a shower, write a letter to Shannon, and take a nap.

At about 3:00 PM, as Jason and several other troops lay asleep on their cots, a ridiculously loud siren caused them to abruptly awaken. Jason jumped out of the cot and scrambled to find his gas mask. He found it and put it on. He looked around for the rest of the troops in his squad, finding only three of them; the rest were somewhere outside of the building, checking out the base. After about two minutes of standing around with a mask on, the all clear signal was given. As Jason took off his mask and tried to calm himself down, everyone in the unit who was not in the building began filtering back in. When everyone was back together, a formation was held to inform the troops of what happened. The commander told them that this was one of what would be many practice drills to come for potential incoming chemical weapons. This statement really made the troops realize that they were in a war zone. Following formation, Jason got dressed in his uniform and decided to get something to eat. So he and a few other soldiers went to the chow hall, where they would wait in line for about an hour.

Although they did not know it at the time, Jason and his buddies quickly found out that chow was a big deal around here, and the lines began forming very early. Jason stepped out of the line to get a better view of just how many people were in front of and behind him, and he guessed that there were about four hundred, at least, in the entire line. This was the norm, and the lines would get longer as the days went by and more troops arrived at the base. This base was the main staging ground for incoming troops coming into the country. Once the hall opened, the chow line seemed to move rather quickly. Jason soon found out why. Besides a salad bar and a few deserts, the main menu was hot dogs, hamburgers, fries, and baked beans. Jason didn't mind, and when he got his food, he sat down and ate it rather quickly, as he wanted to find a phone to call home. This too would be a problem. At the time, there were not very many phones, and a lot of people were waiting to use one. The typical wait was at least an hour. Jason actually waited for about an hour and a half before his turn finally arrived. Jason grabbed the phone and punched in the numbers on his calling card. After about a minute, the phone began to ring.

"Hello," a muffled voice answered.

"Shannon, it's Jason."

"Jason! Oh my gosh! How are you?" she said, the sound of Jason's distant voice arousing her from her slumber. "Is everything okay?"

"Yes, sweetie, I'm fine. How are things back home?"

"What?" she asked, as static broke up his words.

"I asked, how are things back home?" he yelled.

"They're okay, I guess. We really miss you."

"I miss everyone, too. Tell them I am fine and so is everyone else."

"I will," she replied. "Jason, I want you to ..." Shannon's voice stopped.

"Want me to what?" Jason asked frantically. "Shannon? Shannon?" He waited for a response but heard nothing.

Jason hung up the phone and tried to call her back. The first time, he heard nothing after dialing the numbers. The second and third times he heard busy signals. Realizing there was a problem and cognizant of the long line waiting behind him, he gave up. *These damn phones,* Jason thought to himself. As he walked by the person in charge, Jason asked if problems with the phones were common.

"They sure are," the sergeant replied. "Welcome to the Middle East."

Jason walked away shaking his head in disappointment. "The phones are not working," Jason said to the line of soldiers waiting. "But good luck," he said as he continued his walk. *I wonder what she was going to say*, he pondered.

He returned to the warehouse, where the NCOs were getting ready for a meeting. During that time, they discussed the latest news about the war and what training they would be doing. Since the units could not leave the base, their training would be limited to maintenance, strategic and tactical planning, and short trips driving around the base. They were told that President Bush had given a deadline for Saddam and his regime to step down and that if they did not, the U.S. was going to invade Iraq. This news circled quickly, and the troops were getting anxious for that time to come.

For the next three weeks, the soldiers of the 132nd Transportation Company sat through briefings about potential scenarios that could occur in the war, did daily trainings with their trucks, went through several mock gas drills, ate a lot of hamburgers and hot dogs, and endured many frustrations about the phones, hot weather, and blowing sand. It seemed that day in and day out, sand was blowing everywhere, and when there was an actual sandstorm, everything was a mess. Visibility was very limited, activity came to almost a complete halt, and the sand got into everything, including packed gear and clothing. The troops quickly became experts at cleaning their weapons, which had to be done several times a day. As the days went by with the usual activities and the same news coming in, everyone was getting bored and irritated. They were sick of the daily routine and ready for some action. Finally, on March 10th, some meaningful news finally came in.

Captain Hillock called a formation and informed the troops that they were moving out tomorrow. They would be going to a makeshift base near the border for final preparations before moving again. They were told that for the rest of the day, they would be loading their trucks with supplies: food, water, hygiene products, and ammunition. The excitement was evident. Jason was elated. He was now one step closer to that hero's parade he had been dreaming about since he was a kid. But there was little time to fantasize, as there was a lot of work to do. Jason gathered his squad and gave individual instructions to each as to what he or she needed to do.

There were lines forming at all of the supply points, clearly demonstrating that almost everyone was getting ready to move out. By the end of the day, the troops were tired and weary, but they had all of the trucks loaded and in line, ready to move north. The troops were told to write one final letter home and then take a shower, clean their weapons, and get some rest, as they were moving out before sunrise. Jason followed orders and was in his rack within an hour, ready for some sleep. But sleep he could not. He lay in his cot, thinking about Shannon and how worried she must be. He was also getting a little nervous himself, for he had no idea what to expect. He eventually fell asleep, but by 3:00 AM, he was out of the rack and waking other troops. It was time to start their big day.

Everyone was awake and moving toward their trucks with all of their gear by 4:30 AM. Once everyone's equipment was loaded and ready to go, a quick formation was held and the troops were told that they would be driving through the desert until they arrived at their staging ground, at a makeshift base basically in the middle of nowhere but just south of the Iraqi border, which was being operated by components of the 3rd Infantry Division. They would be given further instructions upon arrival. The troops then loaded their trucks and were off for a long, bumpy ride through the desert, finally arriving at the base around 8:00 AM. Once through the gate, they drove to their parking spaces and then began setting up their tents. This would be home for a while. But for exactly how long was anyone's guess.

For the next several days, briefings were held with the company commander and the NCOs. They would discuss potential missions to carry out once in Iraq, as well as what to do if something was to happen to any of the soldiers. Jason and the rest of the NCOs would then brief their troops with some of the information and encourage them to be ready at any moment. This became the norm. There would be more briefings, information would change, and the soldiers would grow frustrated with receiving fresh news every day with nothing happening. Time was passed playing games of cards and Risk, cleaning weapons and equipment, and rereading letters they received while at Camp Arifjan. One day, they even played a game of football with their gas masks on. This gave them an idea of what it would be like in combat if they were forced to wear the masks and be active. Some of the troops enjoyed it; Jason hated it. It was very difficult for him to breath. Aside from these activities, the time was spent hanging out in the tents, sweating, stinking, and literally collecting dust. It seemed as if the big day would never come. Well, come it would, and come it did.

On the morning of March 18th, Captain Hillock gathered his troops. He informed them that President Bush had given Saddam forty-eight hours to comply with his demands or Iraq would suffer the consequences. Although he gave a warning, all of the troops set up near the border were informed that they were definitely crossing. In fact, as the country would later find out, Special Forces were already operating in Iraq, taking out strategic points and gathering intelligence for the air strikes that would soon be devastating areas in the country.

There were mixed emotions among the soldiers. As they glanced at their buddies, pale faces of fear were seen. Some had smiles, and others just stared at the ground. Jason, on the other hand, was ready. He had been awaiting this chance for years. He wasn't smiling, but he was clearly not scared, either. His face, with eyes focused and jaw clenched, demonstrated determination—determination to get the job done and determination to get himself and everyone else home safe. The formation ended with instructions to get everything cleaned, packed, and loaded on the trucks. Jason ensured that the troops in his squad were doing okay and that everything they needed to get done was done accordingly. He gave each of them a talk, letting them know that he was proud of them and that it was okay to be scared. One soldier in particular, SPC Kennedy, appeared very upset, like a puppy who just lost his favorite toy.

"What's wrong soldier?" Jason asked.

"Well, sarge, to be honest, I'm a little scared. I haven't been until this point. Maybe I thought it would never happen, but I don't want to get hurt or killed."

"None of us do, Kennedy," Jason replied. "And we're all scared. Heck, I wouldn't want to be around a guy who wasn't a little scared. You'll be fine. Your truck will be close to mine, and your buddy in the truck will help you watch out. You were trained for this, soldier; the rest is instinct."

Those seemed to be the magic words. Kennedy looked up at Jason. "You're right, Sergeant Henson; I am trained for this. Thanks for letting me talk. And by the way, please don't tell anyone about this."

"Don't worry about it. It's between us. Now go get your truck and gear ready." And with that, both of them headed for their respective trucks and prepared for departure.

The day seemed to last forever. Jason and the rest of the troops had nothing to do but sit and wait for further instructions. Late that evening, however, they did receive word that they would be moving out tomorrow and would follow the elements of the infantry, ensuring that they had all of the supplies that they needed for the fight. Once the infantry had taken an area, they would set up a temporary base and wait for further instructions. The commander ensured them that they would not be in harm's way.

That night, the troops slept in their trucks, as all of the tents were packed. No one really slept, though. Jason was very anxious, a little nervous, and, like the rest of the soldiers, he hadn't showered in over a week. They were all very uncomfortable but determined. When the next day arrived, Captain Hillock called the section sergeants and squad leaders together to give final orders.

"Soldiers, listen up," he ordered as they gathered together. "We're going to be moving out tonight. We'll be following elements of the infantry, pulling up the rear. I know many of our soldiers are anxious for a fight, but we are truck drivers, and our job is to haul supplies to those leading the way. I'm not ruling out contact, but it looks doubtful, at least from the intel I've received. Go and inform your troops. Have them ready."

A collective, "Yes, sir," followed, and the sergeants gathered their troops. Jason passed along this information to the soldiers in his squad and then headed to his truck for a nap. It was really early, and a long night appeared imminent. The troops spent the rest of the day cleaning weapons and simply bullshitting with one another, talking about home and their families as they awaited nightfall. As the sun began to set, the troops had one last formation. The commander reiterated the instructions he gave them the night before, and then gave a speech, one they would never forget.

"Soldiers of the 132nd, I want all of you to know how proud I am of you and how proud the citizens of the United States of America are of you. Without men and women such as you, our nation would not be the great nation that it is today. What happens over the next several days, weeks, and maybe even months will be with you forever; you will never forget it. But know this: no matter what we do or don't do while in this place, what you have done already has taken a lot of courage, and you are true Americans for that. Be safe, God bless, and good luck. Now fall out to your trucks."

The journey was about to begin. Jason was more than ready, and he knew that he could handle whatever might take place. After about an hour, the tanks and other armored vehicles of the 3rd I.D. were rolling out, and it was only a matter of time before Jason and his company were on their way as well.

When they finally crossed the border, there was a little sign on the side of the road that read, "Welcome to Iraq." The soldiers of the 132nd Transportation Company were on their way to making history.

Chapter 8 The Invasion Begins

AS THE SOLDIERS DROVE THEIR trucks over the border, their adrenaline levels were the highest they have ever been. Jason, who was an assistant driver in one of the large Heavy Equipment Tactical Trucks, or HETTs, was pumped. He had been waiting for this moment for about thirteen years now, and at one point never thought it would happen. Well, it was happening, and Jason was sitting back, taking it all in. But it was not as if he were sitting back, enjoying the ride. When the soldiers crossed the berm into Iraq, they weren't exactly driving on nicely paved roads. There were roads made by the heavy equipment before, so in a sense, they were bumpy paths through the desert sand. And to add to the discomfort, the trucks were blowing sand all over the place, which made visibility almost nothing. If not for the goggles Jason was wearing, he would have had to ride with his eyes shut; it was that bad.

As they continued making their push, not knowing what was going to happen, Jason was taking in all of his surroundings. Although they were basically in the desert and sand was about all anyone could see, there were a few other interesting sights placed sporadically throughout the trails northward. The evidence of the war back in 1991 was still in place, as there were old tanks, trucks, regular cars, and busses, along with various other pieces of rusted metal, scattered all over the place. Clearly, the Iraqi soldiers never made an attempt to recover their equipment and try to restore it. Since there were no signs of any type of life in this area, expect for the occasional Bedouin and his family, Jason assumed no one really cared. But it was interesting for him to see these artifacts now, as he thought for a second that former members of this company probably saw the same vehicles. What a story he would have to tell, and he had only been in Iraq for about thirty minutes.

The journey continued northward for about another hour before they hit some pavement. Although this was damaged pavement, it was not as bad as the bumpy desert. When the commander received word that all of the trucks were out of the desert, he ordered the convoy to stop.

Just as they were coming to halt, Captain Hillock came back over the radio with some orders.

"I want all squad leaders and above to exit their vehicles, check on all of their troops and the trucks, and report back to me as soon as that's finished."

Jason immediately exited the vehicle, did a quick walk around the truck, and checked in on the soldiers in his squad, who were in the four trucks behind him. His section sergeant was parked a few trucks ahead of him, so he headed in that direction. Once Jason found him, he reported as directed. "All soldiers accounted for and everything is in good shape," he explained.

"Roger that," Staff Sergeant Hamilton replied.

Jason then returned to his truck to wait for the order to move out.

After about fifteen minutes, another call from the commander came over the radio.

"I need to see the platoon sergeants at my truck now."

So Jason and the rest of the soldiers in the convoy waited about another ten minutes for further instructions. Specialist Clark, from the truck in front of Jason, came back to Jason's door.

"SFC Freeman needs to see us now, sergeant," Clark informed. "Pass it along."

Jason exited the truck again and walked to the next truck.

"SFC Freeman wants to see us; pass it along."

Jason then walked to SFC Freeman's truck, where many of the soldiers had already gathered. They waited there for about five minutes, at which point everyone had gathered in anticipation of some news.

"Listen up," SFC Freeman ordered.

Everyone fell silent and all eyes were on the sergeant.

"The first elements of the infantry have made contact about thirty clicks up the road. We have been informed of possible chemical weapons and were told to be on full alert just in case. We also have to look out for possible artillery."

Not sure how to respond, Jason began looking around at the other troops, many of whom were looking at Jason for the same reason. Their faces were blank. Not an emotion could be pinpointed. Jason looked back at SFC Freeman, who continued with the information.

"If and when a chemical attack does occur, you will be warned by a series of horn blows by first the lead trucks and then by each truck following. When these horns are heard, you continue doing the same to warn the others, hoooaaahh?"

Everyone replied, "Hooooaaaahhh!"

"Squad leaders and section sergeants, it is your job to check on your troops if this happens to make sure they are aware of what is happening and have the appropriate gear on, especially their masks. We'll pass the word along when the all-clear is given. Now return to your trucks and get ready to move out."

The soldiers returned to the vehicles and waited for the convoy to begin moving. While they waited, Jason ran back to each soldier in his squad to make sure they were okay. When he was satisfied that they were, he returned to his truck. The convoy began to move almost immediately.

As they moved forward, the troops began to hear and eventually see some of the fighter jets that were on their way to Baghdad. The barrage of air strikes on Baghdad had begun as this war was in full swing. As the soldiers continued forward in their trucks, they finally saw some signs of life. The occasional Bedouin could be seen walking along the road, begging for whatever the troops could give. Some gave water, while others gave some food. Some of them gave nothing at all and harassed them.

It seemed as if the convoy was slowing again, but for what reason Jason did not know. Shortly after stopping, Captain Hillock came over the radio once again, stating that the convoy was being forced to stop due to fighting that was occurring not too far ahead. Everyone now realized they were approaching the outskirts of some city, town, or village. The commander followed this update by telling the troops to exit the vehicles and take a defensive position. *On what?* Jason thought to himself, looking around at nothing but desert sand. Although this was clearly the behavior of an anxious leader, Jason and the other soldiers did as ordered, understanding that it was better to be safe than sorry.

When all of the trucks had shut down, a faint noise, coming from not too far off, grabbed the attention of almost everyone. At first, no one could make it out, but they soon realized that it was the sound of tanks firing and artillery slamming. The fight was close, maybe too close for this group of weekend warriors.

About thirty minutes passed before the commander finally disseminated some information over the radio.

"We will be moving soon, so be ready. We're going to head towards the city but around the fighting. We will be going on some bumpy terrain for a short while, but we should be back on track soon after that. Just follow the vehicle in front of you."

Once they were back in the trucks and rolling, Jason went over the map again and realized that if they did exactly what the commander said, they would be ahead of the fighting, thus putting them in front of the infantry, which was not something that should be happening to a reserve transportation company. This scared the shit out of Jason.

"Can you believe this shit?" he asked his driver. "We're headed for a mess. Get ready." He then settled into a mode that he had never been in before—he was ready to fight.

As the convoy headed forward, the fighting could be seen more clearly. Jason couldn't really see anything definitive, but he could make out some of the tanks and explosions. The company then drove far enough out into the desert that they could no longer see or hear the fighting. They drove for about twenty or thirty minutes, straight into the desert, before making a shift back towards the road. When they finally approached the road, they were back in a desolate area, with nothing but Bedouins and camels around. They would later find out that the fighting consisted of about two hundred American soldiers and one hundred Iraqi Republican Guardsmen, who had taken over a small village of four hundred civilians. The fight only lasted thirty minutes, with the Iraqis surrendering and no American fatalities, although a few soldiers were said to be wounded. These types of battles would soon become commonplace.

The soldiers of the 132nd continued up the road for another thirty minutes. They had now become a part of a long line of army and marine vehicles waiting to move north. Jason thought, *Great. A traffic jam in the middle of a war.* But that was the case, and the soldiers would be there for a while. Jason exited his truck and went to each of the trucks assigned to his squad to check on everyone. They seemed to be doing okay, but they were obviously hot and tired as the sweat poured off of their faces.

"Make sure you're drinking water," Jason reminded all of them. "Keep up the good work. I know you're tired, but we have to keep going."

Even though the soldiers were drained, they would never admit it. After all, they were warriors, and they were motivated. Most of the soldiers were exhausted by this time, but a break would soon come. They received orders that they were going to be moving to a safe area about ten miles north, where they would set up a perimeter for the night. Jason was looking forward to a break, however short it may be.

They finally arrived at the rest stop, and after the trucks were parked, the commander called each of the platoon sergeants together for a briefing. While this was going on, the soldiers took a few minutes to just sit in any shade they could find and drink some water, even though the water was rather warm. There was no ice in the desert. The troops didn't seem to mind as they sucked the water down. After about ten or fifteen minutes, SFC Freeman returned and called a platoon gathering. He proceeded to tell the platoon that if nothing changed, they would be in this location for a couple of days. He told them that the infantry was expecting some heavy fighting, so they would wait until it was safe before they moved any farther north. Although this news disappointed the war-hungry bunch, they took the information for what it was worth and went back to their vehicles, where they could complete a little personal hygiene.

Taking care of personal hygiene in a war zone, in the desert, is a very unique task. Each individual soldier does it differently, and some really do none at all. Although today's military is very advanced, there has yet to be a portable shower integrated into the army's warehouse. Also, the chances of finding a laundromat are nonexistent. One of the greatest inventions that almost every soldier makes sure he or she has in a war zone, especially when there are not any established bases, is something almost everyone is familiar with, something that each soldier cannot do without— the baby wipe. Yes, these little moist towelettes quickly become a soldier's best friend in the desert. Water has to be rationed, and the extra is used to wash clothes, so baby wipes are the only way to ensure a little bit of freshness.

Once the wipes were used in the different crevices of the body, the soldier would apply a little baby powder, which would momentarily cool the body; then the sensation would go away, allowing the powder to do its magic and keep things dry. The soldiers would usually wear a uniform for five to seven days (in 120-degree weather, with gear on) and then get out a new one. And what a feeling that new uniform brought. The little things go a long way for a soldier in a war zone.

Although changing uniforms was optional, changing socks and underwear was not. Socks (and feet) had to be dried out or else trench foot would set in. This term came from the days of WWI, when the soldiers would stand in trenches full of water. Their feet would be wet for hours, sometimes even days on end. The result could be very bad, looking similar to hands and feet after being in the bathtub or pool too long. So the feet become the most important part of the body for the soldiers to maintain. A soldier who couldn't use his or her feet was worthless in a war. Once these areas were semi-clean, it was on to the rest: shaving with lukewarm to cold water (a real treat), brushing teeth, and washing faces and hands. That's about it. All fresh. Yeah right. But after a while, these opportunities made a soldier feel brand-new.

Most of this would take place in a matter of about ten minutes. The soldier would then clean his or her weapon, if time permitted, and then it was on to perimeter guard, truck maintenance, eating, or trying to take a power nap before one of the proceeding duties would take place. And this is what the next three days consisted of for the troops of the 132nd. There was the occasional scare of artillery and gunfire, as well as jets and helicopters flying over, but after a while, when they realized there was no direct threat, these events were paid little attention. It became a part of everyday living.

On the third day, which was March 24, 2003, the company was given orders to clean up the area, load the trucks, and get ready for a road trip farther north. When everything was ready to go, the commander pulled the company together for an informational briefing.

"Soldiers, listen up. Elements of the marine and army infantry are rapidly moving through the cities of Iraq and, as such, are in great need of some supplies, especially food and water. There are no safe landing zones for the choppers to make a drop, so supplies need to be driven in. They need us. The risk of enemy contact is going to be very high, so be ready. You were trained for this, so I have all the confidence that each of you is up to this challenge. Let's make our families and ourselves proud. Fall out to your trucks."

Everyone was now keyed up, especially Jason. As he sat in his truck, staring off into the desert sand, anticipating the order to move out, he couldn't help but think about his life back home and how everyone must be feeling. In particular, he thought of Shannon, who was probably alone at home, glued to the television, hoping for just a glimpse of him or his unit, or some news about them. Unfortunately, there was no way of knowing where any one particular troop was located at any given time, so news of anyone dying or getting wounded sent almost every family back home into a panic. It took about two months before any news could be sent back to the States, unless someone was hurt or killed. Two months is a long time for loved ones, who spent many hours pacing around in front of the television. Jason's only hope was that everyone in his unit would make it unscathed, so when it came time to contact home, there would be no bad news.

Chapter 9: Contact

WHEN THE TIME CAME FOR the unit to finally move out, there was a directive given over the radios that surprised most of those listening in.

"Soldiers," Captain Hillock stated, "there's been a slight change in plans. We are going to divert away from the army and resupply the marines. They need our help now. Just follow the vehicle in front of you, and keep your space."

Jason, and everyone else, was about to find out that the marines had established contact in the southern city of An Nasiriyah, and before they could form a secure perimeter around the attacks, several of the supply vehicles were destroyed, leaving them with very little in stock. What the commander failed to tell them, which they would quickly realize, was that the fighting was still in full force in and around the city. Nevertheless, the need for these supplies was imperative if the marines were going to sustain the fight.

As Jason's truck approached the city limits, he could clearly see the remnants of fighting everywhere. Armored vehicles were destroyed and some were still burning; buildings were on fire; artillery and marine helicopters were flying overhead, pounding multiple places within the city; and tanks could be seen in the distance, firing into various buildings. The more he saw, the harder Jason's heart pounded. Fighting seemed imminent at this point, and this was not the ideal situation for a transportation company.

The convoy finally came to a halt about a mile outside the city, and as each truck stopped, the troops inside jumped out and got on the ground alongside the road in fighting positions. Jason followed suit.

As Jason glanced over the perimeter, he could see, off in the distance, people walking away from the city. But he could not tell if they were the enemy or innocent civilians, so he warned the soldiers near him to keep an eye on them. It came down from the top that the enemy forces were not fighting conventionally and that they were dressing in civilian clothes with hopes of deceiving the allied forces. It worked well. Many friendly forces were either wounded or killed as they hesitated to fire on people dressed in regular clothes, who would often hide a weapon inside their shirt, pants, or robes. The allied forces suffered many casualties early on as a result of this tactic. So these people who Jason and the rest of the unit could see in the distance could have easily been enemy forces, but because they were not firing and appeared to be no direct threat, no one could fire on them. Jason did not seem to mind. He was not eager to take the life of another human being unless it was absolutely necessary.

The soldiers lined the streets, lying on the roadside curbs with weapons pointing outward, for what seemed to be a couple of hours. In fact, darkness approached before they were called together for a brief directive. By this time, the fires had calmed to nothing more than a little smoke, and the fighting seemed to have moved to another part of the city, or at least calmed in the area closest to the 132nd. Once the soldiers gathered, the commander began.

"Soldiers," he yelled out, "you've done well so far. But the mission is far from complete. We've been given orders to move into the city, just north of where the fighting is taking place, so we should be safe. When we make it through the city, there will be a secure area on the other side for us to set up. There, we will distribute the supplies. No further details have been given, so we'll be playing it by ear from there. Be safe."

The troops headed back to the trucks, where they waited for the order to move out.

Within about fifteen minutes, the first truck began to move. Jason was very nervous. He was biting his nails and shaking his legs. Although the unit was told that their road was to be secured, the potential for danger would still exist, and he had a bad feeling about the whole trip. But he did not verbalize that. He continued as every other soldier would. As the trucks entered the city walls, it quickly became clear that the road was not yet secure and that the marines still had a tough battle going on. Jason quickly got into position from inside the truck in case he needed to fire.

Before Jason's truck even entered the city walls, the commander's voice came over the radio with a frightening statement. He was in the lead vehicle.

"Soldiers, listen up," Captain Hillock quickly called out. "Fighting is still in full force. I repeat, fighting is still in full force. Be ready for anything."

He then called back to the first sergeant, who travelled in the last vehicle. The problem was, they were supposed to change frequencies before talking to each other. This time they forgot.

"Get the body bags ready; we may lose a few here," Captain Hillock relayed.

"Can you believe this shit?" Jason said out loud.

He quickly grabbed the radio and relayed to the commander, "Sir, you're not on your secure line. I repeat, you're not on your secure line, idiot."

"Who is this?" the commander asked.

Jason did not reply. The radio fell silent. *At least it worked*, he thought to himself.

Jason couldn't believe what he had just heard. If at any time in his life he felt intense fear, it was nowhere close to what he was experiencing right now. He checked his weapon to make sure the magazine was fully engaged and that a round was loaded into the chamber. With his weapon ready and his truck now entering the city, Jason pointed his gun out of the window and was ready to fire. As his truck approached the first set of buildings, Jason, despite being exposed to graphic sights as a physician, was not prepared for what he was now seeing. Maintaining his fighting position, Jason momentarily took his eyes off of the buildings and alleyways to look at the dead enemy fighters lying all over the place. Some looked as if they were simply sleeping, while others were completely shot up and dismembered by the extensive fire power used on them. The marines were using every weapon they had to fire at every target; whether it was a round from an M-16 machine gun or a 120-millimeter round from an M1A1 Abrams tank, it did not matter. The goal was to kill the enemy by any means possible. And kill they did. The bodies were everywhere.

As Jason stared at the carnage before him, he had feelings of horror and shock that he had never before felt. This seemed very surreal. The destruction was something he was not prepared to encounter. He was never taught how to handle the sights and sounds of combat. However, he could not get caught up in what he was witnessing. Jason had to maintain focus on the mission at hand. He could only take the sights in for a few seconds before he realized that he needed to be on the lookout.

As he was looking at a group of dead Iraqi soldiers, he heard a bullet zip over his truck, and this quickly brought him back into the reality of the moment. Jason looked in the direction of a house directly in front of him and saw a man firing rounds from and AK-47 in his direction. Jason hesitated but quickly returned fire. The man dropped out of sight, and Jason's truck continued down the road. Unsure of whether he hit the man or not, Jason quickly rechecked his weapon and immediately began zeroing in on the next set of houses. Again he set his sights on a man firing in his direction, but before he could return fire, an armored vehicle sitting by the road began firing on the building, hitting the man and apparently killing him instantly. Jason continued scouring the area for possible targets but found none. Surprisingly, he felt a little disappointed. He was so into what was happening, he didn't want the rush to stop. But his truck and the rest of the trucks in the unit finally made it through the city and into a relatively safe zone, not needing the body bags that the commander so terrifyingly warned about.

This area was safe because the marines had already cleared the roads and houses. The dead bodies were evidence of that. Apparently, the marines had been given orders to fire upon any moving object. And that they did, as many of the dead were women and children. This sickened Jason. *Why would our marines fire on innocent people?* he thought to himself. *Did they not realize that there were women and children on those busses? Perhaps not.* He would later discover that the Iraqi soldiers were using the civilians as shields with the false assumption that they would not be fired upon. They were clearly mistaken. The marines fired at everything, assuring that no combatants made it through to assist the fighting in the city. This whole situation sickened Jason, but there was nothing he could do about it. This was a part of the war, and he had to accept it, for the damage was already done.

By the time the 132nd made it to an area to park and reassemble, it was nightfall. No one could really see where he or she was parking. Soldiers using flashlights with red lenses guided the trucks into position to park. At this point, the night vision goggles barely worked. The sky was filled with smoke and ash resulting from the battles in nearby cities and villages. This would become the norm for the next several weeks, and since tactical driving in a war zone did not permit the use of headlights, driving at night became very dangerous. Nevertheless, Jason and his fellow soldiers were glad to be in a resting zone and out of harm's way, if only for a short period of time.

When Jason's truck was finally parked, he quietly sat in it for a few moments, pondering the horrific sights he took in today. He became a little emotional, allowing just a few tears to dribble from his eyes. But he quickly regained his composure, as he realized that emotions could not be a part of battle and could not be witnessed by other soldiers, especially someone of his rank. However, when he exited the truck and began searching for the troops in his squad, he realized that the incidents of the day were too overwhelming for some people. When he approached the vehicle occupied by Specialist Kennedy and Private First Class Helms, he found two soldiers clearly affected by the combat. Both of them were crying hysterically. When Jason asked them to exit the vehicle, they did not move. They appeared frozen in their seats. Jason realized that it was his responsibility to ensure that these troops regained their composure before the commander called upon them.

After two or three minutes of reassuring them that they were in a safe environment and that it was okay to be afraid, they slowly began to exit the vehicle. Once both of them were out and standing in front of Jason, he guided them behind their truck and sat them down for a talk.

"I want each of you to know that what you are feeling is normal. Remember what I said, Kennedy? It is okay to be afraid, and it is normal."

"Yes, sergeant," Kennedy replied as he wiped a tear from his left eye.

"It's important to understand that when you are faced with this kind of crap and know that it will probably come up again, it is normal to feel whatever you are feeling, and you shouldn't be ashamed of it. Nobody ever gave us a training manual on how to feel," Jason said with a faint laugh, which also garnered chuckles from the two soldiers.

"Just don't jeopardize the lives of the other soldiers," Jason emphasized.

The more Jason talked, the more calm the soldiers felt. They soon regained full composure, but that did not last long.

"What exactly bothered you guys?" Jason asked.

The soldiers hesitated, and the renewed presence of tears exemplified the impact of what happened on that day.

"We were fine, sarge, until bullets started hitting our truck and we couldn't see where they were coming from to fire back. We felt helpless."

Private Helms simply nodded his head as if he were unable to speak.

"I thought I could handle things after the bullets stopped. Then we came upon that bus, and ..." He began to cry again, as did Helms.

Jason, realizing he could not let this go on for long, interrupted, "Look, feeling this way is okay, as I said. I can see how those things would bother you. But look, you're here now, safe and sound. We have to be strong. It's okay to be bothered, but you have to keep in mind that we have a job to do to. There will be plenty of time later for figuring all this stuff out. I gotta report to the commander and first sergeant. Take care. I'll be around."

Jason felt that it was safe to leave them, so he went to find the platoon sergeant and commander to report on the status of the troops and vehicles in his squad.

This would prove to be a difficult task. The darkness was inhibiting Jason's ability to make his way through all of the vehicles and actually locate his leaders. In addition, between all of the commotion from the artillery, gunfire down the road, and vehicles running, communication was severely limited. To make matters worse, amidst all of the commotion and inability to see clearly, it began to rain.

Although it does not rain much in the Middle East, at times it will and does so very hard. This made Jason's walking difficult as the fine sand quickly turned to mud, causing him to slip and slide in certain spots. However, after about fifteen minutes, Jason was able to locate his platoon sergeant and commander and give them the report on his squad. He was also able to get an update on the status of the situation. After informing them his squad was good to go, Jason received some news that brought the reality of this situation to the forefront.

First Sergeant Williams pulled him aside from the commander and told him that he needed to talk to him about something. Jason knew immediately that something bad had happened. He took a deep breath, sighed, and asked, "What is it, top."

"SFC Colson and his driver, Specialist Jones, took some rounds to their truck."

Jason hesitated. "Are they okay?"

Unsure of how to answer that question, First Sergeant Williams replied, "They were hit, and Jones didn't make it. SFC Colson sustained a shot to the neck, and we don't know his status. They were taken away as soon as we pulled into this area."

Jason didn't know how to respond. He just stared back at the first sergeant, shaking his head in disbelief. Although he didn't know Jones all that well, he had been in the unit with Colson for three years. And regardless of how well he knew them, these were guys in his unit and the impact was the same. Jason paused and took a deep breath, "Was anyone else hurt?"

"No one else was hurt, but a couple of trucks were severely damaged. Now we're going to have to find some way to transport those troops."

Not really knowing how to react to this news, Jason asked, "Any other news?"

"Well, actually, Henson, we're going to stay put until we're given further orders. But that's all I know for now. Do you have anything else, sergeant?"

"No, top. Nothing here."

Jason then retreated back to his truck, clearly impacted by this gut-wrenching news. When he reached his truck, he began heaving as he grabbed the door for balance. When he finished, he sat on the ground and took a drink of water as he stared off into the distance, at nothing in particular. Just then, a couple of his buddies, Sgt. Adams and SSG Alderson, who were each standing nearby and heard the noise from Jason, came over to check on him.

"What's up, sarge?" Alderson asked, realizing it was Jason.

"Didn't you guy hear the news?"

"No. What happened?"

"Jones and Colson were hit. Jones didn't make it."

"What!?" they both replied.

"Yeah, and Colson was shot in the neck. Don't know his status."

The two of them just stood there for a minute with their heads down and hands on their hips, processing what they had heard.

"This shit is getting crazy already," Sgt. Adams said.

"You got that right," Alderson stated.

"You all right, sarge?" asked Adams. "I know we haven't had a lot of time to get together and talk, but you know we're here for each other. Always have been."

"Yeah, I know," Jason replied. "I'm all right. We gotta keep an eye on each other, you know that?"

"We know that for sure, Jason," Alderson said as Adams nodded in confirmation. "We gotta get back to the truck. Let me help you up," Adams ordered.

"Thanks, guys. Take care. I'll see you soon enough."

They left, and Jason jumped into the truck and sat there, silently, pondering what the next days and weeks would hold. He also thought about Colson and Jones's wives and how they were going to feel when they got the news. And then he thought about Shannon and what she would do if something were to happen to him. With this thought, he pulled out a piece of paper, a pen, and his red-lens flashlight and began to write a letter.

> *Shannon,*
> *I don't really know where to begin or what to say, but I want you to know that I love you and miss you very much. Things are getting pretty crazy over here, but I'm doing fine. I'm sure by the time you get this letter, you'll have heard that Colson and Jones were shot, and Jones didn't make it. I am so sorry that this had to happen. Everyone is doing okay with it, and we are fighting on in their names. How are you? How are my parents? Probably nervous wrecks. Try not to watch too much TV; I know how you get, and that won't help. It's been a long day, and it's nighttime right now. It's even raining a little bit. I want you to know that as each second goes by, I am thinking about you. You are what's keeping me going and what will continue to make me go. Tell everyone I miss them and that I love them. Most important, I love you. Say a prayer for us.*
>
> *Yours truly, Jason*

Jason wasn't sure when Shannon would get this letter, but with the events of the day, he needed to make sure he wrote something to her. He would later find out that he wasn't the only one thinking about this, as most of the soldiers in the unit wrote similar letters within the next few days.

When he finished the letter, he folded it neatly and put it in one of the pockets of his rucksack. He then did his best to get comfortable in the truck and decided to try and doze off for a bit. By this time it was almost one in the morning. He hadn't had any sleep in over two days. He finally fell asleep, amid all of the artillery explosions and distant gunfire, and was awakened at about five by SSG Alderson knocking on his door.

"We're having a formation in five minutes," he told Jason. Jason stretched and jumped out of the truck, following Alderson to the meeting. They arrived just in time for the commander to begin his briefing.

Although Jason and his buddies, Alderson and Adams, along with a few other soldiers, knew about the losses sustained over the night, most of the troops did not know anything severe had happened.

"I'm just going to get down to it," Captain Hillock stated. "We lost a couple of our soldiers last night, Colson and Jones. Jones's wounds were fatal."

Everyone fell silent.

"I know this is going to be hard for some of you, but we have to continue with the mission. We're going to be moving out soon. We've also been issued some new weaponry from the marines that need to be distributed. We're going to be in some hot spots, so we informed them that we needed at least some AT-4 rocket launchers and a few MK-19s. They also gave us some grenades and a couple more grenade launchers. Be sure they're distributed evenly throughout the convoy. Before you go, let's have a moment of silence for our lost soldiers."

Everyone bowed their heads. A few shed some tears. He then handed the briefing over to 1SG Williams, who continued with instructions.

He gave orders for the squad leaders to pick two troops from their squads to retrieve the new weapons from the ammo supply area, the back of a marine five-ton truck. Once this was ordered, the soldiers fell out, and Jason picked the two from his squad to get the new weapons, which consisted of the AT-4 rocket launchers and several hand grenades. *This is a sign of some bad things coming,* Jason thought to himself. When all of the weapons were retrieved, everyone was ordered back to their trucks to get ready to move out. A new mission was upon them.

As the trucks began to move out on the morning of March 26th, a sandstorm that had developed during the night was picking up in intensity. In fact, the unit did not get too far along in their journey before they received word that the marines leading the way had stopped. The storm had become so intense that visibility was limited to almost nothing. The 132nd, having traveled only about one mile, was forced to pull off of the road and wait the storm out. Never before had a war come to a complete standstill because of inclement weather. But because of the rough terrain and the amount of ground that had already been covered in just a few days, as well as the fact that bombings by the air force had to stop, the powers-that-be determined it was not necessary to further risk the lives of the soldiers and marines at this time; the ground could be made up when the storm passed.

The storm lasted for several hours before it gave way to a severe rainstorm. By the time it was all over, every piece of equipment was covered in sand and mud, and even the soldiers inside of the trucks were coated with a thin layer of sand. The troops would later find out that this storm was the worst of its kind in Iraq in over one hundred years. As the rain gave way to hot, sunny skies, the U.S. military was back in full swing. Airplanes and fighter jets could be seen overhead on their way to bomb strategic targets. Artillery could be heard in the distance, pounding buildings and other enemy locations, and the radio was full of chatter about what was going on with the elements of the Marines Corps. Because there had been no movement by anyone for several hours, the enemy forces had more time to assemble and prepare for what was coming their way. As a result, it took a little longer than expected for the marines to get through the smaller cities on their way to their ultimate destination.

Jason and his unit were forced to set up a perimeter again until they were able to safely move forward. Once they had their vehicles in place, they gathered with the commander for a short briefing. He informed them that they would only be staying in this location for a short period of time until a clear path was made to move farther north. After instructions to clean their weapons and check their vehicles, the troops were dismissed to complete the assignments and wait further orders.

When Jason returned to his truck, he did a thorough inspection around it to ensure everything was secure and intact. He started from the front passenger side and worked his way around the back and up to the front on the driver's side. After completing his round and finding that there was no damage and that everything was in its place, he decided to double check it just to make sure he didn't miss anything. As he passed by his door, around the back, and towards the front again, he noticed something near the bottom corner of the fuel tank. Upon further inspection, Jason noticed that there were three bullet holes on the frame just below the fuel tank, which was located on the side just behind the driver's door. He was stunned. If one of these rounds had been about an inch higher, the truck would have been blown to pieces. A sick feeling quickly developed in Jason's stomach, and he took a seat on the ground.

As he sat there, realizing how close he was to death, his buddy SSG Alderson walked by and saw him sitting.

"What's up, sarge?"

Jason did not reply.

"Are you okay?" SSG Alderson asked as he walked towards Jason, realizing something was wrong.

Again, no response. As he got closer to Jason, he too noticed the bullet holes in the truck.

"Holy shit," he said, leaning in to get a closer look. "You guys were lucky."

Jason looked up at him and expressed his appreciation for recognizing the obvious.

"No shit."

Realizing the impact this had on Jason, SSG Alderson sat down and did his best to reassure him.

"It was a close call, Jason, but nothing more than that. C'mon, we need to get our stuff ready; we'll be moving out any time."

Jason continued to sit motionless for about another minute, then gathered himself and gave Alderson a hug.

"This shit is crazy man," Jason said, fighting back tears."

"I know, but somebody's got to do it, and who better than us?" Alderson stated confidently.

Jason simply nodded and continued his inspection as Alderson left for his own truck. After finding no other damage, Jason checked the fluids and finished up. Everything was good to go. He then cleaned his weapon and moved on to check on the rest of the soldiers in his squad. Everyone else was good to go, too. He ordered his driver, who was bullshitting with some of the other troops, back to the truck to clean his weapon and check all of the gear. He also made him do an inspection, even though he had already done a thorough one himself. Jason figured that since the private was nowhere to be found when he was doing the inspection, this would be a good way to keep him busy and focused on the mission.

Soon after Jason ordered the private to check out the truck, orders came down to load up and get ready for movement. It turned out that the marines made it through a few of the smaller cities and were in need of some more supplies. Since the 132nd had already resupplied a lot of the marine units, their extra supplies were running low. So their thinking was that this might be their last mission for a while until some of the other transportation units came and resupplied them or some helicopter drops could be made. Nevertheless, they had to get ready, so everyone loaded up and the convoy was on its way farther into enemy territory.

It was approaching dusk. The soldiers of the 132nd Transportation Company had been driving for about two hours now, with little action along the way. There was the occasional artillery round explosion and some sporadic small arms fire, but nothing that directly affected the progression of the convoy. Most of the occupied areas that they passed along the way were nothing more than a few buildings and some small huts, but rarely did they pass an area that was occupied by more than maybe fifty people. It was a much-needed break from action.

As they were driving along, the troops had a pretty good feeling about what they were doing. This was the first time that they were able to drive along for more than an hour consistently and take time to reflect on what had happened and what they were doing for the good of our nation. Jason was no exception. Although he was sad about the loss of fellow soldiers and still a little startled about the bullet holes in his truck, this current trek enabled him to process his feelings and take in the scenery, as unsightly as it was—not much more than some mud huts, lots of sand, and a few blown up cars, along with a few filthy kids running around. During this two-hour period, there had been only a few messages sent over the radios, but they mostly consisted of the commander checking on the rest of the convoy, ensuring that no one was having any problems with the trucks.

As Jason sat in his seat, somewhat relaxed at this point, carrying on small talk with the private driving the truck, the commander came over the radio with a message that quickly brought Jason back to reality.

"Soldiers, listen up," Captain Hillock ordered. "We're approaching a city of about three thousand people. The marines quickly went through here about three hours ago without any problems. However, chopper intel stated that they saw some armed people in the streets getting into firing positions. They said they were not able to fire because the armed men were surrounded by women and children."

The next thing that came over the radio was gunfire and then silence. Jason made sure that his weapon was locked and loaded and then pointed it out the window. He could not yet see what was up ahead because of the large contingent of trucks in front of him, but he knew it was trouble.

As Jason's truck slowly moved forward, he began to hear the trucks in front of him firing their weapons. He was ready. Jason screamed out, "Here we go!" and took up a firm position with his weapon still pointed out of the window. Just as he saw the first person firing at the trucks, his truck began to speed up and he fell back in his seat.

"What the fuck are you doing?" Jason irately asked the private.

"The trucks are speeding up, and I'm just keeping pace, sarge."

Jason glanced ahead and noticed that the trucks were rapidly moving forward. The commander came over the radio shouting, "Get on it. Put the pedal to the floor!"

Jason reiterated to the private what the commander said and then regained his position out of the window. Just as he was pointing his weapon outward, Jason quickly fell back into the truck in response to a bullet flying right past the windshield. Regaining his composure, he went back into attack mode and began firing his weapon. Although he did not have anyone or anything in clear sight, he was firing at a building where he had just seen bullets come flying out of a window. He then quickly shifted his weapon to the next set of buildings ahead.

As his truck approached a set of four bullet-ridden shops, three men jumped out of the doorways and began firing directly at him. Because his truck was moving at such a high rate of speed, none of them hit him. However, as soon as he saw the men come out of the door, he opened fire and immediately one of them fell down. He got one—his first confirmed combat kill. *No time to think about it; have to stay on point.* He continued firing at the men, and just as his truck passed by them, a woman came running out of the building holding a small child, screaming and crying. Because it happened so quickly, Jason got off a few rounds before he recognized the woman and was able to pull back. But it was too late. At least one of the rounds hit the woman. But Jason wasn't sure if more had hit her because she fell to the ground.

He immediately stopped firing and pulled his weapon back into the truck. He sat still, staring straight ahead, not knowing what to think or how to react. The convoy was soon past the city and into safe territory again. They drove for about another fifteen minutes when they found a large enough, safe area to pull over and assess the situation. Jason continued to sit, motionless, not knowing what to think about what just happened.

How could this have happened? he asked himself. *Did I really just kill an innocent woman and possibly her small child?*

As Jason thought more about it, he started getting mad. He was mad that she came running out when there was gunfire. He was mad because he realized the men in the building probably forced her outside, hoping her presence would cease the firing. And most of all, he was mad because he felt that his unit should not have been in that type of situation. After all, they were just a reserve transportation company, not some active duty, training every day, shoot-to-kill infantry unit. No. They were a reserve unit that was supposed to move into areas after they were safe and secure. But that hadn't been the case. This group of weekend warriors was in the middle of an invasion, fighting as if it was their primary job, and losing soldiers along the way. And just how many troops would they have to lose before someone realized that they shouldn't be in these situations? Well, Jason would soon get the answer to that question.

This stop wasn't like any of the other ones that the 132nd had to make. Sure, there was the same confusion, but it had not been like this before. Once Jason gathered himself enough to begin checking on the troops in his squad, he got out of the vehicle and immediately noticed that something bad had happened. Several of the soldiers gathered around a couple of the vehicles in an obvious state of pandemonium, throwing their arms in the air, yelling and cursing. Jason ran towards the vehicle closest to him. He saw the front bumper and the number written upon it and right away knew that it was SPC Jennings and PFC Upshaw, two of the soldiers in his squad. As Jason frantically looked around to see what had happened, around the truck came a bloody SPC Jennings.

"What happened?" asked Jason.

"They got him."

Just then, the medic screamed, "Make a hole!" As the area cleared, the medic and another soldier carried a blood-soaked PFC Upshaw, who had clearly been hit by several bullet rounds. When they made it through the crowd, they laid him on the ground and began first aid and CPR. Jason assisted. As they worked on the severely wounded soldier, one of the other medics and some other troops headed towards the same area, carrying another wounded soldier. This area was probably the safest place to work on them, surrounded by several trucks. They laid him down and began first aid.

While the two soldiers were being tended to, waiting for one of the Blackhawk medical helicopters to arrive, Jason let the medics do their work and got some of the higher-ranking NCOs to try and calm the other soldiers down and assess the situation. Many of the younger troops were in a state of frenzy, pacing and stomping around, spewing obscenities at the air. They did not expect to be in these kinds of situations, and it was not getting any easier to handle what was going on.

"Everybody calm down, just calm down. We need to focus here. Get yourselves together. You're soldiers, damn it," Jason said. He was successful at getting most of the frantic soldiers calmed down.

Soon, the helicopter arrived to take the wounded soldiers away.

Once the chopper was gone and while most of the soldiers were gathered in the same area, Captain Hillock called them in for a brief discussion.

"Listen up," he said with an empathic tone.

"I know things have gotten a little rough, and I know there is some concern for the soldiers who just left us, but we need to stay focused on the mission. I know that we didn't plan on being exposed to some of this stuff, but it's happening, and we need to be poised. We're going to stick around here for about another thirty minutes or so to regroup; then we need to get these supplies to the marines. They're counting on us."

The commander walked away, and 1SG Williams gave the order to get everything ready. Jason called his squad to a quick briefing.

"Listen up," he said, sounding stable. "You're all doing a good job. I'm proud of you, and your families would be too. Private Upshaw will be counting on you to do the squad proud. Now head back to your trucks and get ready. Specialist Jennings, I need to talk to you for a minute."

"Yeah, sergeant"

"Hang in there, buddy. Things will get better. I know Upshaw is your friend. But we have to get our job done. If you have any other problems, don't hesitate to come and get me, okay? We need you, buddy."

Jennings nodded and was off on his way. As he walked away, Jason told him to change his uniform and bring it to him. Again Jennings nodded and was off to get ready. Shortly after, while Jason was making final preparations and doing a quick truck inspection, Jennings approached him and handed over the blood-soaked uniform. No words were exchanged; none were needed. Jason put the clothes in a bag and shoved it in one of the storage bins on the truck. He would properly dispose of it when the opportunity permitted. After finishing up the inspection and quickly cleaning and reloading his weapon, Jason told his driver to saddle up and get ready to go. Soon after, a call came across the radio. It was now time to go.

Because of the previous unexpected incidents, everyone was now fully on guard. They were not going to take any chances. After about fifteen minutes of driving at a pretty steady pace, the trucks began to slow, almost to a crawl, and eventually they came to a complete stop. Jason jumped out of his truck to see what was going on, but he could see nothing out of the ordinary. As he saw some of the other soldiers get out of their trucks and slowly start walking toward the front of the convoy, he too began walking in that direction. Jason had taken no more than ten steps before he heard several of the soldiers yelling, "Don't move. Don't move!"

Jason froze in his place, wondering what was going on. He then heard some troops yelling something again but couldn't quite make it out. Jason could also hear something coming in over the radio, so he rushed back into the truck to get the message.

"Landmines! There are landmines spread out all over the place," someone screamed over the radio.

Not knowing exactly what to do, Jason paused and then confirmed the message. The person on the radio repeated himself.

The unit had been warned about the possibility of this kind of situation, but they received no formal training prior to crossing the border. As Jason stood at the truck, pondering his next move, the word was passed back from the troops ahead for everyone to get back in their trucks and to not move until further notice. The same order came over the radio. So Jason and the rest of the troops sat motionless in their trucks for about an hour, with no word about anything, pondering what was going to happen next.

Finally, the commander came over the radio with the message, "All clear. Now let's move out." With that, the trucks revved up and were on their way again.

What Jason would later find out was that, thankfully, the recent sandstorm had uncovered dozens of landmines that would have otherwise gone undetected and potentially cost the marines, and possibly some of these reserves, their lives. The marines noticed these mines on their way north and called in the Explosive Ordnance Disposal Team to diffuse them. What was left were the remnants of the mines, but none of them were still active. Stopping the convoy was a precautionary measure. As these troops saw it, it was better to be safe than sorry. One more obstacle had been overcome, and now the 132nd could continue their mission.

Chapter 10: Now What?

IT WAS APPROACHING NIGHTFALL ON the eve of March 26th, 2003, as the soldiers of this war-weary and sleep-deprived transportation company continued their trek along Highway 7 toward their destination, an area south of Al Kut. The marines were engaged in heavy fighting south of that city and were poised to be there for several days. The Iraqis had several thousand soldiers nestled in and around the city, as well as in various smaller villages and towns along the way. The marines were spread out over several of these areas, and a large contingent of them was finishing up the fighting in Nasiriyah in preparation of the British forces taking control of the city. So it was the responsibility of the 132nd to get close enough to establish contact with the marines, who were waiting for their much-needed fresh stock of supplies.

The soldiers of the 132nd had been driving their vehicles for about an hour now at a relatively fast pace and without any problems, when the commander came over the radio, stating that they were approaching their rendezvous point. Jason had actually fallen asleep and was awakened by this transmission.

After stretching out as much as he could and letting out a bellowing yawn, he began surveying the surroundings, trying to determine what type of area they were about to settle into. Although the sun had set by now and most of the sky was darkened by the smoke from the fires that had been burning in the surrounding area, there was just enough moonlight illumination to see through his night vision goggles. It appeared that they were pulling in to a soccer field. Yes, that's exactly what it was Jason was seeing.

Although Saddam did not allow too many privileges to his people, he did allow soccer, and fields were scattered throughout the country. Some of them were well put-together, while others were simply areas of cleared ground with makeshift goals. This one appeared to be one of the professional fields, as there were light posts and bleachers surrounding it. This sight brought Jason a little excitement. This would be a great location for the unit to set up temporary shop and get some much-needed rest. Maybe there would even be locker rooms to get a little freshened up. Regardless of what was in this area, simply getting off of the road and into a somewhat safe perimeter was enough for Jason.

The trucks slowly filed, one at a time, through the main entrance to the field, careful to stay in a straight line. Although the marines had cleared the area for occupancy, there was still the possibility that they may have missed a landmine somewhere in the area. Once the unit had all of the trucks filed in and set in place, they would send their own team out to make sure there were no active mines left in the vicinity. Jason's opportunity finally came, and his driver pulled the truck into the area to which they were guided. Once the truck was parked and shut off, Jason got out and immediately headed in the direction of the commander and the first sergeant. He wanted to find out what the plan was and if they were going to be in this area for an extended period of time.

As he was walking along, he was glancing around, trying to see what was in the area in addition to the trucks. But it was so dark that he could barely see the ground more than five feet in front of him without light. He knew that they would be near the center of the field, positioning themselves in a location that made them easy to find. After walking for about five minutes or so, Jason finally found the commander and 1SG Williams. They were talking back and forth about when the supplies were going to be picked up and what they were going to be doing once this mission was completed. It was clear that although these two guys were in charge of this unit, they had no idea what the next step was going to be. They would have to sit and wait for an order from the marines.

Before Jason even spoke a word, 1SG Williams turned to him and told him that they would be in this location at least until morning and that there was no further information available at this time. The first sergeant also told him that some marines were coming in to provide security so they could get the rest that they so desperately needed. This news was music to Jason's ears. *Finally*, he thought to himself, *I'm gonna get some sleep.*

As Jason walked away, he saw some of the other squad leaders and passed along the information. It wouldn't be long before most, if not all, of the troops in this company were fast asleep. It was about one in the morning on March 27th when Jason finally settled into his truck to get some sleep. He was out like a light.

As the sun began to rise in the morning, so did Jason. Although it is very hot during the day in Iraq, it can become very cold overnight, so Jason was bundled up in his sleeping bag. Since this was the first morning in Iraq he was able to sleep and wasn't awakened by the fighting, he continued to stay wrapped up in his sleeping bag and enjoy watching the rising of the sun, one of the few beautiful scenes he witnessed.

As he sat there, he reminisced about his life back home. He thought of all of the things that he missed, not the least of which was Shannon. He could not wait to get back to the life he left behind, although he knew that probably would not happen for quite some time, or at least not until the war was over.

This period of relative tranquility did not last long. Word came down over the radio that all of the NCOs were needed at the commander's Humvee for a briefing. Jason slowly removed himself from his little cocoon and got out of the truck. Before he headed towards the briefing area, he did some stretching and some quick personal hygiene, mainly washing his face and brushing his teeth. He then grabbed his rifle and was off to the meeting.

Jason was the last to arrive and was greeted promptly by the commander.

"Nice to see you could make it, Henson."

Jason simply nodded and the commander began the briefing.

"Okay," Captain Hillock began, "here's the latest. A convoy of marines is expected to arrive here in a couple of hours to pick up their supplies, so some of the soldiers need to unload it and prepare it for the pickup. Now, I know this area doesn't look like Harrisville, but it is going to be our home for the next few days. We don't have any more orders for supplies, and since the army and marines are still fighting their way to Baghdad, we are safe to stay put."

"What the hell are we going to do here, sir?" SFC Freeman asked.

The captain glared at him over the top of his sunglasses for a second, as if he were irritated about being interrupted. He did not answer Freeman directly, but continued with his expectations.

"We're going to establish a perimeter around the field and take over security for this area. The few marines who have been here will be joining the rest of their unit. We need to supplement the sandbag fighting positions with foxholes and concertina wire. The area also needs to be swept for land mines. I expect to have a roster for security detail within the hour. Any questions?"

No one responded, so the commander dismissed them. The section sergeants and squad leaders knew what to do, so they started tracking down their soldiers to inform them of the orders and set the security roster. Jason knew his troops would not be happy. He knew that after coming this far, they would not like the news that they had to stop. But, orders are orders, and they had to do what they were told.

When all of the troops were informed of what to do, little time was wasted in completing the tasks, although there was some moaning and groaning. Jason just ignored it. When they were done unloading the trucks, they would be left with nothing to do but sit and wait, with the exception of a few hours of guard duty. It would more than likely be a long few days before they were able to leave this area.

After Jason informed the soldiers in his squad of what was to take place and what each of them needed to do, he decided to scope out the area and see exactly what was around them. He headed in the direction of a set of bleachers that had a building underneath of them. Upon arrival, he found a building that had

R. JEREMY HARRISON

been completely emptied of all of its belongings, with the exception of a rake, a few rusty nails lying around, and a beat-up ladder, which if stepped on would probably completely fall apart. He then headed to the other side of the soccer field to another building. Again, he found nothing other than a few scraps of what was once a supply building of some sort. Although he found nothing useful inside, he thought for a few minutes about the buildings themselves and tried to figure out the best way to use them.

One thing Jason learned early in the army was that soldiers have a way of figuring out how to use anything they may find, whether it is building supplies or just a plain building. He remembered that some of the guys in the unit were carpenters and plumbers and came up with the idea that these building could pose as makeshift shower houses. Excited and proud of himself for being so innovative, he headed back to the commander and 1SG Williams and told them of his proposal. They both agreed that this would be a great idea, so now it was Jason's responsibility to make it happen.

He headed down the line of trucks in search of Sgt. Brown, the carpenter; SSG Mullen and SPC Welch, the plumbers; and some troops who were not busy who could help with the project. After about fifteen minutes of searching, he found who he was looking for.

"Listen up guys," Jason ordered. "I know that no one is really happy about having to stay here, and that includes me. But we need to try to make the best of it. That shack sitting over there could help make things a little better for us. With your help and a little innovation, we could make it into a shower house, and do the same to the other one—have one for the males and one for the females. I think the troops would appreciate that, and it would improve morale a little bit. What do you say?"

"Do you really think we can make a shower out of those heaps of crap?" SPC Welch asked.

"Damn right we can," replied Sgt. Brown. "Top okay with this?"

"Yeah," Jason responded. "He gave me the go-ahead to do what I needed to get it done."

127

"Let's get to it then," Brown stated enthusiastically.

They were eager to have something like this to do, as it would give them some feeling of being back home again. They headed for one of the shipping containers that they were hauling, which was filled with all of the lumber and building materials they needed. Once they had everything gathered, they were off to start work on what would be the female shower.

Obviously this was not going to be a typical shower house, with tile floors, heating and air-conditioning, and regulated hot and cold water. They were going to be field showers. They did have some flooring to put down, but it was going to be wood. The water would flow from a fifty-gallon drum operated by a string. But it would provide some privacy and a chance to get relatively clean. The men spent most of the day on these projects. When they were finished, the water supply truck filled the water drums and troops began rushing towards the showers to get in line. However, there was a wait, as the building constructors would have the first opportunity. Jason was ready and excited to get in there and get clean.

By the time dusk came around, every soldier had had the opportunity to use the newly built facilities and was quite appreciative of what the men had done to make this happen. For a short period of time, the soldiers felt somewhat normal again, thanks to Jason and his ever-present wisdom. But the reality of the situation came to the forefront quickly. That night, the marines arrived, clearly fatigued and war weary, to get the basic supplies they so desperately needed. Once they loaded the water, food, medical equipment, and other supplies into their trucks, it would be back to the front lines for them. For the soldiers of the 132nd Transportation Company, the next several days would consist of on-and-off security duty and waiting for the next set of orders, one of the last things any soldier in the field wants to happen. Boredom, monotony, and anticipation could be detrimental to soldiers' morale.

The next two days were relatively uneventful. Although there was the threat of enemy attacks and possible artillery rounds coming into the area, nothing happened. At one point there was a bus filled with Iraqi men that came down the road, which sent everyone into a momentary ruckus, but it turned out to be a contingent of enemy prisoners of war, who were being guided to the next camp for containment. Other than that, everything else was normal, considering the circumstances.

Many of the soldiers took advantage of the time to write some letters home to let their families know that they were doing okay. They were informed that a helicopter was coming in to bring them some food and water and that it was going to take any mail that needed to be delivered. Jason wrote letters to both his parents and Shannon. He kept them short and sweet, as directed, careful not to write anything that may upset them. He wrote about the hot days and the cool nights and the shower that he was so proud of, and let them know that he was in good spirits. He ended the letters by telling them that he loved them and that the unit was going to be safe. This was just enough information to ease some of the stress they may be feeling about the current situation. Ultimately, he decided against sending the first letter he wrote. Keeping them upbeat was more important to him.

After writing his letters, Jason walked the perimeter to make sure everyone was doing all right and then headed back to take a short nap before his turn came for guard duty. He slept for the better part of an hour—enough time to enjoy a few dreams of home and be rested enough for his two-hour shift. When he awakened, it was approaching dusk and the temperature was quickly dropping. He made sure he had enough clothing on to keep warm and then headed for the foxhole. In about thirty minutes, it was completely dark, and Jason had to get his night vision goggles out in order to see. He would scan the area for about thirty seconds, take a break for a few minutes, and then scan again.

After about an hour or so, at approximately 10:30 PM, Jason heard a faint whistling noise. He scanned the area but could see nothing. The noise became more distinct, eerily resembling a mortar round flying through the air. Just as Jason rescanned the area, he heard yelling from the trucks on the north end of the perimeter. "Incoming! Incoming! Take cover." His suspicions were right; there was a mortar round headed straight for their camp.

Jason relayed the message as loud as he could and then ducked into his hole. As he lay in the hole, covering himself the best he could, he heard everyone in the perimeter yelling to take cover. The explosion hit, crashing into the ground like trains colliding, shaking the entire area, sending dirt, debris, and shrapnel all over the place.

When the shaking ceased and the debris had settled, Jason exited the hole as fast as he could. He climbed out to the yells and screams of many in the unit, but it was so dark that it was almost impossible to determine immediate damage. There was a fire burning about one hundred feet from Jason, which gave him ample illumination to use his night vision goggles and see in which direction he needed to go. Just as Jason approached the area where the mortar round landed, a soldier came crawling out from underneath one of the trucks. With Jason's limited vision, he surmised that the soldier was covered in dirt and blood. He ran over to check for sure and realized he was correct. It was Private Wickowski.

Apparently the mortar round struck between Wickowski's truck and the one next to it. Wickowski was relieving himself outside of his truck and did not have enough time to take cover before the impact. Several other soldiers who ran to assess the damage soon surrounded Jason. Although Jason was a doctor, he did not have the appropriate medical supplies to do anything for the soldier. He shouted out for the medic, who was on sight within seconds. Because of the magnitude of the situation, several of the soldiers were told to turn on their flashlights and begin looking around to assess the damage, even though doing so could further endanger the unit. When there was enough light to clearly see the precise extent of Wickowski's wounds, it was clear that he was going to need serious medical attention.

From the looks of the damage to his legs, it appeared that he was hit as he was diving under the truck. The shrapnel from the explosion had taken off a piece of his left foot and part of his right calf muscle. As the medic and Jason worked frantically to dress the wounds, the commander showed up to see what he needed to do. He realized immediately that he was going to have to call in a helicopter to take the man to a hospital, so he ordered one of the troops to get the radio.

Meanwhile, even though the commander was standing right at his side, Jason started shouting at the surrounding troops out of frustration.

"Anyone who's supposed to be on guard duty get back to your security positions, now!" he screamed. "Everyone else, help get this place cleaned up and check around for further damage. A couple of you stay here with me and put some light on this area."

The commander said nothing. The soldier returned with the radio, and the commander made the emergency call for a medical evacuation. Within fifteen minutes, the helicopter was on site and Wickowski was on his way out, further reducing the number of troops the 132nd had in the field. Once the helicopter was out of the area and Jason calmed himself down, he assisted the troops in cleaning the area and determining the extent of the damage.

While he was walking around the area, Jason saw the shadow of a soldier squatted down alongside one of the trucks.

"Who is that?" Jason asked.

The soldier did not respond. Jason then decided to move in and see what was going on. As he got closer, he distinguished that it was SPC Miller, who was Wickowski's assistant driver. Recognizing that Miller was crying and obviously shaken from the explosion, Jason sat down next to him and did his best to console him.

"Everything's going to be all right, soldier. Wickowski is going to be fine," he continued. "At least he doesn't have to stay in this hell hole any longer. Look, buddy, I know this stinks, but it happened, and he would want us to be strong for him and carry on, right?"

Miller nodded as he wiped away a tear. "He is a great guy, sergeant," Miller said.

"I know," Jason said reassuringly. "He'll still be a great guy; he just might be a little moody for a while," Jason said, trying to get a smile out of the soldier.

Miller did chuckle a little but quickly stopped. Jason stood up and patted Miller on the back.

"Everything will be all right; we'll be just fine. If you need anything, I mean anything, just find me, okay?"

"Yes, sergeant."

"I gotta get going," Jason stated. "Try and get some rest. We have a lot of work ahead."

Jason caught up with some of the troops in his squad who had been looking for him. SPC Jennings informed Jason that one of the trucks in their squad received some minor damage but nothing that would make it inoperable. Other than that, all of their trucks were fine. Jason then told them to go back to their vehicles and get some sleep. He continued walking around the perimeter, trying to determine if anything else had incurred any damage. As it would turn out, only two trucks received minor damage and no other soldiers were injured.

Since Jason's guard shift had passed by now, he made his way back to his vehicle, got himself a drink of water, and jumped into the cab. He had had enough. He sat in the truck for a few minutes, thinking about what had just happened. Not having any true outlet for his frustration, Jason hit the door with his elbow a few times. He stared straight ahead for a few minutes and realized there was nothing else to do at this point. He realized that although Wickowski was injured, overall the unit was lucky, considering what could have happened if that mortar round had directly hit one of the trucks. With all of the night's excitement, Jason was completely exhausted, so he made himself as comfortable as possible and shut his eyes. He was able to fall asleep within a few minutes. The rest of the night was uneventful, so most of the soldiers were able to get some much-needed sleep.

It was about 5:30 AM on March 30th when Jason woke from his sleep. He got out of the truck and did some stretching before making his way to the makeshift port-o-potty to relieve himself. He returned to his truck and freshened up a bit before reporting to the first sergeant to receive orders for the day. Now that the sun was up, he could see exactly what damage the mortar round had caused. He walked over to the truck where he had found Private Wickowski, careful to avoid stepping on any fragments that may be lying around from the explosion. When he rounded the front of the vehicle, he saw the blood where the private had been lying. There was also a large black hole in the ground where the round made its impact. Jason stood motionless, replaying the previous night's events in his mind. His buddy SSG Alderson soon interrupted him.

"You all right?" he asked empathically.

"Yeah, I'm fine," Jason replied. "This has just been a crazy ten days so far, and I'm wondering what's going to happen next."

"We can't get caught up thinking like that, Jason, or we'll never get through this."

"Yeah," Jason hesitated. "I guess you're right. I just wasn't expecting this much shit to happen to our company, especially this early in the war."

"I agree, but it has, and we need to keep going, if for no other reason than for the younger troops."

With that being said, the two of them walked away from the area and continued their search for the commander and 1SG Williams.

When they found the first sergeant, they immediately recognized that something was wrong. The commander looked as if he was trying to hold back tears and he could not say a word. Jason looked at 1SG Williams.

"What's going on, top?"

"We just got word that PFC Upshaw didn't make it."

Jason was speechless. The first sergeant told Jason that one of the bullets went through the side of his body armor and struck an artery, resulting in excessive blood loss. When the commander finally gained his composure, he told Jason and Alderson that they needed to gather the troops so he could inform them of the news. When all of the troops were gathered, the commander told them what happened, and many of the troops in the unit immediately broke down crying. Even though they knew it was a possibility that this would happen, nothing could prepare a soldier for the loss of a comrade—nothing. It's a gut-wrenching feeling when someone who has trained day in and day out to protect you, himself, and everyone else is killed. It seemed so unfair. The commander gave a speech about the sacrifice of PFC Upshaw and how he would want everyone to go on doing what they had to do for their country. He concluded with a prayer before 1SG Williams took over the briefing.

First Sergeant Williams always had a way of getting his troops refocused on the mission, and today was no exception. He said nothing else about PFC Upshaw.

"Many soldiers have lost their lives already in this war, and many more will before it's over. We have a responsibility to complete any job we are given, and that's what we will do. And if we lose soldiers along the way, we will continue to do our job and do it successfully. We are at war, and we will win this war. Now go back to your vehicles and get everything checked out. We have to be prepared for a new mission at any time."

This speech got everyone fired up. But a problem existed: there was no mission to complete. There had been no new orders passed along directing them to do anything, so the speech led to nothing more than a temporary sense of pride and then disappointment and sadness again. The troops continued with their guard shifts, doing basic maintenance on their vehicles, weapons, and themselves. Most actually tried to get some sleep and write some letters. It was as if the war had been put at a standstill within this unit. There was still fighting going on all over the country, but this group was, for the moment, without work.

This is what happens. Soldiers get all revved up for a mission and the beginning of their combat tour, but quickly adjust to the environment and lose some of that momentum, especially when they are left without a specific mission. Even the fear of attacks dissipates to little more than a faint concern. So this group of soldiers, who had successfully completed several missions and had lost a few of their comrades, would spend the days waiting for a new mission, grieving and pondering, hoping and wishing.

The rest of this and the next three days were relatively uneventful. Although the fighting involving the marines could be heard in the distance, the threat of danger to this unit was now basically non-existent. The enemy had, in fact, learned the position of the 132nd, as evidenced by the mortar round hitting a few days ago, but because of the large contingent of American forces zeroing in on them, there was no time to worry about a small amount of non-threatening soldiers. One of the soldiers in the unit had a shortwave radio that he had been using to keep up with the news. A lot of the news was initially inaccurate, but the correct news would eventually come over the radio. Because there was not a whole lot for the soldiers to do, they spent a lot of time at this soldier's vehicle, listening to the progress of the army and marines fighting just north of them. Deep down, they were hoping that the United States would win this quickly, which would increase their chances of going home soon.

By now it was April 2nd, and the marines were setting the stage for the overtaking of Al Kut, a major city en route to Baghdad, which was sure to be a tough fight. Once this city was secure, the path to Baghdad would be relatively smooth. The soldiers of the 132nd listened intently for hours on end, even through the night, in hopes of hearing that the marines were gaining control of the city. The fighting was intense. In the early morning hours, the marines made it into the city. The Fedayeen and Republican Guard soldiers were putting up a good fight, knowing that this may be the last opportunity to save their precious capital city. However, when they realized that they were largely outmatched and were losing soldiers at an alarming rate, thousands of them began to surrender. The soldiers of the 132nd were responding to every bit of success the marines were having, clapping and high-fiving one another. Throughout the day and night, except for performing guard duty and trying to get some sleep, most of the soldiers did nothing but listen to the radio. In fact, Captain Hillock and 1SG Williams eventually made their way over to listen in as well. Everyone was excited. One would not have even thought that this unit was in a war zone but rather at some sort of training, oblivious to what was really happening. The fighting was taking place only about ten miles or less up the road, but that was of no concern to this group. Thoughts of home were in everyone's minds.

It only took about a day before elements of the marines were moving north of Kut and fighting their way to Baghdad, meeting small pockets of resistance, but nothing of much concern for this group of marines, who had made it through the desert cities at a record pace. With every victory came increased hope that the 132nd may get to go home soon. No new missions came their way, which led them to believe that they were not going to be needed. And with the country being relatively secure, transporting goods and supplies could easily be accomplished by helicopter and plane.

Chapter 11: The New Mission

BY APRIL 7TH, THE MARINES and army soldiers had Baghdad surrounded, and some fighting in the city had begun. Still, with no mission coming their way, the troops of the 132nd, although hopeful of going home soon, were becoming disappointed that they had been waiting around with nothing, except guard duty, to do in over a week. Several units had passed by their position over the days, but none were in need of their assistance. The arduous task of guarding virtually nothing was weighing heavily on the minds of these troops. Realizing someone had to step up and do something about this situation, Jason took it upon himself to go to 1SG Williams and Captain Hillock to address his concerns for the unit. When he walked into the operations tent, both were sitting at a table, talking.

"What's up, sergeant?" 1SG Williams asked.

"Well, top, I was hoping I could talk with you two about some issues with the soldiers," Jason replied.

"What's the problem?" asked Captain Hillock.

"Sir," Jason said, followed by a brief pause as he gathered his thoughts, "the troop morale is really low, and there are a lot of negative attitudes developing."

"Go ahead, sergeant. Continue."

"Several of them, even the ones who were close, have begun arguing with one another. Several have been caught sleeping on guard duty. They're complaining almost every time they're asked to do something, and we even had a couple of fights."

First Sergeant Williams stood up. "You having problems controlling your troops, sergeant?" he sternly asked.

"No, top," Jason responded. "It's just that, with the heat, sand, sand fleas, and other discomforts, and not having anything significant to do, the morale is busted, and I'm afraid if we don't do something soon, things may get ugly. We need some kind of mission, even if it's going back to Kuwait to get supplies. At least they'll feel they are contributing."

"Although I don't like hearing these things about the soldiers, sergeant, you do have a point," the commander stated. "Top, why don't we get on the radio and see if there is someone out there in need of some supply runs. Sergeant Henson is right. We need to keep them busy."

"I agree, sir. I'll get on it," the first sergeant replied.

Jason waited around patiently as the first sergeant made some calls on the radio, trying to contact first sergeants from the marines and army. The commander left the tent, more than likely to do a round to check on the troops himself.

After an hour or so of basically begging, 1SG Williams finally found a taker. Once he was informed of the orders and passed along the information through the proper channels so everything and everyone was in line, he got off of the radio and relayed the information to Jason and Captain Hillock, who had just returned to the tent.

"Good news," he said with a smile. "We got ourselves a mission."

With a sigh of relief and a regained feeling of confidence, Jason responded, "What is it?"

"The Saddam International Airport has been taken, and there are going to be military flights delivering supplies. But because Baghdad is obviously the goal, only a few units were left to secure the airport. They need some transportation elements to come in and start delivering the supplies and they'll take anyone to help secure the base. We fit both needs, so it looks like the airport is going to be our new home for a while," 1SG Williams explained.

"Sounds good to me," the commander responded. "Let's inform the soldiers."

This was both good and bad news to Jason. The good news was that they were leaving this desolate area for a more established location. The bad news was that since they now had a mission and were moving to the airport, which was going to be a busy place, they may not be going home as soon as hoped. Nevertheless, this news was certainly going to be welcomed by the troops and very much needed to break up the commotion that had developed over the previous few days.

After the commander informed the soldiers of the news, 1SG Williams had Jason gather all of the NCOs for a briefing of what needed to take place in order to get out of this area and on their way to the airport. Once the news was disseminated throughout the unit, everyone's attitude immediately improved.

It took the better part of the day to get everything ready for the move, but once everything was packed and the area was returned to its previous condition, the 132nd hit the road for their trek to the airport. They drove through the night, using the cover of darkness to help protect them from any danger that may arise along the way. The problem with driving at night, though, was that they could not use their headlights. The only lights that could be used at night were the black lights, which are tiny red lights located on the rear and front of the vehicles, which can barely be seen without the use of night vision goggles. In addition, because they had to drive during the night, no one would get any sleep, and focusing on these little lights while being tired was not an ideal situation. Nevertheless, it had to be done.

Although the trip was only a little over two hundred miles, with the driving conditions and the number of vehicles involved in the convoy, it took the better part of the night to arrive at the airport. In fact, the sun began to rise as they made their way to the entrance. Exhausted and cranky, the troops were eager to get inside, establish camp, and get some rest. Although they were able to get into the airport with no delays, it took several hours before everyone had their vehicles in the unit's assigned area and were able get camp set up. They were given a decent-sized portion of ground in the northwestern corner of the airport to park their vehicles and set up their tents. Iraq was going to be home for a while, and this seemed like a good place to be while there. Everyone knew it would soon be a strategic location to set up key operations in the country, meaning there would eventually be significant security forces to keep it safe and plenty of supplies to make the stay tolerable.

The soldiers were given the rest of the day off to set up their living area and get some rest. It did not take long before most of the troops were asleep. However, Jason was not one of them. Being at an airport, he assumed that there would soon be a chance to get some mail out, so he decided to write letters to his parents and to Shannon, ensuring them that things were going okay and that he was getting along fine. He was careful about what he wrote, for he did not want to give them any indication that he was having some difficulty, especially with the recent loss of troops. He figured it best not to give them any additional reasons to worry about him. After he finished the letters and packed them away until he could mail them, he took off his boots and lay down to get some sleep. He knew that he would soon be busy, and he wanted to be well rested for whatever mission was to come their way.

By early evening, now April 8th, most of the soldiers, including Jason, had awakened from their slumber. Jason was hungry, so he pulled an MRE (Meal Ready to Eat) from his rucksack and commenced eating it. *Great,* Jason thought to himself, *chili macaroni again.* It was the third time this week he had this particular meal. The only part of this meal he still enjoyed was the package of M&Ms.

By now Jason and probably almost everyone else in the unit had grown weary of eating these every day. Hopefully, they would soon be able to get a hot meal. After he finished eating, Jason decided to venture around the airport. As he did at their previous locale, Jason set out to find anything that may be of use to the men and women in his unit. It was amazing to him that only two days ago, heavy fighting had taken place here. The remnants of fighting were everywhere, from the large craters in the ground, to the destroyed airplanes and tanks spread out all over the place, to the holes in the terminal and hangers. The aroma of the explosions and burning could still be smelled in the air. It was astounding that the army could be in and out of this battleground in such a short period of time.

Jason was unsuccessful in finding anything that his unit might be able to use. Actually, after taking in all of the scenery, he really did not put much effort into looking at anything else. He was now feeling a little overwhelmed by the sights, so getting back to the unit was probably the best idea. When he returned, he found 1SG Williams, who again was with the commander.

"How's it going, Sergeant Henson?" 1SG Williams asked.

"Fine, top," Jason replied.

"Just received some good news, Henson," Captain Hillock stated. "The army has not received much resistance in their quest for the capital city, which means the war should be over soon."

"In fact," 1SG Williams interjected, "I won't be surprised if the war is over in a few days; and after running a few pickup and delivery missions, we just might get to go home."

"Seriously?" Jason asked, trying to hide the already gleaming smile on his face.

"That's right," Captain Hillock assured. "Maybe sooner than later."

"That's great news," Jason responded. "Thanks for the information."

Jason was elated at this news. He went back to the troop area and immediately sought out SSG Alderson.

"Guess what, sarge?" Jason asked. "I just talked to top and the commander, and they think we might get to go home soon. They said we've almost taken Baghdad and there's been little resistance."

"That's awesome," Alderson exclaimed. "When do you think we'll get out of here?"

"Top thinks after a few missions," Jason informed him.

"Man," Alderson said, "I can't wait to get home. I'm going on vacation as soon as I get there. No stinking beach, though; I've had it with sand."

"Me, too," Jason replied, "I'm going to take Shannon to New York City, maybe see a Broadway show or something. Go to the

ESPN Zone and catch a game. Yeah, that sounds good to me. Have a few drinks, make a little love ..."

"Okay," Alderson interjected. "Enough, already lover boy. I just want to get the hell out of here. I'll figure it out when I get back there. But your idea sounds pretty good, I must say."

"We shouldn't get everyone worked up, though; who knows what will really happen," Jason stated.

"Okay," said Alderson. "I'll try and keep it quiet."

Jason rolled his eyes at him. Even though he and Jason were good friends, Jason couldn't trust Alderson to keep this kind of news to himself. He loved to spread the rumors.

"What?" Alderson asked. "I'll keep quiet."

Well, the word of this possibility spread quickly, and soon the rumors began to swirl. By the end of the night, some of the troops actually believed they were leaving within the next month.

Once nightfall arrived, the troops once again prepared themselves for a night of rest. Artillery and gunfire could be heard off in the distance, but it was nothing that they had to worry about. Safe and secure in their perimeter, the soldiers went to sleep. At approximately 5:00 AM, the captain awakened the soldiers.

"Let's go," he shouted. "We have work to do."

Within fifteen minutes, everyone was awake and standing in formation, awaiting orders for their next move. First Sergeant Williams called them to attention and gave the formation over to Captain Hillock, who explained what was going to happen next.

"Listen up, troops," he ordered. "I hope everyone is well rested, because we have some work to do. Elements of the 3rd Infantry Division and the 1st Marine Division are engaged in battle in Baghdad. They have not been receiving the resistance everyone expected and, in fact, a lot of the civilians are welcoming them. But nevertheless, there is some still fighting going on, and we have lost some men. Now, it is expected that we will have full control of the city by nightfall, but it is believed that Saddam and his sons have escaped, meaning the search and the potential for battles will continue for a while. However, we have been informed that as the push continues to take over cities to the west and north of Baghdad, the fighters will need supplies. Although there will be some supplies delivered to this airport by plane and helicopter, runs back to Kuwait and deliveries to the north and other parts of this country will need to take place by ground, and we have been tasked to be a part of these missions. Make sure you are taking care of your trucks and yourselves. We will have a lot of work to do."

He then gave the formation back to 1SG Williams.

"Now for the bad news," the first sergeant stated. "I was informed only a short time ago that what many of you, and even I, thought to be true, is not going to happen. We will not be leaving any time soon," he said with a clearly disheartened tone.

"I was told from the powers that be that even if we have no missions for a while, we will still need to stay because we could be needed at any time. We will be here until told differently."

The heads immediately dropped and shook. But 1SG Williams continued with the orders, ignoring the disappointment of the soldiers.

"Our first mission is going to be convoying back to Kuwait in two days to pick up food and water, along with some other odds and ends, and return immediately to this base. Any questions?"

"Who will go?" asked SFC Freeman.

"We'll let you know all the details when we figure them out. You're released to go back to doing whatever you were doing. Start checking the trucks, too," he finished.   The soldiers went back to their vehicles, heads hanging and hearts broken. They began to prepare their trucks and their equipment for the mission, which ended up taking most of the day. Later that night, they received word that Baghdad was formally declared secure. Everyone was elated. With this new information, the troops gained a newfound sense of motivation that redirected their focus towards the importance of what they had to do. The intensity of the disappointment decreased, and the sense of pride went back to a level not present since the first week of the war. They were once again ready to go to work, a timeline for departure home no longer important.

The rest of the night and the next day were spent resting and ensuring everything was ready to go. Before nightfall, on what was now April 10th, 1SG Williams called a meeting for all of the NCOs to discuss details of the mission.

"Listen up, sergeants; we will only be taking fifteen of the trucks and their drivers. The soldiers who do not go will stay and pull security. The soldiers going on the mission will be leaving in the early morning hours and will head south to Kuwait, where they will pick up supplies and immediately return. You all need to figure out who will be going and report back to me with the list," he concluded.

First Sergeant Williams left the area, leaving the sergeants to themselves to figure out who would go. This was going to be a tough decision, as most of the soldiers had complained of boredom. The sergeants knew they were going to have some very unhappy soldiers to deal with. However, it only took about ten minutes to decide, and when the NCOs were done, they informed the first sergeant that Jason and SSG Alderson's squads would go, along with a few other soldiers. This way, it would be easier to determine who would go in the future, as the squads would just switch each time. First Sergeant Williams agreed with the idea. He then released them to inform their squads and prepare the trucks that would be going on the mission.

As expected, many of the troops were disappointed. However, they liked the idea of switching and figured that there would be plenty of missions to run in the near future. Everyone who was going on the trip was ordered to get their trucks lined up near the front gate so they could leave immediately after clearance was given. After the trucks were in place, they returned to their cots to get some sleep. By 4:00 AM, they were awake and getting dressed to go. First Sergeant Williams was going to lead the convoy and wanted everyone in their trucks and ready to leave by 4:30. Just before 5:00 AM on April 11th, 2003, they headed out of the gate for their first of what would be many long-haul missions to Kuwait.

As the convoy of vehicles from the 132nd Transportation Company headed south to pick up much-needed supplies, other American forces were headed north and east, fighting to capture new areas of Iraq. Iraqi Kurdish forces, working along with elements of the U.S. Army, were also fighting in the north. In fact, on April 10th, they captured the major city of Kirkuk. These Kurdish soldiers turned out to be a great asset to the coalition troops. For years, they waited for the opportunity to seek revenge on the Iraqi soldiers who had terrorized their people for years. They were the main fighting force in the north, which alleviated some of the pressure on the coalition to get troops into that region.

For the next several days, as they had done all along, the American forces captured each city they entered, encountering very little, if any, resistance. Some casualties were sustained during the fighting, but only a very small number lost their lives. By April 21st, most of Iraq was fully secured. However, some cities to the east, particularly Fallujah, put up a tough fight, and it would take some time before that area was under the control of the coalition. Over the course of several months, the United States would perform many operations going into and back out of Fallujah. Several U.S. soldiers would lose their lives there, but it was a location that had to be secured. It was a hotbed for insurgents and anti-American sentiment.

As the fighting in the north and east continued, the soldiers of the 132nd went on with their missions from the airport to Kuwait and back, retrieving supplies that would prove vital for the success of the operations of the fighting forces. Their trips, as arduous and tiresome as they were, went on with very little trouble. There was the occasional truck breakdown and sporadic flat tire, but no resistance was encountered while performing their missions. In fact, soldiers started looking forward to their trips south, as they were afforded an opportunity to relax for a day once they arrived in Kuwait, and they could also get a hot meal and shower. Eventually, these accommodations were established at the airport, but it took a while before that occurred. Additionally, more phones were put in place in Kuwait. Although the connections were never that great, each soldier was able to call home. Even if it was only once every few weeks, it was nonetheless a great perk of the trips. Jason was able to talk to both Shannon and his parents. Although this made him miss home even more, it was great for all of them to know that everything on both fronts was okay and that everyone was safe.

By the end of end of April, the 132nd had made several trips to Kuwait and back. It got to the point that they knew how to get there without directions. Jason was among the contingent of soldiers who arrived back at the airport on May 1st. As they drove through the gates and toward their company area, they began to hear screaming and yelling from various points around them. Jason looked around to try and pinpoint where the sound was coming from, and when he laid eyes on the first group of yelling troops, he realized they were cheering with joy. When he got back to the company area, SSG Alderson came running to Jason's vehicle.

"Have you heard?" he asked Jason.

"Heard what?"

"We won the war," Alderson said excitedly. "President Bush declared victory today while he was aboard the *USS Abraham Lincoln*!"

This was fantastic news, by far the best yet. Jason hoped that this meant an early return home. The days immediately following the announcement were filled with optimism. Missions to Kuwait were put on hold for a few days while the commander and first sergeant found out what the near future was going to hold.

On May 5th, the commander finally returned to the unit with some information to pass along. The anxious and hopeful troops were eager to hear anything, as the past four days seemed quite long with no work and nothing to talk about, other than what everyone was going to do once they returned home. When the commander had everyone gathered together, he began.

"Soldiers, I have some good news. I just spoke with a general who told me that there is no reason we should be here for more than two or three more months, pending any unforeseen roadblocks."

Everyone was elated to hear this news. There were smiles and high-fives throughout the formation.

"Now," Captain Hillock continued, "knowing this, the next few weeks are going to be very busy. We've received more missions to Kuwait, and we have to prepare things here as well and keep guard duty going."

The news of the continued missions didn't seem to bother anyone, now that they were going home soon.

"That's all I have for now," the commander continued. "Just be ready for the next mission, which will be in two days."

The excited troops headed back to their respective areas and began preparations for the missions.

For the next two months, with no updated news about anything, the soldiers of the 132nd continued their missions up and down the dusty desert roads, transporting various supplies, everything from water to toilet paper, ammo to food. Progress was being made on the condition of the airport, and it was shaping up to be a decent-looking base of operations. Telephones and some computers were put into place, and there was even a makeshift chow hall built, so now the soldiers on this base had some of the comforts of home. It seemed as if the entire military in Iraq was busy, working to build, rebuild, and improve the quality of life for both the coalition forces and the Iraqi civilians.

There was the occasional threat of violence from radicals in the areas surrounding the base, but overall things seemed relatively safe. Sporadic fighting took place in various parts of the country. However, the casualty count was very low. Most of the civilians seemed pleased with the presence of the coalition forces, and as time passed, many bonds were established between the two sides. The situation in the country seemed to be headed in the right direction, and most of Iraq's citizens, along with the rest of the world, held similar feelings. The overall morale of the soldiers in the 132nd was positive, although it was dissipating with each passing day as they anticipated the order to go home.

It was now late June, and there was still no word as to when these soldiers may get to go home. The missions to Kuwait and back continued, and it appeared as if there was no end in sight to the trips. Several bases in Iraq had now been taken over by coalition forces, and it seemed as if they were now going to be permanent bases from which to stage operations, meaning a more demanding need for additional supplies. The number of trucks that the 132nd was sending had increased to about three-fourths of their company, meaning less rest in between trips for many of the weary troops. But they did not seem to mind too much, as the trips made the days go by faster, and they really felt that they were a vital part of the effort to establish democracy in this war-torn country.

At the end of June, while the entire 132nd company was at the airport, an army general made his way over to their area to brief them on the latest news and recognize them for their efforts.

Once the troops gathered around, the general began.

"Soldiers of the 132nd," the general shouted, "you have been doing some great work for our effort, and for that I, and the people of Iraq and America, thank you. There's still a lot of work to do, however, and I encourage you to continue with the same pride and enthusiasm you have displayed all along. Your work is very important, and the forward soldiers appreciate every effort you have made. Because of the work of you and many others like you, all of our operations have been a success. We've encountered some tough resistance, but we've prevailed every time. We're fighting hard. Now, before I leave you to your work, are there any questions?"

There was silence for about twenty seconds. Then, Sgt. Adams, Jason's buddy, presented the general with the obvious question.

"Do you know when we might get to go home, sir?"

The general hesitated as first, and then replied, "There are some changes in command coming up soon, and no one knows for sure what the next commander will want to do. However, you should get to leave within the next couple of months."

Everyone was excited to have this information confirmed, but because it was not the first time they heard it, the soldiers did not set their hopes too high. No other questions asked, so the general left the area. First Sergeant Williams said a few words about their hard work before giving the troops the rest of the day off. Jason and the rest of the company went back to what they were doing before the formation. Some slept, others wrote letters, while several of them went to wait in the long line to use the phone and computer, Jason included.

Jason stood in line for the phone for about an hour, which was typical. When his turn finally arrived, he sat down to call Shannon. She picked up on the first ring, as if anticipating his call. It was about 11:00 PM in Pennsylvania, 3:00 PM in Iraq.

"Hey, baby," Shannon said with an excited tone. "Happy birthday."

Jason paused. He had been so busy lately with running missions and taking care of his troops that he forgot his own birthday, not that he could really celebrate. "Thanks," he said, rolling his eyes.

The two of them talked for about fifteen minutes. She gave him updates on what was happening back home, and he told her what the general had just said a few hours earlier. This news excited her, although Jason was sure to remind her that it was not the first time they were given redeployment timelines. Shannon told him how much she missed him and that she could not wait for him to get home. He felt the same. They concluded their conversation with the usual, "I love you." Jason headed back to the company area. Now he knew it was time to go home. Forgetting his own birthday made him realize that he was becoming a different person, as the important things in his civilian life had taken a backseat to what was going on in Iraq.

Chapter 12: Change of Plans

ON JULY 7TH, SOME NEWS WAS passed along that would impact everyone in Iraq. The general who had recently briefed the 132nd was right; the command was changing. General Tommy Franks was stepping down as CENTCOMM commander, and General Abizaid was taking over. With a new commander came new tactics and missions, and the 132nd would soon find out their ultimate fate.

No other news was passed along, and the 132nd continued their missions. However, on July 22nd, some exciting events did occur that would definitely impact the current state of Iraq. An interim government was established, and following that news, the announcement was made that soldiers from the 101st Airborne had killed the sons of Saddam, Uday and Qusay. Apparently, Iraqi civilians were getting more comfortable with the presence of the Americans and other coalition forces to the point of giving them information as to the whereabouts of many of Saddam's loyalists. This was a huge moment for the troops and the closing of a chapter for the Iraqis, as two of the men who had tortured and killed so many innocent civilians over the years were now gone. The next big step would be capturing or killing their father, but that would not occur for a while.

Following the killing of Uday and Qusay, things in Iraq began to change, almost overnight. Although sporadic fighting persisted from the onset of the war, this now relatively peaceful country was about to turn in the other direction. Insurgent attacks were beginning around Iraq, particularly in the eastern section, which was referred to as the Sunni Triangle. This violence would change the way everyone functioned, especially the 132nd, as they were frequently on the road, which was becoming more dangerous by the day. As a result of these new attacks, Central Command realized that the reconstruction and reestablishment of the country may not move as quickly and smoothly as once thought. They now recognized that fighting forces may be there for a while. This was a demoralizing blow to the soldiers on the ground, many of whom thought they would be going home soon.

The commanders of the army announced that all soldiers in the country, with the exception of those already on their way out, would have a mandatory minimum of twelve months deployed. This news was devastating. Even though several high-ranking officials had told them that they were leaving soon, the 132nd Transportation Company was now going to be there until at least February of 2004. Anger and depression set in almost immediately. Morale dropped, and the soldiers wanted an explanation. No other details were given, other than that their help was needed because this latest wave of violence was spreading; sending troops home now was not an option. The soldiers were given a chance to call home before the next mission to let family know they were not leaving soon. But the family members already knew, as they had seen it on the news.

When Jason called Shannon, she was crying and weeping.

"What's wrong, honey?" Jason asked.

"We heard that you have to stay for at least an entire twelve months," she replied as she continued to cry.

"I know, Shannon. It stinks, but things will be fine, and we'll be home soon enough."

Shannon tried to respond but continued crying. Jason heard a faint voice in the background.

"Are my parents there?" he asked.

With no immediate response, Jason asked to talk to his dad.

"Jason. It's Dad."

"Hi, Dad," Jason said, sounding disappointed.

"Hey, buddy. What's going on?" Ray asked.

"Well, obviously you know by now that I won't be home anytime soon. We're going to continue running missions for what looks to be several months now. This new order sure is pissing everyone off. So much for coming home soon."

"Are things going okay other than that?" Ray asked, not knowing what else to say.

"I guess," Jason replied. "We seem to have a pretty strong hold on the place. A lot of our soldiers are really upset, though. Please try to reassure Shannon. I know she's going to have a tough time, especially with this news. Damn it."

"You hang in there, son. We'll take care of things back here."

Jason began to respond, but as he did, he began to tear up.

"Gotta go, Dad; people are waiting. Tell Mom I love her. Bye."

"Love you, son."

Jason's resentment towards the military was building, and he was so angry that he did not want to talk to anyone. It was not that he minded being there; rather, he was upset that everything kept changing. He now felt that he could not even trust the government that sent him there. Nevertheless, he kept his opinions to himself and continued the mission. Showing his true emotions to the troops would do nothing more than upset them further, and that would be a bad thing for everyone.

On August 19th, something happened that solidified that things were getting worse. Although the U.N. did not approve of the United States going to war with Iraq, they eventually sent people into the country to show support for the reconstruction and reestablishment of a new government. Their headquarters were located in the Canal Hotel in Baghdad, specifically in an area presumed to be a safe zone. However, safe it was not, for on this day, a truck loaded with explosives made it through checkpoints and to the front of the hotel, where it was detonated, killing several U.N. officials and wounding dozens more. Among the dead was Sergio Vieira de Mello, the top U.N. envoy in Iraq. This heinous act of violence against a non-threatening group of people clearly demonstrated that the insurgents would attack anyone cooperating with the reestablishment of the country as a democratic state.

As a result of this attack, the U.N. eventually pulled its entire force out of the country, a small victory for the quickly growing terrorist insurgency. This was just the beginning of what would turn out to be a major battle against these types of attacks. But the Unites States was warned that this would happen. During an interview with Dan Rather on the eve of the war, Saddam Hussein stated that although the coalition may not get tough resistance during the invasion, they would suffer gravely over the duration of the occupancy. It was clear that he was right, and that this was just the beginning of this type of violence. The soldiers of the 132nd Transportation Company would soon find out how serious the insurgents were about wreaking havoc in the country.

By the end of August, the protocol for doing convoys along the roads of Iraq had changed, and anyone traveling outside of the safe zones was now going to have to be extra cautious. Over the past several months, the trips to Kuwait and back had become so routine for the soldiers of the 132nd that they were not even wearing their body armor. They were so accustomed to the terrain and the people along the way that fear was no longer felt. But that attitude quickly changed, as many convoys were finding themselves in the middle of ambushes and firefights. These trips were no longer leisurely, as the pace of the war was beginning to pick up once again. Improvised explosive devices, or IEDs, were now a common, almost everyday occurrence along the roads of Iraq, and each month they became more deadly and precise. The insurgents' methods were growing more sophisticated and strategic, and by mid-September, they were a force to be reckoned with, especially for the convoys traveling throughout Iraq. Although the attacks were occurring more often, they did not slow down the pace of reconstruction. Supply runs did not cease, and missions did not change.

The soldiers of the 132nd were by now one of the more experienced groups to carry out the supply missions, and therefore knew the roads better than anyone. They became the focal point of all transportation briefings, particularly because they knew what was where along the way and where the most vulnerable areas might be located. New units coming to do these missions would frequently consult with 1SG Williams to determine the best times and routes to conduct their operations. But simply because they knew the routes better did not mean that they were always going to be safe. In fact, because they were on the road so often, the locals came to expect them, which could prove deadly for them.

Soon, word spread throughout the base that insurgents were targeting many of the incoming and outgoing convoys. Some of them were being ambushed by small arms fire and rocket propelled grenades, while others were running into IEDs. Some casualties did occur, and as a result, the commander of the base held a mandatory meeting with all company commanders to discuss what precautions and new trainings should be implemented. Not much changed as a result of the meeting, but extra precaution would definitely be taken.

Convoys would be supported by military police and some infantry Humvees, who had .50 caliber guns at the front and rear of each convoy. Additionally, many of the units who did not have armored vehicles began cannibalizing old, damaged vehicles and welding the metal to their trucks. Although this practice was not authorized, units were willing to take the risk of getting in trouble if it meant saving a life or two. Besides, most of the commanders ordered their soldiers to do this. The 132nd was no exception. They scrounged up as much extra metal as they could and began welding pieces to the truck doors and undercarriages. Any extra protection was welcome. They even cut pieces off of the blown-up Iraqi airplanes that were destroyed during the invasion. Whatever they could find, they used. They also added sandbags to the floorboards of the trucks, which could lessen the impact of an explosion or maybe stop a bullet. It only took a few days to get the necessary upgrades completed, and it was a good thing, as a new mission was handed to them on the eve of completing the work.

Chapter 13: The Final Blow

MUCH TO THE SURPRISE OF everyone in the unit, the new mission was not going to be to Kuwait. Instead, they were going to be headed to Camp Anaconda in Balad, which was home to a large airbase that the United States now controlled and was going to make a major staging point for operations. It is located about forty miles northeast of Baghdad and was home to many Saddam sympathizers. This would be the most dangerous post-invasion operation to date for the soldiers of the 132nd. Most of the runs to Kuwait consisted of picking up food, water, and various building and vehicle supplies. This mission was going to be very different. Since there was such an increase in the insurgent attacks, many of the units on the base found themselves in firefights almost every time they left the post. As a result, there was now a shortage in ammunition for just about everyone, meaning that the soldiers from the 132nd going on this mission were tasked to pick up a resupply of various munitions. This would be dangerous for many reasons.

First of all, insurgents were attacking everywhere, especially in and around Baghdad. Second, the 132nd never received any training on how to handle ammunition. And last, carrying ammunition would make them a prime target, not to mention the extent of an explosion if one of the trucks were hit by an RPG or IED. First Sergeant Williams wanted his best soldiers to perform this mission, and it did not take long to decide who would. Jason was one of the first on the list, followed by his buddies SSG Alderson and Sgt.

Adams. Volunteers were plenty, but sending everyone was not an option. Only ten trucks were going to go, meaning twenty people. This was to be a quick, one-day mission, picking up the ammo and immediately returning to base. Once it was determined who would go, that group was given a briefing on what to expect and what to do if something were to happen. Following the briefing, the soldiers were released to make final preparations and get the trucks lined up to leave. Jason, his buddies, and the rest of the crews were going to leave before daybreak.

At 4:00 AM on September 14th, 2003, the trucks headed out the front gate to the airport and were on their way to Balad. First Sergeant Williams lead the convoy, followed by SSG Alderson and Sgt. Adams. Jason was in the next to last vehicle. Although the journey was only about forty miles, due to the darkness and extra precaution being taken, it actually took about two and a half hours to arrive at the base. There were no problems along the way, and as the sun was rising, the soldiers of the 132nd were driving through the gates of Camp Anaconda, anxious to pick up the ammo and get back to the airport. Once they were on the base, 1SG Williams had to contact the base commander to inform him that the convoy had arrived and find out exactly where they had to go to get the munitions. While he did this, he directed the rest of the trucks to pull off of the road and wait for him to return. Jason took advantage of this time to take a quick nap, as did most of the others.

First Sergeant Williams returned about an hour later and ordered the trucks to follow him. They pulled into a fully fenced and fortified area surrounded by armed soldiers and a few tanks. The guards at the main gate directed them exactly where to go. In front of them were huge, covered stacks of boxes and crates, filled with just about every type of weapon and ammunition one could imagine. Before they began loading the trucks, Jason wanted to get a picture of him, SSG Alderson, and Sgt. Adams standing in front of one of the mounds of weapons and ammo. There had not been many opportunities to take pictures together on a mission, so this seemed like a perfect chance, even though the guards would have taken the camera if they caught them. Pictures of this sort were forbidden, as the ammo dumps were considered classified.

Nevertheless, they took a picture, and they even smiled as it was taken. Following the picture, they began loading the trucks with as much ammo as they could. Even though they had never handled this much ammunition before, there was no one there to give them instructions. They were on their own in figuring out how to load, stack, secure, and transport the stuff. It took about an hour to get all of the crates loaded onto the beds of the trucks. By now it was about 9:00 AM and the soldiers were hungry, so before they left the base, they found a chow hall and got some breakfast. At 10:30, they were headed out of the gates and on their way back to the airport. Barring any unforeseen problems, they would arrive just in time for lunch.

The trip started out good. The weather was nice and the traffic was unusually light. Locals were greeting them as they passed by, and there were no signs of trouble. However, about ten miles into the trip, a call from 1SG Williams came over the radio.

"Soldiers, listen up," he stated before a brief pause. "We just received word that, about an hour ago, a convoy was hit on this same stretch of road. It was mainly small arms fire. The area is coming just ahead. If you begin receiving fire, do not slow down. I repeat, do not slow down. Continue through as fast as you can. Make sure you report the activity over the net. Over."

Several "Rogers" were heard over the radio.

"First Sergeant out."

The convoy continued along the highway for about another ten minutes before Jason realized that the farther along they went, the fewer people he was seeing. This seemed very suspicious. Jason got on the radio and told the rest of the convoy what he had noticed. Just as he was finishing his transmission, bullets started flying from up ahead. They were approaching one of the many underpasses, which had now become prime locations for insurgent attacks and ambushes. As they drew closer, the gunfire increased. The convoy continued as directed, but soon it came to a complete halt. Apparently, 1SG Williams noticed that one of the gunmen was fixing an RPG launcher on his shoulder, and so he floored the gas pedal and got past the underpass, out of sight of the insurgent.

However, the next truck, the one being driven by SSG Alderson and Sgt. Adams, was not so fortunate. As 1SG Williams and his Humvee sped through the ambush, he looked back to make sure everyone was keeping pace. Just as he turned, he saw out of the corner of his eye the RPG flying through air, headed directly at the truck behind him. What immediately followed was a tremendous explosion, followed by continuous gunfire coming from several directions. He turned his vehicle around and went back. As a result of this explosion, the entire convoy was halted, and now a full-fledged gun battle was taking place. First Sergeant Williams reported what was going on over the radio, but he received no response. He had no time to wait. His troops needed his help.

Witnessing the explosion, Jason knew that someone was going to be hurt, if not killed, but he could not tell from his location which vehicle was hit by the RPG. He immediately stopped his truck and jumped out to return fire. This fight was going to go on until one side decided to give in or until everyone was dead. There was no way to maneuver around the exploded truck, and they were not about to leave it. As Jason took up a fighting position, he saw a man with another RPG launcher pointed at the truck in front of him. The men in that truck did not notice, as he was firing in another direction. Jason immediately fixed his weapon on the guy and fired, hitting him in the head and dropping him instantly. There was no time to think about this, as bullets flew right past Jason's head. He shifted his weapon towards the culprit and unloaded in his direction, dropping him within seconds. Everyone in the convoy was now involved in the firefight.

Intense fighting continued for the next fifteen minutes. Jason and the rest of the soldiers involved in the fight immediately killed several of the enemy combatants and surrounded them, herding them into one location. But like ants in an anthill on fire, they kept coming out. One by one, they would appear, fire their weapons, and almost immediately get shot. It was evident that these particular insurgents were not well trained in this type of fighting, at least not to the level of this group of soldiers.

Eventually, the few insurgents who were left ran to a truck and retreated, probably going back to regroup and return to ambush another unit another day. Under most circumstances, the troops would have followed them until they were either killed or captured, but because one of their vehicles was still burning, they all headed in its direction to assess what happened. As Jason drew near the burning vehicle, he stopped dead in his tracks. As soon as he saw which truck it was, he knew who was in it. He knew SSG Alderson and Sgt. Adams were dead or seriously wounded. Jason ran the rest of the way to the truck, and when he managed to pry open the passenger door, the charred body of Sgt. Adams was before him, almost unrecognizable. Jason jumped back and put his hands over his mouth, then let out a few screams of profanity. He quickly came to and realized he had to keep working, so he continued to check on his other buddy.

The front of the truck was still burning, and while a few of the soldiers were spraying it with fire extinguishers, Jason ran to the other side to check on SSG Alderson, although he knew he was probably dead, too. When he opened the door, SSG Alderson's body was leaning against the steering wheel, badly burned and covered in blood. However, as Jason worked to remove his body from the truck, SSG Alderson made a groaning noise.

"He's still alive!" Jason shouted.

Jason immediately laid him on the ground and yelled for the medic to bring the first aid kit. Jason was more experienced than the medic in dealing with burns, so he removed the clothing that was not attached to the skin, and then he began applying ointment and bandages to the cuts and burns. He also administered a morphine shot to ease some of the pain. Although Jason was working diligently to try and save SSG Alderson, he knew that it was not going to be enough. Alderson was so torn up that Jason knew there was almost no chance of survival, but it was not in Jason to give up.

"Come on, buddy, hang on. Help is on the way," Jason said to his dying friend. "Just hang in there; don't you die on me now," he continued as he applied bandages and injected more morphine.

But it was all for naught. Within five minutes, SSG Alderson was gone. Jason continued working on him, even though he knew his buddy was dead. It took three of the soldiers, including 1SG Williams, to pry him off. As Jason was working to gain his composure, a helicopter came flying in, followed by some Humvees on the ground. But they were too late. The battle was over, and two soldiers were dead.

The helicopter landed, and with the help of Jason and the first sergeant, the crewmembers loaded the two soldiers onto the helicopter and took them away. The five Humvees with manned .50 caliber machine guns scoured the area, assessing the dead insurgents and making sure the threat was gone. In all, the soldiers of the 132nd killed twenty-three of the attackers. No one else in the unit was injured, so by military standards, it was a good fight. Soon after the area was deemed secure, a wrecker was brought in to tow the damaged vehicles, and a couple of five-ton trucks and a military fire truck arrived to clean up the area. Once the remaining soldiers of the 132nd were checked and questioned, they got back in the trucks and began the journey back to the airport. This was a day none of them would ever forget, especially Jason.

In less than an hour, the convoy arrived at the airport, now safe and out of harm's way. The commander of the base was already aware of what had happened, so he had a crew ready to take the trucks to the drop off area and unload them so the 132nd soldiers could get back to their area. A five-ton truck took them the rest of the way. When they arrived, the rest of the soldiers in their unit were all gathered together to greet them. The distress that the drivers were experiencing must have been evident, for when they exited the truck, heads hanging and speechless, the rest of their unit remained motionless. Recognizing what was happening, the commander ordered the unit to assist the returning fighters in removing their gear and help them to their personal areas. As one of the soldiers, SFC Green, attempted to grab Jason's arm to assist him, Jason immediately ripped it away and pushed the sergeant.

"Get the hell away from me! I can do it myself."

SFC Green looked away and noticed that 1SG Williams was watching Jason. He looked directly at SFC Green and shook his head, gesturing to just let Jason go about his business. Everyone knew that Jason was close to SSG Alderson and Sgt. Adams, so they did not bother him for a while, knowing he needed some alone time to calm down.

After about half an hour, 1SG Williams, fresh from a shower, made his way to Jason and recommended that he take a shower as well. Jason did not respond to the request at first, but when the first sergeant repeated the order, Jason grabbed his stuff and went to the newly renovated shower facilities. He was alone in there. Not physically, but psychologically. He looked at no one, and he said not a word. When he finished, he went back to his cot and lay down. First Sergeant Williams returned and sat down next to Jason.

"I'm sorry for the loss of your friends, Jason. They were good soldiers, and they would want you to go on fighting for them," he said as he patted Jason on the leg. "I'm going to give you a break from the missions for a while. In fact, I was just informed that we were given permission to send some troops to Qatar on R and R, and I want you to go. What do you say?" Jason continued lying motionless with his hands behind his head. He did not respond to the first sergeant.
"In fact, sergeant, I'm going to go along with you. You deserve it. Hell, we all deserve it. You in?"
Jason continued staring straight up, but he did nod his head a little bit.

"Good," 1SG Williams replied. "I'll get back to you with the details later. Get some rest."

Jason did not sleep well. In the little amount of time he did sleep, he kept seeing the bloody, burned faces of his friends. He awoke from his slumber screaming and sweating, and immediately drew the attention of the rest of the troops around him.

"Are you okay, sarge?" one of the soldiers asked.

Jason nodded his head and tried to get back to sleep. But he could not quit thinking about what happened that day. He began to cry. *How could this be?* he asked himself. Frustrated, he got out of his cot and decided to take a walk. SFC Green saw him walking out of the tent and decided to try and talk to him. When he caught up with Jason, he asked him to stop for a minute. Jason complied, and listened to what Green had to say. SFC Green, who was older than most in the unit, had served with a tank unit during operation Desert Storm. During that time, he received the Purple Heart, resulting from an incident in which an enemy tank hit his tank and the entire crew, except for him, was killed. He sustained multiple burn and shrapnel wounds.

"Listen, Jason, I know you're upset, and I know you're mad, but I want you to know that we are all grieving. This sucks, but we have got to go on. We have a mission to complete, and that's what Alderson and Adams would want us to do. The other soldiers need your guidance."

Weeping, Jason put his head down.

"We need to get the hell out of this place. We've lost enough men already, and we don't need to lose anymore. We've done enough; don't they see that?"

SFC Green agreed, but reiterated to Jason that no matter what, they had to complete the mission, as other soldiers depended on them. Jason did not respond, and he continued his walk toward the phones. SFC Green followed.

"I need to call Shannon," Jason said.

"I think that's a good idea."

Jason waited silently in line for about thirty minutes before his turn came. He got through on the first try, and Shannon answered on the first ring, again as if anticipating his call.

"Hey, it's Jason, baby."

"Hi, honey. How's it going?" she asked.

Jason did not respond.

"What's the matter, Jason?" she asked.

Trying to focus and keep from crying, he responded, "Some of the guys were killed today, and I was there."

"What happened? Who was hurt?" she asked.

"I don't want to say over the phone yet, but they were good friends of mine," Jason responded.

"How are you holding up?" Shannon asked.

Jason hesitated, unsure of the answer, "I don't know. I'm so sick of this place. We should have been out of here by now. We fulfilled our duty and then some, and we're still here doing crap we shouldn't be doing," Jason vented.

Shannon wasn't sure how to respond. She had never heard Jason this upset. The worst she ever heard was when he was complaining about tests in medical school, and that was nowhere near this.

"Things will be okay, Jason," she stated, "and you'll get through this."

"Enough about this place," Jason stated. "What's going on back there?"

"Things are going fine back here. We sure do miss you, though. Your dad talks about you a lot to other people. He's so proud of you. I've been spending a lot of time with your parents, and we've been discussing plans for your return."

"Don't get your hopes up," Jason mumbled.

"What?" Shannon asked.

"Nothing," he replied.

"I really miss you, Jason Henson," Shannon said.

"I miss you too, Shannon. I love you, and I can't wait to see you again. But I have to get going for now," he said as he struggled to hold back his tears. "Tell everyone I'm fine."

"Bye, Jason. I love you."

Jason hung up the phone and headed back to the company area. He tried once again to get some sleep. This time was a little better. He was able to get in a few hours before dawn and was up before most others in the unit. He lay in his cot for a while, fantasizing about getting home, but those thoughts kept getting mixed with feelings of sorrow for his friends' families. Frustrated again, Jason got up and decided to go for a run. First Sergeant Williams was already awake, so Jason went over to tell him he was headed out. "Hey, top, I'm headed out for a run," Jason said.

"Sounds good, sergeant. By the way, there's a trip going out to Qatar today, and I was hoping you would be going," 1SG Williams said. "I'm getting out of here for a few days, too."

Jason stood silent for a few seconds, pondering what he was going to do.

"All right, I'll go," Jason replied.

"Good," 1SG Williams said. "Now go for that run."

Jason nodded and then was on his way. When he returned from his run, he found most of the unit awake and getting dressed. Some of them were packing clothes. Just after Jason got in, 1SG Williams appeared.

"Those of you that are going on R and R, the plane is leaving in an hour, so you need to get your stuff ready," he shouted.

Most of them were already doing that.

He continued, "For the rest of you, I just received word that we are needed for another supply run. We need ten volunteers to make a run to a nearby base to deliver food and water. It should be safe and not take very long."

Hearing this, Jason snagged his towel and a clean uniform and headed for the showers. On his way out, he passed SFC Green, who could tell by the scowl on Jason's face and the stomping of his feet that he was very angry.

"What's up, sarge?" he asked Jason.

"We just got handed another fucking mission. Can you believe this shit?"

"To do what?" SFC Green asked.

"Running supplies, as usual."

SFC Green did not know how to respond, so he simply stated, "Well, we're going to Qatar, so hopefully whoever has to go on the run will be okay."

Jason, clearly not appreciating that remark, turned away and continued to the shower house. When he got back to the company area, he packed his bag for the trip and headed to the truck that was taking them to the plane. Although there was nothing he could do about the mission, he was still not happy about it, especially right after his friends were killed. He sat silently in the five-ton truck and did not say another word to anyone until they arrived in Qatar several hours later.

When they arrived at the base and got situated in their living quarters, Jason found 1SG Williams and expressed his discontent.

"Top, this is ridiculous," Jason said. "After the shit we just went through, we get another mission the next damn day. What the hell?"

First Sergeant Williams knew it was coming and was prepared to give an answer.

"Jason," he interrupted, "I know what you are going to say, but I can assure you that I did everything I could to prevent our unit from doing this mission. They needed someone immediately, and we were the only ones available."

"This is bullshit," Jason responded, and then he turned to walk away.

"You want to get a beer, sergeant?" 1SG Williams asked.

Jason stopped in his tracks. "Are we allowed to do that?" he asked.

"While we are here, we are allowed to have two beers a day," replied the first sergeant.

Jason thought for a moment and said, "Yeah, that sounds like a good idea. Let me get changed."

When they were ready, the two men went to a nearby building that was set up for the troops on R and R to relax and have a couple of drinks. They were given two drink tickets as they entered the building, and off to the bar they went. For the first time in about ten months, Jason felt human again. He was finally able to relax. He and the first sergeant stayed for a couple of hours, reminiscing about past trainings, good times at home, and the people they had waiting for them when they returned to the States. Towards the end of the day, as the two soldiers seemed to be ready for some real sleep, 1SG Williams turned to Jason.

"I have some good news, Henson," he said, "but you can't tell anyone, okay?"

"Roger that," Jason said. "What's up, top?"

"Well, during the briefing about this new mission, the base commander informed me and the captain that this was going to be our last hauling mission and that for the rest of our time at the airport, unless an emergency occurs, we will only be performing base duties and getting our things ready to go home. He recognized the extent of our losses and the large amount of missions accomplished. In fact, he said that, to date, no other company has logged as many miles as we have in that amount of time. He said that it was now someone else's turn. The commander also said that new units are already arriving that will take over the new missions."

By the time the first sergeant finished saying what he had to say, Jason was grinning from ear to ear.

"This is great news," Jason said.

First Sergeant Williams reiterated the secrecy component and then told Jason to go get some sleep. Jason headed back to his room a changed man, at least temporarily. This was the first good news he'd had all year. Although the excitement kept him awake in his rack for a while, Jason eventually got his best night's sleep since he was deployed and started the next day with a brand-new attitude.

Jason spent the next two days mostly by himself, which was fine by him. He was alone with his thoughts and fantasies about returning home to Shannon. He thought about all of the things he wanted to do, in particular take a vacation, somewhere nice and quiet, like a cabin by a lake. He told himself that this deployment would change him forever. *I am going to appreciate everything I have so much more*, he thought. To pass some time, Jason went to the base theater to catch a movie. *Terminator 3* was showing, so he decided to see that. He also spent time in the gym exercising and a lot of time trying to get some sleep. When his three days of R and R were up, he was well refreshed and ready to go. He met up with the rest of his unit where they were dropped off three days prior and waited for the ride back to the airport, where they would take a flight back to Iraq to finish out their tour. Jason was eager to get back and find out how that last mission went, as well as to get any fresh news.

When they finally arrived at their company area, everyone seemed relatively upbeat. *They must have heard the news*, Jason thought to himself. Jason looked around for some of the troops in his squad and first saw SPC Jennings, who immediately began walking toward Jason.

"Have you heard, sarge?" the specialist asked.

"Heard what?"

"We're done with the hauling missions and we're only going to be doing stuff on the base and getting ready to leave this shit hole."

Jason, acting as if he knew nothing about this, responded, "That's great news."

He then asked about the mission that took place the day he left.

"They took some small arms fire," Jennings said, "but no one got hurt and nothing was damaged, except for a couple of tires."

This was a great relief for Jason. He continued to his personal area to get things situated. About half an hour had passed when the captain appeared and said that there would be a formation in five minutes. Jason finished getting dressed and lined up. When everyone was in place, 1SG Williams called them to attention and the commander stepped in front of the unit.

"At ease," he said. "I have a bunch of things to say, so listen up."

Everyone was dead silent.

"Our days of hauling missions are over. We're going to be focusing on base security and prepping the equipment for a trip to Kuwait, a one-way trip to Kuwait," Captain Hillock said with a smile.

The soldiers cheered, gave high-fives and hugs, and then fell silent for some more information.

"However," Captain Hillock continued, "if for some reason we are needed for another hauling mission, we will comply and provide whatever manpower and equipment is needed for the job. But we would only be used in an emergency. I'm proud of all of you. Your sacrifices have helped to protect the people of the United States of America and those who have suffered in this country. Great job."

He then handed the formation over to 1SG Williams, who provided details about what they would be doing over the next couple of months. He basically repeated what the captain had to say and then told them how the security operations would work.

"I know everyone is delighted with this news. But we can't forget where we are and the dangers that still exist. Let's make sure that we are doing everything right and are continuing to be vigilant. We are not home yet," 1SG Williams concluded.

He then dismissed the troops so the section and squad leaders could work on the security roster. Once that was finalized and the shifts began, the only other focus of the soldiers in the unit would be working on fixing damaged trucks, repairing any other broken equipment, packing stuff in their storage containers, and performing random base operational tasks, such as helping in the mess hall and assisting in building up the base. Things were finally looking up for the 132nd Transportation Company.

Over the next month and a half, which seemed like a year to most in the 132nd, things were relatively peaceful and calm, with the exception of occasional mortar rounds coming into the base. However, none of them ever came close to the soldiers, and so far there had only been a few injuries reported throughout the base related to these types of attacks. The days were very monotonous— rotating guard shifts, working on equipment, and doing menial tasks throughout the base, like watching the phone lines and doing head count at the chow hall. But they did not seem to mind too much as they had already done a lot during this year. Jason spent a lot of time writing home and using the phone. He was counting the days when he would get to see his beloved Shannon again. Although the days were pretty boring, everyone seemed content, and because things were relatively calm throughout the rest of the country, they were okay with what they were doing at this point.

However, by mid-November, terrorist attacks were increasing and the death toll of the coalition forces was going up. It seemed as though the insurgents had been quietly regrouping and planning their attack strategies. In fact, November concluded as the deadliest month yet for the coalition. Not only were American casualties increasing, other countries were losing troops as well. In Nasiriyah, for example, a suicide bomb attack on an Italian police base took the lives of at least twenty-three people, among them the first Italian casualties. It was not just the Americans the insurgents wanted to kill, but anyone working with them.

Along with the increased violence came increased security measures, so doing security at the airport became much more focused—and dangerous. The airport would surely be a prime target for an insurgent attack. All these new events brought the reality of the situation to the forefront once again for the soldiers in the 132nd. Mortar attacks on the airport increased slightly, as did small arms fire on the guard positions in the towers. The tension began rising, both because the dangers were increasing and because it was happening just before they were getting ready to go home. Losing someone is always a bad thing, but losing one so close to going home and around the holidays would be really dreadful.

Chapter 14: Good-bye Iraq

THANKSGIVING CAME AND WENT, AND there was still no final word on when they would leave. Everyone was getting anxious. On December 1st, a mortar round hit about fifty feet from the position of the 132nd, blowing windows out of some of the trucks and knocking a couple troops off of their feet. Jason was among many who were beginning to feel like sitting ducks. It seemed that it would only be a matter of time before their luck ran out. Many of the soldiers, including Jason, began requesting hauling missions just to get out of their fixed position. But because all of the trucks had been repaired and were ready to ship home (with the exception of the recent window blowouts), getting a new mission this late in the game was not going to happen.

The next several days were tense. Many of the soldiers began arguing with one another about petty things: making too much noise, being in each others' space—things that were never before problems. They all needed to hear some kind of news about leaving, or getting a mission—anything. Fortunately, on December 10th, they finally received some news. Just after breakfast, when everyone except those on guard duty was present in the company area, Captain Hillock gathered the troops for a quick briefing.

"I know the past couple of months have been stressful for all of you, not knowing what to expect from day to day. But believe me, if I had any useful knowledge passed along to me, I would have given it to you immediately. However, I have finally received word

173

of a departure date. We have been given authorization to depart for Kuwait on December 23rd."

Everyone cheered following this announcement. Although the past couple of months had been emotionally draining for Jason, this news brightened his spirits. At last, this deployment was going to end. What a great Christmas gift. When everyone settled down a bit, the captain continued.

"Now, that gives us about two weeks to get things in order. I know that most of the preparation is completed, but a few more things have to happen, and we also have to continue our guard duties until that date."

The captain ran down a list of tasks that had to be done before they left the airport, and most were standard procedure for departing troops. There would be briefings from various personnel about what to expect when they returned home, the medical procedures that had to take place, the mandatory paperwork process, and what needed to be done with the trucks, equipment, luggage, and so on. By the time the captain was finished, almost no one was listening, as they were solely focused on what they were going to do once they got home. When the formation ended, everyone dispersed and began their daily routines. Some of them went to the phone and computer tents; some took a nap, while others began work on the laundry list of tasks to be completed prior to leaving the country. Although a lot of the tasks were done, 1SG Williams wanted everything double- and triple-checked to ensure nothing could preclude them from leaving on time. The briefings would start within a week and everything needed to be finished by then. Additionally, work needed to be done on the trucks that were damaged during the recent mortar attack. There would be plenty of work to keep everyone occupied until they had to leave.

The next couple of days were quiet around the base. There were no mortar attacks and no mention of engagements with the enemy by the soldiers on guard duty. It seemed as if the insurgents were taking a break. However, on December 13th, In Ad Dawr, near Tikrit, which is located in northern Iraq and is the hometown of Saddam Hussein, members of the 1st Brigade of the 4th Infantry Division, working on tips from the locals, located a spider hole near a farmhouse. The hole was not much larger than the size of an average man. Cautiously, they removed the cover and peered into the hole. They discovered a little surprise. Covered in filth and masquerading in an uncharacteristic full beard was none other than Saddam Hussein himself. The man who was frequently seen wearing a sharp-looking military uniform and holding a rifle in one arm, demonstrating his power, had been reduced to nothing more than a rat in a hole. This was a great victory, not only for the soldiers who captured him, but also for the entire coalition and, most important, the people of Iraq.

Once word and pictures of the capture spread, celebrations ensued in the streets and on the bases. It seemed as if every citizen in the country was outside, chanting, praying, and firing their guns. However, there were also those people who remained faithful to Saddam, who were not so happy about his capture. There were some attacks that took place on those who celebrated in the streets and some sporadic mortar attacks throughout the country as a result of this news. But in spite of the capture and the following commotion, few deaths were reported. The Saddam loyalists and anti-American insurgents would eventually gain strength and use the capture of Saddam as a catapult for their destruction.

Once the celebrations subsided, it was back to the norm at the airport. Although Saddam's capture did lead to increased security, the soldiers of the 132nd continued preparations for their departure. The next several days went by quickly. By December 20th, everyone and everything was ready to go. Various personnel who dealt with transitioning units filled the last two days at the airport with briefings. They discussed some common issues that arise when reintegrating with families, such as role confusion and detachment. They discussed the importance of taking time before jumping back into work, and they talked about what services would be available to the soldiers if there should be any problems, such as Vet Centers and the Veterans Administration Medical Centers. However, because each soldier was so focused on what he or she was going to do upon arriving home, no one seemed to pay attention to this important information.

By the night of the 22nd, all of the briefings were done and the troops were ready to go. All tasks had been completed, and the 132nd Transportation Company was given the green light to leave for Kuwait in the morning. Understandably so, no one could sleep that night. The excitement of getting out of Iraq was overwhelming. But there were periods of sadness. The soldiers could not forget that several of their friends would not be joining them on this trip home. Jason seemed most upset by this, and rightfully so, for two of the men lost were his dear friends, and he was there when they died. But he would not forget them, and he was going to try to enjoy life when he got back to Pennsylvania. The troops headed out before sunrise for one last trip south. It was going to be a great day.

If everything worked out according to plan, they would be settled in Kuwait and able to relax by Christmas day. The first couple of hours went smoothly. By now, the sun was rising and their night protection was fading. But the soldiers stayed focused. They remained vigilant yet anxious to get to Kuwait. About halfway through their trek, they came to a sudden stop. They were just outside of a small village that appeared to be harmless. Jason thought maybe someone was having vehicle problems. There was no way they could be lost, as they had made this journey so many times during the past year.

After about fifteen minutes and no movement, Jason decided to get out and go to the front of the convoy to see what was going on. As he drew closer to the lead vehicle, he saw what the holdup was. There was an IED right in the middle of the road. If the convoy had not stopped when it did, someone would have been hurt, or worse yet, killed. Jason asked the captain what they were going to do, and the captain said that a team was coming to take care of it. They would stay put until the situation was resolved. About two hours later, the team arrived to take care of the IED. Within thirty minutes, the 132nd was given the go-ahead to resume their trip.

It was now almost noon, and the soldiers were growing even more uneasy, desperately wanting to get to Kuwait and away from any more threats. This close call made everyone realize just how dangerous this country was becoming. It was clear that anyone could be a target at any time. This potential incident reminded Jason of that awful day when his buddies were killed. He became very upset, cursing and constantly readjusting himself in the seat. When asked by his driver what was wrong, he said nothing. Jason decided the best thing to do was to try and get some sleep. Maybe this would help alleviate some sadness.

Although it took a while, Jason did manage to fall asleep. And even though sleeping while in a moving vehicle was against regulation, Jason did not care. He needed a break. He managed to sleep for about a half an hour, and when he awoke, he did feel a little better. About an hour before reaching the border, the convoy stopped again. But this time it was to make sure all of the vehicles were running properly and to refuel. This stop lasted about an hour.

"We're almost there," Jason said to his driver.

The trucks began moving again, and in no time they finally reached the border, free from any real threat of danger. The alleviation of stress was imminent. Although some terrorist threats existed in Kuwait, it was, by most accounts, a safe place. They were now one step closer to home.

Chapter 15: Camp Arifjan - Again

THEY ARRIVED AT CAMP ARIFJAN in Kuwait in the early evening, feeling much different than they had the first time they were here. The feelings of uncertainty and fear that once consumed their thoughts were replaced by relief and joy. They were one step closer to home.

By sunset, they had all of their trucks parked in the designated area. The morale of the soldiers in the unit was at its highest point yet. They had a quick formation to discuss what was to take place within the next twenty-four hours and then headed to the tent city, where soldiers in transit were housed until their departure.

Once they had their personal areas set up and their bags unpacked, most of them headed for the shower trailers. Feeling clean and being able to sleep in a real bed (bunk beds were set up in the tents) was going to be a real treat. Jason took his time getting his area set up, and when most of the troops were in the showers, he headed for the phone tent. He could not wait to call Shannon and tell her where he was.

There was a line to use the phone, but he did not mind. It gave him a chance to calm down and focus on what was happening to him and his unit. The entire time he stood in line, he had a smile on his face. *I'm finally here*, he thought to himself. After standing in line for about thirty minutes, his turn came. He rushed to the phone and quickly began dialing the numbers. He got through on the first try, and Shannon answered the phone.

"We're in Kuwait, honey; almost home," he said with great joy.

Speechless, she immediately began to cry. She, like Jason, at one point felt that this day would never come. But it did, and they were both at a loss for words. When they settled down, they began talking about when he might actually be home and what his unit had to do before they could leave. They also talked about what they were going to do once he did get home. They fantasized about taking a cruise or maybe going to Hawaii. They also talked about lazy days at home, doing absolutely nothing. Their conversation lasted for about twenty minutes before Jason looked over and saw the long line that had formed since he got on the phone. Knowing that the other soldiers wanted to call home, too, Jason told Shannon that he would call her again soon and that he loved her.

Jason got off the phone as happy as could be. He headed back to the tent feeling like a new man. When he got back to the tent, he grabbed his stuff to take a shower. By now, most of the soldiers were done with theirs, so he was able to take his time and enjoy getting clean. Afterwards, he headed back to the tent, jumped in his rack, and went to sleep, sure to have happy dreams about being home.

Unfortunately, Jason's sleep was not as pleasant as he had hoped. He tossed and turned most of night, and when he did sleep, he kept seeing the faces of his buddies Alderson and Adams. In fact, he awakened at one point screaming for help. Well, this woke up most of the tent, and when he realized what was going on, he got out of bed and went outside for some fresh air. SFC Green joined him.

"You okay, buddy?" he asked Jason.

"I thought I was," he replied. "I went to bed feeling good about being out of Iraq and going home," he explained. "I was surely not expecting this to happen."

"Unfortunately, Jason, dreams about our experiences are pretty common, but eventually they will subside. When I got home from Desert Storm, I had nightmares almost every night for a while, but as time went by, I had them less and less. They still happen from time to time, but nowhere near like they were at the beginning. You get used to them, sort of. You'll be all right."

SFC Green patted Jason on the shoulder as he stood up to go back to bed.

"Try and get some rest," SFC Green said. "We have a lot to do over the next few weeks."

Jason went in shortly after SFC Green. He went back to his rack and eventually fell asleep. The rest of the night was calm. He awoke the next morning feeling rejuvenated but also a little sad, with images of his friends still fresh in his mind.

The unit was going to have a formation at eight o'clock. Prior to formation, most of the soldiers went to the chow hall for some breakfast. Jason sat alone, reminiscing about the good times he had with SSG Alderson and Sgt. Adams. He was really starting to miss them. When Jason finally finished his food, he headed back to the company area and joined the rest of the unit in formation. He made sure all of the troops in his squad were there and then stood quietly in line. With all of the troops present, 1SG Williams made his way to the front of the formation.

"Welcome back to Kuwait," he shouted.

Most of the soldiers responded with a loud army, "Hooooaaaaaaaaahhhhhhhh!"

The first sergeant began by telling them the rules of the base, which were much different from the airport in Iraq, mainly because there was a significantly less chance for enemy activity. He then informed them of what was going to happen over the next month and a half before they went home. Their duties would consist of doing a lot of paperwork, of course, and cleaning the equipment. There were a few other odds and ends that needed to be completed, but the focus would be on the two aforementioned tasks.

Equipment leaving Kuwait had to be thoroughly cleaned and then inspected by a customs team, which usually consisted of military police personnel, to ensure no contaminants would go back to the United States via the trucks. When the first sergeant finished with the itinerary, he turned the formation over to the captain, who had a few things of his own to say.

"First of all," he began, "I want to congratulate each and every one of you for a job well done. The citizens of America would be proud."

He then reiterated some of the things that 1SG Williams said, and then gave one final word.

"I have one final thing to say," he declared. "I know it's about ninety-five degrees and sunny, and there are no snowmen, lights, or decorated trees around, but I want to wish each and every one of you a merry Christmas. Now let's get to work."

Almost everyone, including Jason, had forgotten that it was Christmas Eve. The surroundings sure did not make it evident, and amidst all of the activity the past few days, it seemed to have slipped their minds. Jason did not even get to say anything to Shannon. All of the excitement overshadowed the holiday. He decided he would call her later, once the workday was finished.

Jason and the rest of the soldiers in the unit spent the day trying to get organized. They knew that there was a lot of work to do, but they also realized that they had plenty of time to get it all completed. As a result, Jason and the other leaders decided to give the rest of the troops the day off to relax and try to enjoy Christmas Eve while they organized the task list and assigned specific jobs to each of the troops. This would ultimately make the process much smoother for everyone. The captain and 1SG Williams were okay with this idea.

So the troops spent the day watching movies, sleeping, lifting weights, and even eating some ice cream and pizza from the vendors on the main base area. The squad, section, and platoon leaders worked diligently throughout most of the day trying to get the itinerary organized in a way that would make completing all of the tasks relatively simple, and by dinnertime, they were finished. They had broken down each day by time, task, personnel, and equipment. Barring any unforeseen distractions or delays, they should have everything completed by the end of January. They even broke the schedule down so everyone would have the weekends off.

Captain Hillock and the first sergeant were so impressed by the schedule that they decided to give everyone Christmas day off, only setting the plan back by one day. After he finished eating dinner, Jason went to the phone tent to call Shannon. Again he stood in line for about thirty minutes. When his turn finally came, he had difficulty getting through. There seemed to be trouble with the satellite system. He tried and tried but had no luck. Eventually, a soldier from the communication company came and informed them that the phones would not be operable until tomorrow.

Although Jason was upset, he decided to go to the main base and catch a movie and get his mind off things. Some of the other soldiers were talking about the movie *Elf* and how funny it was supposed to be, so Jason figured it would cheer him up a little bit, which it did. After the movie, Jason decided to take a stroll around the base by himself. A little time alone was a precious thing. He walked around for about an hour, checking out the scenery, seeing how much the base had changed since they were there last. He then went back to his tent to get a shower and get some sleep.

Christmas morning arrived, and it was just like any other day. It was hot and dusty, and there was no tree surrounded by presents and no lights up on the tents. Jason knew everyone back home was still sleeping, so he got dressed, went to breakfast, and went to the gym for a morning workout. Following that, he took a shower and went back to the movie tent, this time accompanied by SFC Green, who had now become one of his closer buddies in the unit.

They spent most of the day together, playing cards, checking out the post exchange, and doing a little shopping for folks back home. They eventually headed back to the phone tent, where they knew they would have to wait for a while to use the phone. And they were right; they waited in line for almost two hours before their turns arrived. Jason did not get through as easily this time as he had the other times, but he figured it was because of the time of day and the fact that it was Christmas. Soldiers all around the world were probably trying to call home.

After about fifteen minutes, Jason was about at his wits end. He decided to try one more time, and if he did not get through, he would come back later. He dialed the numbers and took a deep breath. Finally, the phone began to ring, and after the third one, Shannon answered the phone.

"Merry Christmas," Jason shouted.

"Merry Christmas, sweetheart," she replied.

An emotional conversation ensued, and the two talked for about thirty minutes. Although there were several people waiting in line, Jason did not care. He was really missing home today, and he needed to communicate with Shannon if he could not see her. They talked about everything: how her job was going, how his parents were doing, how much they missed each other, and most important, how excited they were to finally get to see each other again in less than two months.

They laughed and cried and laughed and cried throughout the entire conversation. Jason finally decided it was time to go so the other soldiers could use the phone, so he said his good-bye and asked Shannon to tell the family Merry Christmas. Feeling very sad and lonely, Jason went back to the tent and took a nap.

He woke up just before dinnertime and decided to get something to eat. The chow hall was decked out in holiday colors and trimmings, which gave him a slightly warm feeling. Dinner was pretty good: turkey, ham, mashed potatoes, and all of the fixings of home. Jason sat with SFC Green and a few other sergeants but did not participate in any of the conversation. He could not stop thinking about home.

When asked if he was doing okay, Jason stated that he was, so the guys went back to their conversation. They understood how he felt; they just chose to try not to think about it. But being the family guy he was, Jason could think of nothing else. When he finally finished dinner, he went back to the tent and lay in his bunk. He looked through some pictures his family had sent to him and reread some of the letters. He eventually fell asleep and dreamed happy thoughts of home. This was surely going to be a Christmas Jason would want to forget.

The next day, Jason awoke feeling good. It was now time for the soldiers in the unit to focus on getting work done to go home. After morning breakfast, 1SG Williams held a formation and went over the itinerary the leaders had recently put together. When he was finished, the soldiers gathered with their respective teams and went over the game plan in detail.

Jason and his team were going to be in charge of the wash bay, ensuring all of the trucks got in at their designated times. They would also assist with the cleaning. Having one team focus on this would enable them to know exactly what had to be done and what little tricks could help the process go a little smoother. The other teams would be responsible for unloading and reloading the shipping containers, making sure they were packed right. But they would only be repacked after the customs inspectors thoroughly inspected the items before they were packed to ship. Personal gear and weapons had to be cleaned, tactical gear had to be in working order, and heaps of paperwork had to be completed. Everyone had a job to do, and they had plenty of time to do it.

For the next month, this group of soldiers had their hands full. Sure, there was some down time to catch a movie or make a phone call, but knowing that everything had to be done and done right before they went home, everyone spent most of their time doing and redoing their assigned tasks. They were going to make sure nothing in their control was going to hold them back from going home.

By the last week of January, everything seemed to be done. All of the vehicles had passed through the wash bay and were parked in a special area, where they would sit until their date to be loaded on ships. Items in the shipping containers were inspected and packed to go. All of the other equipment and personal gear was cleaned, fixed, and in line to ship out.

The last phase would be going through the out-processing stations to get all of their paperwork in line. They had to redo wills, powers of attorney, life insurance, discharge from active duty papers, and all sorts of other paperwork. They even had to do what was called a post-deployment health assessment, which asked questions pertaining to events that occurred in Iraq and how these events bothered them today, if they did at all. The soldiers usually answered that nothing bothered them, for fear that if there were a problem, it could hold up their departure. This whole process was just a formality to ensure everything was in line, and it would be a process that they would go through again once they returned to the States. When all of the paperwork was completed, the last task was to take the vehicles to the shipping yard to board the massive vessel back to the States. Once that was done, it was simply a waiting game. By February 6th, everything was finally done, and now they just had to wait for orders to go to the airport.

The soldiers spent the next several days trying to find things to do to pass the time. Each day seemed longer as the anticipation for their departure grew. There was no hint as to the specific date they would leave, although they assumed it would be around Valentine's Day, which would make one year in the sandbox. There was a newly built movie theater on the base, so a lot of the soldiers spent several hours a day there. There were also a couple of gymnasiums where several soldiers passed time getting in a workout. Other soldiers slept, listened to music, and played cards. They would do anything to pass the hours.

Jason was no exception. He exercised, took in a few flicks at the theater, slept, and made a few phone calls back to the States. Of course, most of those were to Shannon. He did call his parents a couple of times, which made all of them even more excited for his return. Finally, after several mostly boring days, 1SG Williams passed the word along that there would be a formation after dinner. It was now February 12th.

Well, word spread quickly, and by the time the chow hall opened for dinner, every soldier in the 132nd was standing in line. They figured this formation would be the big one, the one they had been waiting for now for several months. The chow hall began serving at five o'clock, and by five thirty, everyone was standing in formation outside of their tent area. Their excitement was evident. Many were laughing and goofing off, things they had not really done in quite some time. Jason stood silently. Although he was excited about the likely news of finally leaving, he had learned from past experience that nothing is final until it is actually happening.

Finally, 1SG Williams and the captain made their way to the formation. By the time they were standing in front of the troops, everyone had gone completely silent. First Sergeant Williams called the formation to attention and then handed it over to the captain. He did not waste any time telling them the good news.

"Well, the time has come. At 1400 hours tomorrow, the busses will be here to pick us up and go to the airport. We're going home!"

He then paused while the soldiers responded. Some yelled, others hugged the people next to them, while others cried tears of joy. The captain gave them about thirty seconds before he called out, "At ease!" He proceeded to tell them once again how proud he was of them and then called the first sergeant back in front. First Sergeant Williams then gave them instructions as to what had to be done prior to leaving Camp Arifjan and what would take place at Camp Wolf, where they would ultimately fly out of. The soldiers were then dismissed to pack their things and to take care of any other necessary preparations.

They were not permitted to call home, for security reasons, until they reached the States. No one really seemed to mind, as they had plenty of other things to do. They finished the night hanging out together at their respective tents, reminiscing, joking, playing cards, and listening to music. It was a great night.

Although they eventually tried, hardly anyone could fall asleep, and for understandable reasons. Most of them, including Jason, lay in their bunks, fantasizing once again about what they were going to once they returned home, as they had so many times in the past year. When they finally awoke in the morning, everyone was out of the rack and finishing their morning routine before packing their stuff one last time and piling it up outside to load on the busses.

After everything was ready to go and everyone had eaten breakfast, the soldiers had to sit around and wait for the busses, which could not come soon enough. Fittingly, on this final day in the Middle East, a sand storm started, along with the near one-hundred-degree weather. Just a little reminder of what they would be leaving. After several hours, the busses finally arrived. The soldiers could not have packed them any quicker than they did, and within about fifteen minutes, they were on their way to the final stop before going home.

When they arrived at Camp Wolf, the same base they were on exactly one year ago, they could barely contain themselves. They unloaded the busses and were directed to a tent, where they were given one last customs briefing before having their bags searched. After that, they were sent to a hangar to wait for the plane.

They waited there anxiously for about two hours, when 1SG Williams came in and said what everyone was waiting to hear.

"Let's go home."

The troops grabbed their bags and got on the busses again to head to the tarmac, where their 747 was awaiting them. As they loaded the plane, most of the troops gave one final farewell wave to the land of the endless beach and headed to their seats. When the plane finally started its engines, everyone began screaming. They were in the air within minutes, headed back home.

Chapter 16: One Last Stop

As one can imagine, the troops on the plane heading home were ecstatic. When they weren't sleeping, they were laughing and joking, reminiscing and planning. They reminisced about the bad times they had in Iraq and the friends they lost, and they planned what their lives were going to be like when they returned home. Jason kept to himself most of the trip. He slept most of the time, and when he wasn't sleeping, he read *Maxim* magazine and listened to music. He spent time pondering what life would be like as a combat veteran and wondered if his expectations, such as the parade and great sense of patriotism, would be worth it. Above all, he and everyone else knew that their experiences in Iraq would have a profound impact on their lives, but exactly how, no one knew for sure.

With the exception of a short stop in Germany, the plane did a straight shot to McGuire Air Base in New Jersey, which is located next to Fort Dix, one of the primary mobilization locations for the reserves and National Guard. The flight took a little over fourteen hours, and when it finally landed, the soldiers were jumping up and down, yelling, "We're home! We're home!" When the doors of the plane opened, the soldiers began filing out onto the tarmac. Several of them stopped to kiss the ground, thrilled to be back on United States' soil.

February in New Jersey is cold, and today was no exception. It was about twenty-five degrees with snow flurries, a far cry from the one-hundred-plus-degree weather that they experienced less than a day earlier. But the soldiers loved it. Although they were not really dressed for this type of weather, it didn't really seem to bother anyone.

There were busses just off of the tarmac waiting to take them the short drive to the barracks at Fort Dix, where they would stay for seven days during the final phase of out-processing. More paperwork, physicals, briefings, and various other formalities had to take place before they could be released to go back to Harrisville, where their families and friends would be awaiting their arrival. The idea behind this week-long stay at the base was to not only ensure that their military affairs were in order before they were released from active duty, but to give the soldiers an opportunity to readjust to the new surroundings. This was also the time when any physical and/or psychological issues would be addressed.

The soldiers in this particular unit did not seem to mind that they had to stay here for a week. It was enough to know that they were out of the Middle East and that they would be home, sleeping in their own beds, in a week. As the busses pulled up in front of the barracks, the soldiers filed off and grabbed their belongings from under the bus. When the busses left, the first sergeant held a quick formation to give them instructions for the remainder of the day. He told them that they had to turn their weapons in to a makeshift armory in the building and put their things in their rooms. He said they should try and relax for a while, either getting some sleep or contacting families. He concluded the formation by welcoming them back to the States and said that there would be another formation at 5:00 PM. They were then released to put their things away and, as expected, most of them rushed to find a phone to call home.

Jason took his time getting his things situated in his room and actually took a nap for about an hour. He knew that everyone else would be dashing off to the phones, so he felt that there was no point getting in a big hurry and then having to stand outside in line, in the freezing cold. Besides, it was only 11:30 AM, so he had most of the day before the next formation to make a call. Because of the excitement on the flight home combined with the eight hours difference between the United States and Kuwait,

Jason was exhausted and fell asleep almost immediately. Not even the commotion from the other troops banging around kept him awake.

He had been sleeping for about two hours before SFC Green woke him up to inform him that he and a few other guys were going to the bowling alley on base to grab a bite to eat and have a few celebratory drinks. Jason hesitated, but ultimately decided to go along with them. When they arrived at the bowling alley, Jason noticed a phone booth that was unoccupied, so he told the guys he would meet them inside in a few minutes. He quickly went to the phone and called Shannon. She answered on the third ring.

"Hello," she said.

"Hey, baby. Guess where I am?"

Shannon paused, but then excitedly yelled, "You're at Fort Dix!"

Jason confirmed that he was, and the two of them continued to talk for fifteen minutes about the details of his next week and when he thought he would be home. They were both very excited. However, while he was talking to Shannon on the phone, he noticed that, for the first time, he was a little nervous about the reality of seeing her again. Although he did not say anything to her about it, he was uncomfortable about feeling this way. He refocused his attention on her, telling her about the last day in Kuwait and the flight home, as well as what it felt like being back in the United States, which he likened to walking into a stranger's home.

Shannon did not say much during the conversation aside from addressing her excitement about seeing him again. She also spent a lot of time crying. The reality of Jason being home after a little over a year was finally setting in. Jason finished the call by asking her to call his parents and give them the news.

"I can't wait to see you again," he concluded. "I love you."

"I love you, too, Jason. See you soon."

Jason walked into the bowling alley feeling a little confused about his nervousness. SFC Green saw him entering the building and could tell immediately that something was wrong. As Jason approached, SFC Green handed him a beer and asked if everything was okay. Jason nodded but did not fool this two-war veteran.

"Feeling a little nervous?" SFC Green asked.

"Yeah. Is that normal?"

SFC Green reassured Jason that it was normal and that it should actually be expected, given the fact that they had not seen each other in over a year.

"It will pass," SFC concluded.

Feeling better after this advice, Jason took a drink of his beer and jumped in on the bowling action.

Jason, SFC Green, and the other guys played three games before it was time to start heading back to the barracks for the formation. When they returned, everyone was in attendance and the formation was about to begin, so they jumped into their positions. First Sergeant Williams began the formation. He went over the agenda for the next six days, explaining exactly what was going to happen and when. He informed them that if they were having problems of any kind, such as with their pay or awards, or physical or psychological problems, that this was the time to have them addressed. He stressed the importance of resolving any problems while they were at Fort Dix, as there may not be another chance once they return to their home station. He then informed them of some of the rules of the base for demobilizing troops and what the repercussions of any forbidden acts could be. For example, an Article 15 would be given for leaving the base without permission, which entailed losing pay and possibly rank. The captain then took over the formation and basically reiterated what 1SG Williams said. He also stressed the importance of getting things done in a timely manner so that there would not be any delays returning to Pennsylvania.

With the conclusion of the formation, the captain released the soldiers for the rest of the night and informed them that morning formation would be at seven o'clock. Once released, most of the soldiers went to the chow hall for dinner, while others went back to the bowling alley for some more drinks and bowling. Jason went back to the bowling alley as well. They stayed there until about eleven, at which time most of them were drunk and knew that they had better get some sleep or else tomorrow would be a rough day.

Morning came, meaning the beginning of out-processing. For the rest of the week, the soldiers would be in and out of briefings, getting checked out by dentists and doctors, filling out more paperwork, and getting new identification cards as well as their release papers. Everything took a while to finish, but all of it was important. Some things were optional, such as talking to a mental health professional and having any physical injuries checked out, so most of the troops bypassed this part. They did so to avoid being held over after the company left while the problem was resolved. But there were some who took advantage of these offerings because they did not want to be refused help later because they denied any issues now. Jason was not one of them. He figured that if he needed help, he would get it once he returned home.

There were also briefings to go through, some of which were lead by individuals from the Department of Veterans Affairs, who informed the new veterans of what services they were eligible to receive once they were released from active duty. Again, because so many of the troops were focused only on getting home, they did not pay much attention to what was being said in these briefings, choosing instead to fantasize about being home or sleeping. Although it is difficult to blame the soldiers in this regard, nevertheless, many missed out because of their anticipation.

By Thursday, two days prior to leaving the base for Harrisville, most of the soldiers had all of the stations completed and all of the briefings done. However, the regulations stated that they must stay for a week, so now they just had to wait. Many of the soldiers spent the last two days at the bowling alley, just about the only place where there was something to do to pass time. Others went to the gym, called home, slept, and went shopping at the PX. Jason made a few calls home and spent the rest of the time between the gym and the bowling alley. He had called Shannon every day since arriving at Fort Dix, and so the nervousness had dissipated. He also called his parents a couple of times, so everyone was on the same page about what was happening and what to expect when he arrived back at the unit.

Friday night finally came, and almost no one could sleep. Everything that had to be done was done, and everyone had their bags packed. Nothing left to do but wait. Everyone was feeling great. Nothing could bring the troops down now. The morning of February 21st finally came, and everyone was up early, making final preparations to get out of there. The busses were not due until around eleven o'clock that morning, but everyone and everything was outside waiting by nine. At around ten thirty, the busses finally arrived—a little early. This was it; they were finally going home. It took less than five minutes before the busses were loaded, and by eleven, they were on their way. The trip could not go by fast enough.

The trip from Fort Dix, New Jersey, to Harrisville, Pennsylvania, on three busses takes about four hours, and today was no exception. However, about ten miles outside of the city limits of Harrisville, the busses pulled into a rest stop. Waiting there were several police cars, fire trucks, ambulances, and multiple cars filled with family and community members. To the soldiers' surprise, they were going home in a parade.

It seemed like it took forever to go the last ten miles in this convoy of vehicles, but they finally arrived. People were lining the streets, clapping and yelling, many holding up signs. The soldiers were waving and yelling back to the people. When they finally pulled into the parking lot of the armory, their long-awaited trip home over, there were several hundred people cheering and clapping. Many were even crying, especially the families of the troops. It had been about thirteen months since the soldiers had seen their husbands, wives, moms, dads, children, and other relatives.

Jason spotted Shannon and his parents immediately. They were also cheering and crying. The busses finally stopped, and the troops exited, each attacked by his or her family. Jason's turn finally came, and when he made eye contact with Shannon, they both paused. They stared at each other for about five seconds before Shannon came running to him, crying and smiling. They embraced one another. The time had finally arrived. This was the happiest moment in the lives of most of these families, Jason's included. The soldiers were finally home.

The arrival at the armory was everything that Jason had hoped it would be. Although they were not walking in the streets of the city, the soldiers received their parade, and the dream that began when Jason was only sixteen years old was finally fulfilled. But as exciting as it was, something did not seem right to Jason. He felt like something was missing or out of place. He could not quite put his finger on it. However, he figured that is was a normal part of returning from combat, so he shrugged it off and continued basking in the moment.

After about ten minutes of hugging, kissing, and crying, the soldiers in the unit were ordered to get into formation. A general was in attendance and wanted to recognize the soldiers with a few words of wisdom.

"I'm so proud of all of you, and I want to thank each and every one of you for the sacrifices you have made for this country," she stated. "I know that not everyone made it back, and we will never forget them. I know they would be proud of all of you as well."

This brought tears to the eyes of most in attendance, especially Jason, who was so close to two of those who were lost.

The general continued, "I also want to recognize and thank the families for their support of the soldiers. They wouldn't have been able to do this without you. I want to conclude with one last statement: reintegration back to civilian life can be difficult, so I want each of you to take things slowly. Don't rush anything. This goes for the families, as well. Take your time. That's all I'm going to say about that. Soldiers, thank you again for a job well done. Good luck."

She turned the formation over to Captain Hillock.

"I'm not gonna keep you from your families any longer," he said. "Just remember, we have drill again in three months. Your squad leaders and section sergeants will be contacting you. Welcome back. Dismissed!"

Everyone scattered as if a bomb was about to explode in the middle of the formation. They could not wait to get out of there and back to their homes and families.

Jason, however, took his time. The speech from the general really hit him hard, momentarily consuming his thoughts. As he slowly walked towards his family, Shannon asked him if he was okay. Jason nodded and said that he was fine. Heading to the car, Jason looked back at the armory, as if he were looking for someone. Again Shannon asked him if something was wrong.

"Just looking," he replied.

What he was really doing was looking to see if Sgt. Adams and SSG Alderson's wives were anywhere around the area. But realizing that this would probably have been too much for them to handle, he refocused his attention back to his family. They got in the car and began the journey back to Jason's parents' house. Jason was about to embark on his new life as a combat veteran, and the road ahead was going to be a long one. It was time to forget what happened in Iraq and get back to the life that he once knew, a life that seemed so wonderful.

Chapter 17: Home?

THEY ARRIVED AT JASON'S PARENTS' house in the middle of the afternoon. As they pulled into the driveway, Jason noticed an unusually large number of cars in the area but thought nothing of it. Just as they were about to enter the house, Ray looked at Jason with a tear in his eye.

"Welcome home, son. I love you."

He opened the door and immediately people began clapping and shouting.

"Welcome home, Jason!"

Jason's parents, along with Shannon, had arranged a surprise party for him, inviting all of his and Shannon's closest friends and family members. Jason began to cry. Shannon put her arm around his waist and walked him into the house. Everyone commenced patting Jason on the back and giving him hugs. Jason continued crying, but eventually regained his composure enough to thank everyone for being there.

The dining room table was full of food and drinks, so once the initial excitement settled, everybody grabbed a plate and started eating. Jason, the disciplined and respectful soldier that he was, waited until everyone else had his or her plate before he took his turn. He piled his plate with a little bit of everything, seeing as how he hadn't touched good pasta, his mom's juicy Cajun meatballs, or his uncle's homemade Italian sausage in over a year. He also made himself a stiff drink, Captain and Coke. Finally, he was home and able to enjoy the little things that he missed so much while he was away. Most of the guests stayed for a couple of hours or so, but by eight o'clock that evening, just about everyone was gone, except for a few friends from the neighborhood.

While they were sitting around, reminiscing about old times and the things that Jason had missed, there was a sudden knock at the door. Jason looked at his dad as if he might know who it was, but Ray just shrugged his shoulders. No other guests were expected this late. Jason sat his drink down and walked over to answer the door. He was not quite prepared to see this guest, not just yet.

When Jason opened the door, a small-figured woman was standing there, shivering and crying. She stood there for what seemed like an eternity to Jason. They stared at each other, neither knowing what to say or do. Finally, Jason grabbed her and gave her a firm hug, holding her for several minutes without saying a word. It was Lisa Alderson, the wife of his buddy, SSG Alderson.

Not yet knowing who it was, Shannon and Ray walked to the door to see what was taking so long. When they realized who it was, they turned and walked away, knowing that these two needed a few moments. Jason eventually brought her into the house, which was dead silent at this point. With compassion in their eyes, each person walked up to Lisa and gave her a hug. No one really knew what words would be appropriate, so not a word was said until she finally spoke.

"I just wanted to come over and say hello and welcome Jason home. I do not want me being here to ruin the mood. I just felt that being around one of my husband's good friends when he returned might be a good idea."

Ray quickly responded, "No, no Lisa, you are more than welcome here. Don't be silly. Can I get you something to drink?"

Lisa glanced at the table to see what was available.

"I'll have a glass of wine."

"You got it."

She sat down on the couch and stated that she did not want to talk about her husband, but she would like to know exactly what happened. Jason, feeling very uncomfortable about this request, was not quite sure how to respond. He looked around the room, as if waiting for someone to come to his side. But that did not happen. It seemed as if everyone was ready to hear the story as well. Jason knew it was not a good idea at this point, especially since they had been drinking. But Jason, feeling a responsibility to assist her in getting some closure and realizing she deserved to hear it from him, relayed the events that he would not soon forget. This was the first time that he retold the story since it happened.

Less than a minute into the story, Jason took the first of many pauses and deep breaths because of the emotions he was feeling. Shannon sat next to Jason with her arm wrapped around him, consoling him through this difficult recollection. For about the next forty-five minutes, Jason went through every precise facet of the firefight. By the time he was finished with each gut-wrenching detail, everyone in the room was in tears. Lisa walked over to Jason and gave him a hug.

"Thank you," she said as she gave him another hug.

She then thanked everyone for being so supportive, and with that, she left. She apparently came to the house for one reason and one reason alone: to hear her husband's story. With the attitudes completely changed at this point, the rest of the friends and family decided it was a good time to go home, leaving Jason alone with his parents and Shannon.

Everyone was now just sitting around in the living room, saying very little.

"You okay, buddy?" Ray asked his son.

"Yeah, I'm just happy to be home," Jason replied in an unconvincing tone.

They spent about another hour talking about meaningless subjects, trying to lighten the mood before going to bed. But no matter what was said, all that Jason could think about was that awful day when two of his best friends' lives were taken.

Since they each had a few drinks, Jason and Shannon decided to spend the night there rather than taking the risk of driving home. Before going to bed, Jason took a long, hot shower, enjoying each and every second of being alone in a shower that was clean and relaxing. When he and Shannon finally lay down to sleep, they talked a little about what had happened that night and the overwhelming emotions of joy and relief Jason felt. Exhausted from the long day's events, Shannon looked at Jason.

"I love you, Jason."

"I love you, too," he replied.

Shannon soon fell fast asleep. Jason, however, did not fall asleep so quickly. In fact, throughout the entire night, he probably only slept for about an hour or less, as he could not stop thinking about everything that had happened that day, especially Lisa showing up unexpectedly. When he did sleep, he kept waking back up, sweaty and scared from the images of his dreams. However, he thought nothing of it, figuring it was normal, as SFC Freeman told him. Besides, he had not slept in a normal bed in over a year and did not have someone sleeping with him. He figured that after a couple of days, everything would be normal again. It was just a matter of getting used to his old environment. He vaguely remembered someone saying something about sleep problems when his unit was briefed at Fort Dix, but neither he nor anyone else in his unit had really paid much attention to what was said during their week there. Home was all they could think of at the time.

At about eight o'clock the next morning, Jason and Shannon got out of bed, eager to start their lives together again.

"How'd you sleep?" Shannon asked Jason.

"Not too good, but I'm sure it was from all of the excitement," he replied.

"Probably so," she said.

Thinking nothing else of it, Shannon headed to the bathroom. Jason lay there for a few more minutes, still thinking about what happened the night before. He was feeling really guilty about celebrating being home when some of his friends could not do the same. Shannon then returned from the bathroom.

"Let's go downstairs; it smells like something's cooking," she said.

Jason got out of bed and went to the bathroom to freshen up. They then headed downstairs to the kitchen, where they were greeted by a table full of food.

"What's all this?" Jason asked.

"Well, I know you haven't had a home-cooked meal for a while, so I figured I'd be the first to give you one," his mom replied.

Jason sat down at the table, where his dad was reading the paper.

"Anything good?" Jason asked.

"Well," Ray replied, "take a look at this."

Jason got up from the table and went over to where his dad was sitting. Looking over his shoulder, he saw that the entire two pages in the opened section were about his unit returning home.

"That's pretty cool," Jason said. "I'll read it later."

"Okay," Ray said. Jason sat back down and commenced eating. Within a minute, he had finished most of the food on his plate.

"Jason, slow down," Shannon said.

Without even realizing it, Jason was eating his food just as he had in Iraq and Kuwait, as if he was in a hurry.

"Sorry," Jason responded.

He filled his plate again and ate a little slower. When he finished, he thanked his mother and headed upstairs for a shower. Shannon came into the bathroom while he was still in there.

"What do you want to do today, Jason?" she asked.

"Well, I'd like to go home and get my stuff unpacked," he replied.

"Okay," she said as she headed to the bedroom to gather their things.

Once they were ready to go, Jason hugged his parents and thanked them for everything.

"I'll see you soon," he said to them.

The drive home was relatively quiet. There were signs up on a lot of the homes, welcoming the troops home, and Jason was trying to read all of them as he passed.

"Everything okay?" Shannon asked.

"I'm fine. I'm just checking out the signs."

No other words were said until they arrived at their house. Jason sat still in the car for a minute, hesitant to run in. He knew that this was basically the final step towards being a citizen again, so he was mentally preparing himself for the reality of the situation. As he walked towards the front door, he noticed that the grass was really high and the hedges had not been trimmed.

"Why hasn't this stuff been trimmed?" Jason asked with an attitude.

"I've had a few other things on my mind lately, like getting plans together for my husband's return home. It's winter anyway," Shannon replied.

"Still could have cut the grass," Jason mumbled.

"What was that?"

"Nothing."

They continued into the house. Jason dropped his bags on the floor and looked around.

"Something's different," Jason said.

"You've been gone a long time. A lot is different," Shannon responded.

Shannon sensed Jason had a bit of a chip on his shoulder. He started complaining as soon as he got home, about clothes piling up, boxes of junk piled in the basement, new decorations—things that he never would have gotten mad about before his deployment. But she said nothing about it. She assumed his attitude was normal for a returning soldier and that he just needed some time to readjust. She figured he would get back to his old self soon enough.

Jason picked up his bags and went to his room to unpack. When he was done, he began looking around the house to familiarize himself with his surroundings again. He noticed that Shannon had made some changes: the furniture was moved around, there were new pictures on the wall, and the bathroom was painted, among other minor changes—but this time he kept his comments to himself. Shannon brought up his last bag and dropped it on the floor.

"Be careful with that," Jason said. "There are important things in there."

"Sorry," she replied and headed back downstairs. Jason grabbed the bag and began unpacking it. It contained his camera, paperwork, some memorabilia, and various other things he collected while away. Jason immediately put the things in their place and grabbed his camera as he headed back downstairs.

"I want to get my pictures developed," Jason said to Shannon.

"Okay, we'll go in a little bit."

Jason seemed irritated by this response, sighing loudly.

"I want to go now."

Shannon gave him a dirty look and shut the sink water off, as she was doing the dishes. She grabbed her keys and headed to the front door.

"I don't like your attitude," Shannon said as she passed Jason.

"Sorry," Jason said sarcastically.

On the way to the photo shop, Shannon asked Jason what his problem was. At first he said nothing, but after Shannon asked two more times, he finally responded.

"I'm just a little irritated. I kind of feel out of place, but I don't know why. I'm sure after some time it will pass, so please just bear with me."

"I'll try," she said, "but I don't appreciate your attitude when I did nothing wrong."

Jason did not respond. They arrived at the photo shop within a few minutes, and Jason headed in, leaving Shannon behind. He told the worker that he wanted his pictures developed immediately. He sounded as if he was giving an order. The worker gave him a strange look and told him it would be about an hour. Although Jason was not happy about the wait, he agreed and handed over the camera.

By now it was close to noon, so he and Shannon decided to get some lunch at a nearby restaurant. Within the first five minutes of sitting at the table, six people had welcomed Jason home. This made him feel pretty good and seemed to change his attitude a little bit. Again he ate his food quickly, but Shannon figured this time it was because he was excited to get his pictures. When they went back to the shop, the pictures were finished. Jason thanked the worker and went on his way. He waited to get home to open them. He was very excited, as he did not remember what pictures he had taken.

As he sat on the couch sifting through them, he came upon a picture that caused him to immediately break into tears. It was the picture of him, Sgt. Adams, and SSG Alderson from their last day together, standing at the weapons dump and smiling at the camera. They were killed shortly after. He cried for several minutes. Shannon did not say a word. She simply consoled him with her arm around his back.

"I want to get this enlarged," Jason said.

He continued through the rest of the pictures rather quickly and then headed back to the shop to get the picture enlarged. He bought a frame for it as well, and when he returned home, he immediately sat it on his dresser. He looked at it for a while and then went back downstairs, where he and Shannon spent the rest of the day relaxing and talking.

The next several days were spent going over financial affairs, getting rid of unnecessary paperwork, and sorting through all of their things, working to get everything back to the way it was before Jason left for Iraq. It was as if they were in a hurry to get back to their old lives.

Within a week, Jason and Shannon had all of their affairs in order, and the stage was set to begin with their regular lives again. It was the weekend, so they decided to go to a local bar and have some drinks. Although Jason was a little nervous about this, he obliged because he knew Shannon really wanted to go out. He also figured it would be a good chance for him to relax a little bit. They arrived at the bar around nine o'clock.

There were not many people there yet, so they grabbed a seat at the bar and ordered a drink. Shannon had a beer, while Jason had a Captain and Coke. Since Jason had not had much to drink over the past year, he was feeling a little tipsy within the first hour. The bar began to fill up, and some familiar faces appeared. Jason and Shannon made small talk with the people they knew, many of whom welcomed Jason home. Some stopped and chatted a little, but for the most part, Jason and Shannon were alone.

At around eleven thirty, both Jason and Shannon were drunk, but they were having a good time, so they continued. An old friend of Jason's showed up at the bar, someone he had not seen in over three years. Jason and his friend were excited to see each other as they smiled and gave each other hugs, asking how the other had been. This friend, Eric Bloom, sat with Jason and Shannon and spent the next half hour or so catching up on old times. Everything was going great, until Eric asked Jason a question.

Eric looked at Jason for a few seconds before he said anything. And then it came.

"I gotta ask you something," Eric said, pausing to make sure he had Jason's attention.

"Did you kill anyone while you were over there?"

Jason, stunned by this question, did not know how to respond. He couldn't believe that his own friend was asking such a question. *I guess some people just don't get it,* Jason thought to himself.

Shannon did not hear the question, so she could not interrupt to save him from answering. It took Jason about thirty seconds before he could talk, and as he started to answer, he began to cry. Shannon just happened to turn her head at this point.

"What's the matter, Jason?" she asked as she put her hand on his forearm. "Nothing," he replied as he pushed her hand off of him.

Eric realized that he asked the wrong question and apologized. He then walked away. That set the pace for the rest of the night. When asked, Jason refused to go home and started ordering shots. He figured he could forget about the memories this way.

At around 1:30 AM, a guy walked up to the bar beside Jason and accidentally bumped into him, spilling Jason's drink. Although the guy apologized, Jason was furious.

"Watch it, man," Jason said.

Again the guy apologized.

"Fucking idiot," Jason said.

The guy took obvious offense and asked Jason what his problem was. Jason immediately stood up and hit the guy, instantly knocking him to the ground. Jason did not stop. He jumped on the guy and continued hitting him, until Eric and some other guys grabbed him. After Jason calmed down a little, he shoved the guys off of him.

"Let's get out of here, Shannon," Jason said.

They got a taxi and headed home. Jason passed out on the way, but woke enough to get in the house and get in bed.

The next morning, Jason slowly arose from the bed, holding his head in obvious pain. He asked Shannon what happened the night before but received no response. Shannon now realized that Jason was not the same guy he once was and was unsure if he would be again. Her assumption that things would get back to normal was incorrect, and last night clearly emphasized that. Not knowing exactly where to begin, she started with Eric's question and went from there. Jason stayed silent for the entire story, and when Shannon finished, he apologized.

"That's great that you apologize, but I think that something is wrong with you."

Offended, Jason replied, "Well what do you expect? I just got back from war. The guy obviously pissed me off."

Not sure if she should say anything else, Shannon paused and then decided she needed to get away from the house for a while to think about things.

"I have to go to the store. Do you need anything?"

"No."

Shannon left, and Jason continued to lay there, pondering what Shannon told him. He felt a little upset, but when he looked at the picture of his buddies on the dresser, that went away. He became mad again and actually thought to himself that the guy should not have started with him. He was convinced that the guy spilled the drink on him on purpose. Jason decided to get out of bed and take a shower. He then went downstairs and made himself some coffee and watched a little television. When Shannon returned home, she sat on the chair opposite Jason.

"Jason, I'm a little worried. We had a guy from the Vet Center come to one of the family support meetings, and he talked about some readjustment issues that you could have. He said that if certain warning signs appear, you should go talk to someone. One of those things was fighting and being angry."

Jason immediately responded, "I'm a doctor. I do not need to talk to someone about what is going on with me. I'm smart enough to figure it out myself."

Shannon did not say a word, knowing it was probably useless. She got up and went to the kitchen. Jason continued to watch television for several more hours while Shannon was around the house pretending to be busy to avoid him while he was angry. Early that afternoon, Ray called to see how Jason was doing. He did not know about the fight, and Jason was not about to tell him.

"How's it going?" he asked Jason.

"Fine," Jason responded.

"You need anything?" his father asked.

"No, Dad," Jason replied.

There was silence for about ten seconds before anything was said. Ray then spoke up.

"I'm not rushing you, son," Ray assured, "but I was wondering when you plan on returning to work."

"Well, actually, Dad, I was hoping to return soon. I need to get back to my old self again, and I figured going to work would help."

Shannon heard him say that and was happy to hear it. She figured that it would help him to be around regular people again.

"You can start as soon as you want. I think it's a good idea to start again soon, too," Ray said.

"Yeah, I'm ready," Jason insisted. "Gotta run, Dad. Take care," he said as he hung up the phone.

Jason got off of the phone and yelled for Shannon. When she came in to the room, he again apologized for his attitude and behavior and told her he was going back to work Monday, hoping it would help him get better. Shannon gave him a kiss and went about her business again, as did Jason.

Later that day, Jason received a phone call. It was SFC Green, asking Jason if he wanted to get together that night for some drinks. Without consulting Shannon, he said that he would, and when he ended the call, he told Shannon about it. Before she could say anything, he promised that there would be no problems and that he would not be out late. Not wanting an argument, Shannon said she didn't mind, although she really did. Jason got ready and gave Shannon a kiss as he headed out the front door.

He met with SFC Green and some of the other guys in the unit at a bar about ten minutes away from his house. All of them greeted each other and proceeded to suck down some drinks. Jason had his usual Captain and Coke, along with an occasional shot. They began talking about how their time home had been going, and most agreed that is was different than expected. They felt it was good to be home again but that things did seem strange. Jason told them about the fight last night, and most of the guys said they would have done the same thing.

After a few hours of storytelling, everyone was pretty drunk. They continued to tell stories late into the night, and around midnight, Shannon called Jason. "Is everything all right, Jason?" she asked.

"Yeah, things are great; no problems. If there are, I will call you. Bye," he said as he hung up the phone.

Some of the guys left shortly after the phone call, but Jason and SFC Green stayed. In fact, they were there at two o'clock when Shannon called again. She was clearly upset, but Jason didn't want to leave.

"The bar is closing soon, and I'll be home after that," Jason insisted.

He then hung up the phone. SFC Green overheard the way Jason was speaking to Shannon.

"Why are you treating to her like that, Jason?" he asked.

"That's really none of your business," Jason replied.

"You know, Jason," Green continued, "when I returned from Desert Storm, I was the same way, and that was what led to my divorce. I think that you need to consider going to talk to somebody. Maybe the Vet Center would do you some good."

"I'll be fine," Jason insisted as he threw some money down on the table. "See you later, sarge."

Jason got up and headed out of the bar. SFC Green did not try to stop him. He figured Jason wouldn't listen anyway.

Very drunk, Jason got into his car and drove home. As he pulled into the driveway, he ran over a bush in the yard, which prompted Shannon to come running out of the house. It woke a neighbor, as well, who was peering out of a window.

"Mind your business," Jason said as he stumbled towards the house.

This night ended the same as the last, with Jason passing out as soon as he hit the bed.

The next morning, Jason awakened to see Shannon sitting at the foot of the bed, glaring at him.

"I'm not going to put up with this kind of behavior anymore, Jason," she insisted.

Unsure of exactly what happened and why she was upset, he thought of the only thing he could muster at the time.

"Nothing bad will happen again," he assured her. "I'm going back to work soon, and I'll be past this phase."

"We'll see," Shannon replied. "I'm going to your parents' house to visit. Do you want to go?"

"No," Jason said. "I need to get my things ready for work, and I was thinking about going to the office to get reacquainted with the place—see what's what."

"Okay," she said as she gave him a kiss on the forehead. "I'll see you later."

She stood up and headed for the door.

"I love you," Jason said.

She looked back at him, fighting back tears.

"I love you, too."

Once she was gone, Jason got out of bed and began the same routine as yesterday. He did not go to the office and he did not get anything ready for work. Shannon returned early that evening.

"How was your day, honey?" she asked.

"It was great. I went to the office and got some things done. How was your day?"

"It was nice. I wish you could have gone with me," she said as she put her coat and purse away.

They spent the rest of the evening sitting on the couch together, watching television. Shannon tried to get Jason to cuddle with her, but he did not.

"Why won't you get close to me, Jason, or even give me a kiss? Is something wrong?" she asked.

"I'm not in the mood," he replied.

After watching television, they made their way to bed. Except for their good nights, not a word was said.

The next day, Jason awakened feeling good about starting work again. He took a shower and went downstairs to find Shannon making him breakfast.

"Almost done, honey," she said as she flipped the eggs.

"Thanks, but I'm not hungry. I'll just have some coffee."

Shannon had made him eggs, toast, bacon, and pancakes. Frustrated by Jason's apparent lack of consideration for her work, Shannon threw the food in the garbage can and walked out. Jason poured some coffee in his mug and yelled, "Bye," as he walked out the door. Shannon did not respond.

Jason arrived at work to find a banner on the building that read, "Welcome Back, Dr. Henson." Jason smiled and continued inside. On the way to his old office, he was greeted by the secretary.

"Welcome back, Jason," she said.

"Thanks, Maggie. It's good to be back," he responded.

Jason opened his office door. The place was a mess. No one had been in it or cleaned it since he left. Furious, he went back to Maggie.

"Why the hell does my office look like that?"

With a scared look on her face, she stated, "Your father told everyone to leave it alone and that you would want to take care of it yourself."

Jason walked away and headed back to his office without saying a word. He slammed the door shut and spent the next two hours cleaning and organizing. When his dad stopped in the office, Jason would not say a word.

"What's the matter, Jason?" Ray asked.

"Why did you allow my office to get so dirty?"

"I thought it would give you a chance to refamiliarize yourself with your office."

"Someone could have at least cleaned it," Jason stated.

Ray apologized and left the room. Around eleven, Jason had his first patient. It was a little old lady who apparently had a cold. Jason asked what was wrong, and she said that she had a cough and runny nose. Jason seemed irritated.

"You have a cold; get some cold medicine."

Clearly offended, she walked out of the office. Ray saw her leaving and asked Jason what happened.

"Stupid lady with a stupid cold. Waste of my time."

"That's what you practice for and how you get paid," Ray replied. "Where's the Jason who every patient loved?"

Jason did not respond, and Ray left. Jason had an attitude towards his patients all day. He compared every problem they had to the problems the soldiers and civilians had in Iraq and felt that these patients had no reason to be here and that they were whining.

At the end of the day, Ray sat Jason down in the lobby.

"Are you okay, son ... really okay?"

"I'm fine. I wish everyone would quit asking me that question."

"Do you think everyone would ask if they thought that you were fine?"

This question made Jason realize that something may be wrong, but he was not yet ready to admit it.

"I'll be okay, Dad. I just need some time to readjust. Maybe I came back to work too soon. I'm gonna get out of here for the day. I'll see you later."

Jason then headed home, where Shannon was waiting for him at the dinner table. "Hello," he said as he sat at the table.

"How was your day?" she asked.

"Well, it wasn't what I expected. I snapped at almost all of the patients and was mad about everything, from my dirty office to a little old lady having a cold."

"I'm really worried about you, Jason."

"Shannon, I'll be fine. I just need some time," he insisted.

"You keep saying that, but what about now, when you're snapping and yelling at everybody?"

"If things don't get better real soon, I'll go see someone," Jason said, rolling his eyes.

Shannon seemed content with this response, and the two began eating. Afterwards, they played a quiet game of cards before going to bed.

For the next month, everything seemed to be fine. Although Jason continued with his negative attitude for a few weeks, he gradually improved his personal skills and was getting back into the groove at work. Additionally, things between he and Shannon improved, and they were getting along fine. Jason started to see a gradual increase in patients again, obviously from word of mouth that he had changed his attitude. By late April, everyone thought that Jason had returned to being the Jason of old, and he seemed to be in a good mood all the time, joking and laughing like he used to. But what they did not know was that Jason was only masking his true feelings. He thought that if he pretended that he was doing well for a while, eventually he would get back to normal again. But Jason didn't know what normal was. In fact, so many things had happened to him over the past year and a few months that he forgot what he used to be like—or at least what he used to feel like.

Jason sat at home one night watching television with Shannon, and everything seemed to be going well. They happened to be watching the news, something they had been avoiding, when a piece came on about an ambush that occurred exactly where Sgt. Adams and SSG Alderson were killed. This instantly brought him back to that moment. He sat there in a daze.

"Are you okay?" she asked.

No response. He was gazing at the television. She actually had to shake him before he responded.

"Jason," she asked, "where were you?"

Jason did not say a word and headed to his room. He grabbed the picture of him and his buddies from the dresser and sat on the corner of the bed, crying.

Shannon appeared in the room a few moments after Jason sat down.

"Jason," she said, "why don't you tell me what's going on?"

Jason sat silently. It took several minutes before he finally regained his composure.

"You wouldn't understand," he claimed.

She sat there silent for a moment.

"I can't understand if you don't tell me."

Jason thought about that for a minute and then did what Shannon had been waiting for all along: he told her everything. He spent over two hours talking about all of the casualties in his unit and all of the horrible things he witnessed. Shannon sat there, quietly listening, even crying at various moments. Although this was difficult for Jason, he actually felt a little better when he was done. In fact, he was experiencing a feeling that he had not had in quite some time, like a weight was lifted off of his shoulders.

"I appreciate you listening to me, Shannon. I'm sorry for what I've put you through."

Shannon gave him a hug.

"I love you," she said.

The two sat for a little while longer, talking, and then did something they had not done since he had been home: made love.

Jason had been feeling emotionally numb and that was keeping him from being able to express himself, both emotionally and physically. It was a great night for both of them. They awoke the next day feeling optimistic

Jason continued the facade of being in a great mood all of the time and pretended that nothing was bothering him. Although he had felt that night with Shannon had changed him, he was now realizing that it was only temporary.

One day in the office, on a day when he was actually feeling pretty good, a patient came in and changed everything. It was SPC Jennings, one of the troops from his squad. Jason was excited to see him, but that excitement did not last long. When Jason had him alone in his office, he asked Jennings why he was there. The specialist stated that he had been suffering from panic attacks and not getting any sleep. He said that he was having nightmares almost every night about the night when PFC Upshaw was killed.

"Jennings, these reactions are typical for what you've been through. With time, everything will be okay and back to normal," Jason said, not believing this himself.

He gave Jennings some medicine for the panic attacks and to help him sleep.

"If you ever need anything, you call me, okay, Jennings?"

"Yes, doc … I mean, sarge," he said with a quaint smile. "I'll see you later."

After SPC Jennings left the office, Jason told the secretary to hold his calls, and he shut the door to his office. Jason then had what would be the first of many of his own panic attacks. Seeing Jennings and reliving that awful night with him brought back even more bad memories. When he was finally able to calm himself, he called Shannon and told her what had happened. He told that he was going to leave work early and that he needed a drink. She said she would meet him at the bar in an hour. Jason then hung up the phone and had Maggie cancel the rest of his appointments. Without explaining, he left for the day.

Jason arrived at the bar about thirty minutes before Shannon, and by the time she arrived, he had already sucked down three Captain and Cokes and three shots, so he was feeling revved up. Shannon ordered a beer and sat next to him.

"How are you?" she asked.

"I'm sick and tired of this shit," he replied. "When is it going to stop?"

She rubbed his back for about two minutes before anything else was said.

"Do you think the Vet Center or VA medical center might be an option now?"

Jason immediately responded, "I told you that would not happen. How would it look if a doctor can't even take care of himself?"

"It's not a matter of being a doctor," she replied. "You're a combat veteran, and you need to talk to someone who can help you. That's why they are there."

Jason assured her that those places were not an option for him. He finished his last drink and, now very upset, told her he was going home. Shannon told Jason she was going to the store, but instead went to the Vet Center herself. She was seen almost immediately and told the therapist about her situation. The therapist gave her some information about post-traumatic stress disorder and other readjustment issues and told her that they would be there if her husband needed them. Shannon took the literature home, and while Jason was sleeping, she read through it. She was only vaguely aware of post-traumatic stress disorder from the one meeting at the family support group.

As she read through it, she recognized many of the symptoms in Jason, especially the nightmares and flashbacks. But she was not aware that the anger issues were a part of the disorder as well. She also recognized the hypervigilance, or jumpiness, short-term memory loss, emotional numbing, and intrusive thoughts—Jason was often thinking about his combat experiences. After reading this, she was sure that this was what Jason had. But how was she going to convince him of this and, most important, how was she going to get him into treatment? It was something she would have to really think about and not just spring on him.

Over the next several weeks, Jason's panic attacks worsened to the point where he needed medication. His days mostly consisted of going to work and going home. He had less and less interest in social activities, unless it was going to a bar, which was something that he was now doing pretty regularly. In fact, many of Jason's patients would see him in the bar and see the way he behaved and quit going to his office for treatment. Word spread about Jason's situation, further reducing his client base. But he didn't seem to care. As long as he had work and a place to live and drink, that was all that mattered.

By mid-summer, Shannon had had enough. She grew tired of waiting for the right moment to talk to Jason about PTSD, and everyone else in his life was now avoiding him for fear of his reactions. His parents even started keeping their distance from him. They didn't even come over for his birthday, although they did call him. Every time Ray would try to help Jason, an argument would ensue. His mother gave up a while ago.

The Fourth of July celebration was the tip of the iceberg. Jason drank heavily at the bar, and when the larger fireworks would explode, Jason would almost jump completely out of his seat. He eventually went home, where he felt a little safer. The explosions clearly reminded him of mortars exploding in Iraq. The next day, as Jason again awoke with a hangover, Shannon basically gave him an ultimatum.

"Either you get some help and get this problem fixed or I am leaving. We used to have a great marriage, and you were very well respected, but now neither of those is the case. It's time to get better and stop hiding from your problems."

Jason didn't know what to say. Between this news and his pounding head, he just wanted to go back to sleep. So he told Shannon they would talk about it later. She then stomped out of the room and out the front door. Jason could hear the tires squealing from his bed. She came back several hours later to find him gone. Very upset, she called his dad and asked if Jason was there. When Ray said that he was not, she decided to tell him what was going on. About fifteen minutes into the conversation, she could hear Jason pulling into the driveway, so she quickly hung up the phone. He came through the front door carrying flowers and a bag.

"I'm sorry," he said. "I'll make it up to you."

He gave her a hug and said that he was going to get some help.

"Thank you," she said, tears rolling down her face. "What's in the bag?"

"Nothing," he responded.

She asked again, and when he did not tell her, she grabbed for it. He pushed her away, but that did not stop her. She came at him again, and again he stopped her.

"Fine; here," he said.

He handed over the bag, and when she opened it, she began to cry even harder.

"What's this for?" she asked.

"Protection," Jason said. "I think it will make me feel safer here and it will help me get some sleep and not be so jumpy."

"You're not keeping this in my house," Shannon asserted.

216

"Just for a little while, honey."

"Absolutely not."

Jason said that he would take the gun back first thing in the morning because by now the store was closed. He made his way into the kitchen to get something to eat and ate it in front of the television, which had now became commonplace. They no longer spent any time together at the table. He watched television for the rest of the day and eventually went to bed. Shannon had to leave early the next morning, so she was already in bed when he turned in. She was also awake before him in the morning, and before she left, she told him to make sure the gun was returned. He assured her that it would be, although he had no intention of taking it back.

Once Shannon left, Jason got out of bed and grabbed the gun. He took it out of the case and looked it over, proud of his new purchase. He felt stronger with this in his hands and thought for sure he would feel better with it in the house. He pondered where he would stash it so Shannon wouldn't find it. After a few minutes and still no good ideas, he got up and went down the hall to the bathroom. While he was gargling some mouthwash, he noticed that one of the tiles in the ceiling was not completely connected. He pondered it for a moment and thought this would be a great place. If Shannon hadn't seen the tile by now, she wouldn't see it in the future; and if she did, she probably wouldn't think anything of it anyway. Plus, it would be close enough to the bedroom that if he had to get it quickly, he could.

So Jason ran back to his room, grabbed the gun, went back to the bathroom, and carefully moved the tile and hid the loaded gun in there. He was proud of himself for this idea. He then decided to get cleaned up and head to work.

When he arrived at the office, his father confronted him.

"Jason, I'm fed up with your attitude and behavior. I want you to get help," he demanded.

"I already called the Vet Center to get some info and will make an appointment as soon as I find some time."

"Take time right now," Ray insisted.

"Right now?" Jason asked. "No way. I have a lot to do. I said I would get to it soon."

And that is the attitude he stuck with. He continued to tell everyone that he would get to it soon, but he kept putting it off. All the while, his situation was deteriorating. Shannon had pretty much given up and was now simply going through the motions at home. She was not 100 percent sure that Jason had returned the gun, so she thought that if she left, he would kill himself—or her. She continued to try some of the coping mechanisms she had learned from her own therapist, such as general reassuring, not pushing any issues, and taking time for herself. But nothing seemed to work. Jason continued drinking and living with his problems, and it was getting no better for her.

As the end of summer approached, Jason was only working a few hours a day. The majority of his patients had left for another doctor, and the ones who were still seeing him did not know what was really happening. As a last ditch effort, Shannon called SFC Green and told him what was happening. He had no idea the situation had gotten so dire. Jason had been avoiding all of his military buddies for a while now, so no one knew what he was dealing with. He had not gone to drill since his return either.

Jason came home from work one day to find SFC Green and 1SG Williams at his house. They told Jason to sit down and hear them out. SFC Green went through the same story that he had told Jason before, but Jason let him go on anyway. Then 1SG Williams added his own experiences.

"Jason," he said, "I've been having some problems too since I got home, and it sounds a lot like some of the ones you are having. I decided to go to the Vet Center and then to the VA medical center, and they have helped a lot. If you don't get help now, it's only going to get much worse. And by the way, if you don't get your ass back to drill, you're going to get kicked out of the army."

Jason listened to everything they had to say and finally agreed to go to the Vet Center. He said that he would go first thing in the morning. It appeared that Shannon had made the right decision bringing these two men into the situation. They stayed a little while longer and finally left just around six o'clock that evening. As soon as they were gone, Jason flipped out.

"What in the hell do you think you are doing? I can't believe you would go behind my back and do that."

Shannon, scared out of her mind, replied, "I thought they could help. I love you and want you to get better and be happy. I'm desperate, Jason."

She then ran out of the house crying. Jason, now very angry, grabbed a beer and headed back to his favorite place—the couch. Shannon returned about an hour later and headed straight to the bedroom. When Jason eventually went up, Shannon was asleep, or at least pretending to be asleep. Jason left her alone and went to sleep himself. He did not sleep very well that night, which was normal for him at this point. When he did fall asleep, he dreamed of a life back in Iraq, where he did not have to deal with the things he was dealing with here.

He woke up the next morning, contemplating going back to Iraq in hopes that he could find himself again and everything would be okay. He told no one of this. Jason had these ideas before, but he was not as serious as he was now. He felt that ever since he returned, something was missing, and he started to believe going back could solve everything. Between going to work and stopping at the bar, Jason did some research about volunteering for a unit going overseas and what he would have to do in order to go. It seemed as though it would be an easy task, except for one thing: in order for him to go with another unit, he would have to get released from his current one, and there was no way 1SG Williams would let that happen.

Well, this sunk Jason even deeper into depression. It seemed as if there was no way out. He was adamant about not seeking help for his problems. His attitude was that everyone would see him as weak if he went. Even though he did not have this attitude about everybody else who went, for some reason that belief stuck with him.

By September, just about everyone had given up on him, even his family. Jason was in a world of his own, and no one was going to be able to help him except for himself. Work was not important, and even his bar stops decreased. He spent more and more time watching television and looking through old pictures. Shannon stayed with him. But for how much longer could she tolerate this situation?

As the days of September passed, Jason was getting less and less sleep. In fact, he was only getting about three hours a night. He was going to work every other day and only staying for a few hours. He quit answering phone calls and would not return messages. He suspected by now that Shannon was having an affair, although he had no proof. His father quit trying to call, as did most of his friends.

On September 13, 2004, Jason went to his bedroom for the very last time. He was well aware of what occurred one year ago from tomorrow, and he knew he was going to get no sleep, even though he had partaken in several drinks at home that night. Shannon was not aware of what the next day held, and because Jason had been so out of it lately, she thought nothing of his mood.

Jason lay in his bed quietly, allowing for the occasional whimper and shedding of a tear. He reflected on his life over the past couple of years and felt that he could never get back to normal again, whatever normal meant. He was ashamed of himself for what he had become. He was also mad. Mad because when this dream started thirteen years ago, this was not part of the plan. *Where did it all go wrong?* he asked himself. He reminisced about the good times he had with Sgt. Adams and SSG Alderson, crying over the loss of his close buddies. Jason just never seemed to be able to get over what happened on that awful day in Iraq—not to mention all of the other bad things that had happened since then.

Well, he finally fell asleep, but he had night terrors and frequently woke up sweating throughout the night. Shannon also woke up several times as a result of him hitting her, but by now she was used to this and just went back to sleep. When the sun began to rise the next morning, Jason was awake and preparing to get out of bed. He stretched, looked at Shannon, and slowly got out of bed, careful not to move too fast as a result of his headache from drinking so much the night before. He headed to the bathroom to relieve himself. He took notice of the loose tile in the ceiling, where just a few months ago he hid his gun. He stared at it for a minute or so, but decided to head back to bed and try to get some sleep, which turned out to be a lost cause.

He tossed and turned and finally just lay in one position, looking towards his dresser, staring at the picture of him and his fallen buddies. Eventually, Shannon awoke and saw him looking at the picture and asked if he was okay.

"Yeah," he said, "I just can't sleep."

Shannon was now awake and figured she should just get up, too. She got out of bed and headed for the bathroom. Jason got out of bed, too, although he paused as he walked towards the door. He looked at the picture of his friends, picked it up, and sat back on the bed. He began to cry uncontrollably. Shannon heard him but decided to let him be alone.

Jason heard her leave the bathroom and head downstairs, where she was going to fold some clothes. He wiped the tears from his face and again headed to the bathroom. He stood in there crying for several minutes. Shannon had heard him cry several times before, but nothing like this. She yelled upstairs, asking him if he was okay. He did not reply. A few seconds later, concerned, she put down the shirt she was folding and headed up the steps. She approached the bathroom and shook the doorknob. It was locked.

"Are you okay?" she shouted.

By now she was really worried and continued asking if he was okay. Then everything was silent. She knew something was wrong. She ran into the bedroom and grabbed a hairpin to open the door.

Jason stepped onto the toilet and pulled down the gun. It was already loaded. He stared at it for a few seconds and then turned the switch from safe. As he glared into the barrel, he had some passing thoughts of times when he was happy, when he made Shannon happy. He remembered when he used to go grocery shopping and would bring home flowers to surprise Shannon. She loved it. Doing that hadn't even crossed his mind since his return home. He then moved to thoughts from Iraq, remembering he and a fellow soldier carrying a blood-soaked PFC Upshaw. He remembered the woman carrying her baby, screaming, and then falling to the ground after a single shot. He thought of Alderson … Adams.

Shannon was at the door, screaming, trying to get it open. All of a sudden, she stopped. Her worst nightmare had come true. She commenced screaming again and finally got the door open, only to find Jason lying on the floor in a pool of blood. She ran to the phone to call 911, but she knew they could do nothing. She ran back into the bathroom and sat on the floor, holding her husband in her arms.

The emergency crew finally arrived, and when they got no answer at the door, they came in and heard Shannon crying upstairs. They rushed up the stairs, only to find Shannon covered in blood, holding a lifeless Jason in her arms. She looked at them, trying to find the right words to say. She looked back at Jason and then at them again.

"The war is over for him now," she said as she rocked with her husband in her arms.

"The war is over for him now."

Made in the USA
Lexington, KY
23 September 2013